Kissing Friends?

Lord Carew held Samantha comfortingly against his surprisingly strong and well-muscled body. His left arm was tight about her waist.

She rested her cheek against his shoulder. Samantha felt sheltered and wonderfully comforted. She fitted against him much more cozily than she did against any of the beaux she had allowed to embrace her. Neither loosened the hold as they looked into each other's eyes.

"Kiss me," Samantha whispered. There was no doubt that the voice was hers, startling in its boldness, straightforward in its meaning.

Lord Carew kissed her gently, softly almost tenderly. Samantha kissed him back in the same way and felt relaxation and a healing sort of peace seep back into her body and into her soul.

He was very dear to her, she thought. A very dear friend. But did friends kiss like this . . . ?

D0191357

SIGNET REGENCY ROMANCE
Coming in July 1995

Anne Barbour
My Cousin Jane

Elisabeth Fairchild
Lord Endicott's Appetite

Elizabeth Jackson
Rogue's Delight

Lord Carew's Bride

by
Mary Balogh

A SIGNET BOOK

SIGNET
Published by the Penguin Group
Penguin Books USA Inc., 375 Hudson Street,
New York, New York 10014, U.S.A.
Penguin Books Ltd, 27 Wrights Lane,
London W8 5TZ, England
Penguin Books Australia Ltd, Ringwood,
Victoria, Australia
Penguin Books Canada Ltd, 10 Alcorn Avenue,
Toronto, Ontario, Canada M4V 3B2
Penguin Books (N.Z.) Ltd, 182–190 Wairau Road,
Auckland 10, New Zealand

Penguin Books Ltd, Registered Offices:
Harmondsworth, Middlesex, England

First published by Signet, an imprint of Dutton Signet,
a division of Penguin Books USA Inc.

First Printing, June, 1995
10 9 8 7 6 5 4 3 2 1

Copyright © Mary Balogh, 1995
All rights reserved

Ⓟ REGISTERED TRADEMARK—MARCA REGISTRADA

Printed in the United States of America

Without limiting the rights under copyright reserved above, no part of this
publication may be reproduced, stored in or introduced into a retrieval system, or
transmitted, in any form, or by any means (electronic, mechanical, photocopying,
recording, or otherwise), without the prior written permission of both the copyright
owner and the above publisher of this book.

BOOKS ARE AVAILABLE AT QUANTITY DISCOUNTS WHEN USED TO PROMOTE PRODUCTS OR
SERVICES. FOR INFORMATION PLEASE WRITE TO PREMIUM MARKETING DIVISION, PENGUIN BOOKS
USA INC., 375 HUDSON STREET, NEW YORK, NEW YORK 10014.

If you purchased this book without a cover you should be aware that this book is
stolen property. It was reported as "unsold and destroyed" to the publisher and
neither the author nor the publisher has received any payment for this "stripped
book."

Chapter 1

"Oh, do come with us, Sam," the Countess of Thornhill said. "I know it is only a short walk to the lake, but the setting is lovely and the daffodils are in bloom. And surely it is better to have company than to be alone."

There was a look of concern on her face that made her cousin, Samantha Newman, feel guilty. She would far *prefer* to be alone.

"The children will not bother you, provided you tell them quite firmly that you are not to be romped with," the countess added.

There were four children, the countess's two and Lady Boyle's two. They were perfectly normal, well-behaved—though exuberant—children. Samantha was fond of them and had no objection to being romped with quite frequently.

"The children never bother me, Jenny," she assured her cousin. "It is just that I like being alone occasionally. I like walking long distances to take the air and commune with my own thoughts. You will not be offended, will you?"

"No," Lady Thornhill said. "Oh, no, of course not, Sam. You are our guest here and must do as you please. It is just that you have changed. You used not to like being alone at all."

"It is advancing age," Samantha said, smiling.

"Advancing age!" her cousin said scornfully. "You are four-and-twenty, Sam, and as beautiful as you ever were, and with more admirers than you ever had."

"I think perhaps," Lady Boyle said gently, entering the conversation for the first time, "Samantha is missing Lord Francis."

Samantha hooted inelegantly. "Missing Francis?" she said. "He was here for a week—visiting Gabriel—and left this morning. I always enjoy Francis's company. He teases me about being on the shelf and I tease him about his dandyish appearance. Lavender silk for dinner last evening, indeed, and in the country! But when I am not in his company, I forget him immediately—and I daresay he forgets me, too."

"And yet," the countess said, "he has twice made you a marriage offer, Sam."

"And it would serve him right if I accepted one of these times," Samantha said. "He would die of shock, poor man."

Lady Boyle looked at her in some shock herself and smiled uncertainly at the countess.

"No, if you really do not mind, Jenny, and if you will not be hurt, Rosalie," Samantha said, "I believe I will walk alone this afternoon. Aunt Aggy is having a rest, and this lovely spring weather calls for something brisker than a stroll to the lake."

"You could have gone riding about the estate with Gabriel and Albert," the countess said. "They would not have minded at all. But here I go, trying to manage your life again. Have a good afternoon, Sam. Come, Rosalie, the children will be climbing the nursery walls in their impatience already."

And so finally Samantha was alone. And feeling guilty for spurning the company that had been offered her. And feeling relieved to have the rest of the afternoon to herself. She drew on a dark blue spencer over her lighter blue dress, tied the ribbons of her bonnet beneath her chin, and set out for her walk.

It was not that she disliked either Jenny or Rosalie or their children. Quite the contrary. She had lived with Jenny and Jenny's father, Viscount Nordal, for four years after

her parents died when she was fourteen. She and Jenny had
made their come out together. They had loved the same
man . . . No, that was not to be thought of. Since Jenny's
marriage six years before, Samantha had frequently stayed
at Chalcote with her and Gabriel. If they were in town during the Season, she often stayed with them there. Jenny was
her dearest friend.

And Rosalie, the wife, also for six years, of Gabriel's
closest friend, Sir Albert Boyle, was impossible to dislike.
She was sweet and shy and gentle and did not have a mean
bone in her whole body, Samantha would swear.

The trouble was that they were both very contentedly
married. They were both absorbed in affection for their
husbands and affection for their children and affection for
their homes.

Sometimes Samantha wanted to scream.

And Gabriel and Albert quite clearly shared all those af-
fections with their wives.

Samantha had been at Chalcote since just before Christmas. The Boyles had been there for a month. Aunt
Agatha—Lady Brill—Samantha's constant companion, had
come with her. Lord Francis Kneller, another of Gabriel's
friends, had been there for a week. Everything was so wonderful, so peaceful, so cheerful, so domesticated. Everyone,
it seemed, was in the process of living happily ever after.

Oh, yes. Samantha's steps quickened. Sometimes she
could scream and scream and scream.

And she felt horribly guilty. No one could be kinder to
her than Jenny and Gabriel. At least Jenny was her cousin.
Gabriel was nothing to her, and yet he treated her with as
much courtesy and even affection as if she were his cousin,
too. It was horribly ungrateful to want to scream at their domestic bliss. She did not resent their happiness. Indeed, she
was very happy for them. Their marriage had had such an
inauspicious beginning. And she had felt that it was partly
her fault. . . .

No, it was not that she resented them. It was just

that . . . Well, she did not know just what it was. It was not jealousy or even envy. Darkly handsome as Gabriel was, she had never felt attracted to him herself. And she was not in search of a man of her own. She did not believe in love. Not for herself, anyway. And she had no intention of marrying. She wanted to remain free and independent. She was almost both already—Uncle Gerald had not kept firm reins on her since she reached her majority. But when she was five-and-twenty, her parents' small fortune would be hers to manage herself.

She could hardly wait.

Her life was as she wanted it to be. She was not lonely. She had Aunt Aggy all the time, there were always Jenny and Gabriel to be visited, there were numerous other friends. And there was that group of gentlemen whom it pleased Gabriel to call her court. It was flatteringly large, considering her advanced age. She believed it was so large just because all its members knew very well that she intended never to marry. They felt safe flirting with her and sighing over her and sometimes stealing kisses from her, and even occasionally making her marriage offers. Francis had made her two, Sir Robin Talbot one, and Jeremy Nicholson so many that both of them had lost count.

Her life was as she wanted it to be. And yet . . . She could not even complete the thought. She supposed it was the normal human condition never to be quite happy, quite satisfied. She did not know what it was that was missing from her life, if anything. When she turned five-and-twenty, perhaps everything would be finally perfect. And there was not long to wait.

She did not know where she was walking. Except that it was in the opposite direction from the lake. And again she felt guilty. Jenny's Michael and Rosalie's Emily, both five years old, were intelligent and interesting children. Rosalie's Jane, three years old, was a mischief, and Jenny's Mary, aged two, was a sweetheart. Rosalie was in a delicate way again and was due to deliver later in the spring. Perhaps for Jenny's sake Samantha should have gone with them.

She recognized where she was when she came to the line of trees. She was close to the boundary between Chalcote and Highmoor. They were two unusually large estates adjoining each other. Highmoor belonged to the Marquess of Carew, but Samantha had never met him. He was from home a great deal. He was from home now.

She walked among the trees. There was no real sign of spring yet above her head, though the sky was blue and there was definite warmth in the air. The branches were still bare. But soon now there would be buds, and then young leaves, and then a green canopy. There were snowdrops and primroses growing among the trees, though. And there was the stream, which she knew was the exact boundary line, though she had not walked in this particular place before. She strolled to the edge of it and gazed down into the clear water gurgling over the stones at the bottom of the streambed.

Not far to her left she could see broad stepping-stones that would take one safely across to the other side. After strolling toward them and hesitating for only a moment, she crossed them and smiled to find that Highmoor land looked and felt the same as Chalcote land.

She had no wish to turn back yet. If she returned to the house, Aunt Aggy might be up after her rest and Samantha would be obliged to bear her company. Not that she did not love her aunt dearly, but . . . well, sometimes she just liked to be alone. Besides, it was far too lovely an afternoon for part of it to be wasted indoors. The winter had been long enough and cold enough.

Samantha continued on her way through the trees, expecting that soon she would come out into open land again and would be able to see the estate. Perhaps she would be able to glimpse the house, though she did not know if it was close. On such a large estate it might be miles away. Jenny had told her, though, that it was a magnificent house, with features of the old abbey it had once been still visible from the outside.

The trees did not thin out. But the land rose quite steadily and quite steeply. Samantha climbed, pausing a few times to lean one hand against the trunk of a tree. She must be dreadfully out of condition, she thought, panting and feeling the heat of the sun almost as if it were July rather than early March.

But finally she was rewarded for her effort. The land and the forest continued upward—there was even a quite visible path now—but to one side of her the land fell away sharply to open grassland below. And Highmoor Abbey was in the distance, though she had no clear view of it. She moved about a bit, until finally there was almost a clear opening downhill, with only one tree obstructing the view. There was no seeing it quite clearly, it seemed, and the slope looked rather too steep to be scrambled down.

But there was a feeling of magnificence. A feeling of excitement, almost. It looked wilder than Chalcote, more magical.

"Yes, that tree does need to be removed," a voice said from quite close by, making Samantha jump with alarm. "I was just noticing the same thing."

He was leaning against a tree, one booted foot propped back against it. She felt an instant surging of relief. She had expected to see an arrogant and irate Marquess of Carew— not that she had ever seen him before, of course. It would have been unbearably humiliating to have been caught trespassing and gawking at his ancestral home. Even this was bad enough.

Her first impression that he was a gardener was dismissed even before she reacted to his words. He spoke with cultured English accents, even though he was dressed very informally and not at all elegantly in a brown coat that would have made Weston of Old Bond Street shudder for a week without stopping, breeches that looked as if they were worn for comfort rather than good fit, and top boots that had seen not only better days, but better years.

He was a very ordinary looking gentleman, neither tall nor short, neither herculean nor puny, neither handsome nor ugly. His hair—he was not wearing a hat—was a nondescript brown. His eyes looked gray.

A very unthreatening looking gentleman, she was happy to note. He must be the marquess's steward, or perhaps a minion of the steward.

"I—I do beg your pardon," she said. "I was, um, I was trespassing."

"I will not have the constables sent out to arrest you and haul you before the nearest magistrate," he said. "Not this time, anyway." His eyes were smiling. They were very nice eyes, Samantha decided, definitely a distinguishing feature in an otherwise very ordinary face.

"I am staying at Chalcote," she said, pointing downward through the trees. "With my cousin, the Countess of Thornhill. And her husband, the Earl of Thornhill," she added unnecessarily.

He continued to smile at her with his eyes and she found herself beginning to relax. "Have you never seen Highmoor Abbey before?" he asked. "It is rather splendid, is it not? If that tree were not there, you would have the best view of it from this vantage point. The tree will be moved."

"Moved?" She smiled broadly at him. "Plucked out and planted somewhere else, just like a flower?"

"Yes," he said. "Why kill a tree when it need not die?"

He was serious.

"But it is so huge," she said, laughing.

He pushed away from the tree trunk against which he had been leaning and came toward her. He walked with a decided limp, Samantha noticed. She also noticed that he held his right arm cradled against his side, his wrist and hand turned in against his hip. He was wearing leather gloves.

"Oh, did you hurt yourself?" she asked.

"No." He stopped beside her. He was not a great deal taller than she, and she was considered small. "Not recently, anyway."

She felt herself blushing uncomfortably. How gauche of her. The man was partly crippled and she had asked if he had hurt himself.

"You see?" he said, pointing downward with his good arm. "If the tree is moved, there will be a full frontal view of the abbey from here, perfectly centered between the other trees on the slope. It is all of two miles away, but an artist could not have done better on a canvas, could he? Except to have left that particular tree off the slope. We will be artists and imagine it removed. Soon it will be removed in fact. We can be artists with nature as surely as with watercolors or oils, you see. It is merely a matter of having an eye for the picturesque or the majestic, or merely for what will be visually pleasing."

"Are you the steward here?" she asked.

"No." He turned his head to look at her over his outstretched arm before lowering it.

"I did not think you could be a gardener," she said. "Your accent suggests that you are a gentleman." She blushed again. "I do beg your pardon. It is none of my business, especially as a trespasser." But it struck her suddenly that perhaps he was a trespasser, too.

"I am Hartley Wade," he said, still looking into her face.

"How do you do, Mr. Wade," she said. She extended her right hand to him rather than curtsying—he did not seem the sort of man to whom one would curtsy. "Samantha Newman."

"Miss Newman," he said, "I am pleased to make your acquaintance."

He shook her hand with his right one. She could feel through his glove that his hand was thin and the fingers stiffly bent. She was afraid to exert any pressure and was sorry then for the impulsive gesture of offering the handshake.

"I am considered something of a landscape artist," he said. "I have tramped the estates of many of England's most prominent landowners, giving them advice on how they can make the most of their parks. Many people believe that having well-kept formal gardens before the house and regularly mown lawns is enough."

"And it is not?" she asked.

"Not always. Not often." His eyes were smiling again. "Formal gardens are not always even particularly attractive, especially if the land before the house is unusually flat and there is no possibility of terracing. One would have to be suspended in the sky—in a balloon, perhaps—and looking downward to appreciate the full effect. And usually there is a great deal more to parks than just the house and the mile or so of land directly in front of it. Parks can be extremely pleasant places in which to walk and relax and feast the senses if one exercises just a little care and planning in organizing them."

"Oh," she said, smiling. "And is that what you are doing here? Has the Marquess of Carew employed you to tramp about his park and give him advice?"

"He is about to have one of his trees repositioned at the very least," he said.

"Will he mind?" she asked.

"When someone asks for advice," he said, "he had better be prepared to hear some. A number of things have already been done here to make the most of nature, and to add to it and change it just a little for more pleasing effects. This is not my first visit, you see. But it is always possible to imagine new improvements. As with that tree. I cannot understand how it has escaped my notice before now. Once it is gone, a stone grotto can be erected here so that the marquess and his guests can sit here and enjoy the prospect at their leisure."

"Yes." She looked about her. "It would be the perfect spot, would it not? It would be wonderfully peaceful. If I lived here, I believe I would spend a great deal of time sitting in such a grotto, thinking and dreaming."

"Two very underrated activities," he said. "I am glad you

appreciate them, Miss Newman. Or one might be tempted to sit, perhaps, with a special companion, one with whom one can talk or be silent with equal comfort."

She looked at him with sudden understanding. Yes, that was what it was. That was it. That was what was missing. She had felt it and wondered about it and puzzled over it. And here was the answer, so simple that she had not even considered it before. She had no special companion. No one with whom she could be silent in comfort. Even with her dearest relatives, Aunt Aggy and Jenny, she always felt the necessity to converse.

"Yes," she said, a curious ache in her throat. "That would be pleasant. Very pleasant."

"Are you in a hurry to return to Chalcote?" he asked. "Or is there anyone who will be anxious over your absence? A chaperon, perhaps?"

"I have outgrown the need for chaperons, Mr. Wade," she said. "I am four-and-twenty years old."

"You do not look it," he said, smiling. "Would you like to stroll up over the hill, then, and see some of the improvements that have already been made and hear some of my ideas for new ones?"

It was very improper. She was a lady very much alone in a wooded area of the countryside with a strange gentleman, albeit a very ordinary and rather shabby gentleman. She should have turned very firmly in the direction of home. But there was nothing at all threatening about him. He was pleasant. And he had aroused a curiosity in her to see how nature could be manipulated, but not harmed or destroyed, for the pleasure of humans.

"I should like that," she said, looking up the slope.

"I have always thought the marquess was fortunate," he said, "having the hill on his land, while the Earl of Thornhill was left with the flat land. Hills have so many possibilities. Do you need assistance?"

"No." She laughed. "I am just ashamed of my breathlessness. The winter has been endless, and I have been far too long without strenuous exercise."

"We are almost at the top," he said. His limp was quite a bad one, she noticed, but he appeared far more fit than she. "There is a folly there, in a very obvious place. I normally like to be more subtle, but the marquess has assured me that any guests he brings this way are always thankful for the chance to sit and rest there."

Samantha was thankful for it, too. They sat side by side on the stone seat inside the mock temple, looking down over the tops of the trees to the fields and meadows below. The house could be seen over to one side, but it was not as splendid a view as would be that from the top of the slope where she had stood earlier. He pointed out to her places where trees had been removed and replanted in previous years. He indicated two paths down the steeper part of the slope, each leading to a folly that had been carefully placed for the view it afforded. He explained that there was a lake just out of sight that he was particularly working on this year.

"The secret is," he said, "to leave an area looking as if all its beauty and effects are attributable to nature. The lake must look like an area of wild beauty by the time I have finished with it. In reality I will have made several changes. I will take you down there afterward and show you if you wish."

But he made no immediate move to do so. They were sheltered from the slight breeze where they sat, and the sun shone directly on them. It felt almost warm. There were birds singing in the trees, almost invisible except when one rose into the air for some reason before settling back again. And there were all the fresh smells of spring.

They sat in silence for many minutes, though Samantha was largely unaware of the fact. There was no awkwardness, no feeling that the conversation must be picked up again. There was too much of nature to enjoy for it to be missed in conversation.

She sighed at last. "This has been wonderful," she said. "Wonderfully relaxing. I could have gone to the lake at

Chalcote with my cousin and Lady Boyle, one of her other guests, and their children. At the risk of offending them, I preferred to be alone."

"And I ruined that attempt," he said.

"No." She turned her head to smile at him. "Being with you has been as good as being alone, Mr. Wade." And then she laughed, only partly embarrassed. "Oh, dear, I did not mean that the way it sounded. I mean I have enjoyed your company and been comfortable with you. Thank you for opening my eyes to what I had not even thought about before."

"It is too late to go down to the lake now," he said. "It must be past teatime, and you will be missed. Perhaps some other time?"

"I would love to," she said. "But you are working. I would not want to waste your time."

"Artists," he said, "and writers and musicians are often accused of being idle when they are staring into space. Often they are hardest at work at such times. I have been sitting here beside you, Miss Newman, having ideas for my—employer's park. I would not have sat here, perhaps, if I had not been with you, and would not therefore have had the ideas. Will you come again? Tomorrow, perhaps? Here, at the same time we met today?"

"Yes," she said, coming to a sudden decision. She could not recall an afternoon she had enjoyed more since coming to Chalcote almost three months before. The thought made her feel disloyal to Jenny and Gabriel, who had been so kind to her. "Yes, I will."

"Come," he said, getting to his feet. "I shall escort you as far as the stream." His eyes smiled at her in that attractive way he had—almost the only thing about him that was actually physically attractive, she thought. "I must see you safely off Carew's property."

She was afraid that all the walking would be hard on his infirmity, but she did not like to mention it again. He limped beside her all the way back down the hill to the stream.

They talked the whole while, though she would not have been able to say afterward exactly what they talked about.

"Do be careful," he said as she made her way back across the stones to the other side of the stream, trying not to hold her skirts too high. "Toppling into the water at this time of year might be just too exhilarating an exercise."

She stopped at the other side to smile at him and raise a hand in farewell. One of his arms was behind his back. The other was crooked against his hip. It was his right hand. She wondered if by some miracle he was naturally left-handed.

"Thank you," she said, "for a pleasant afternoon."

"I shall look forward to seeing you again tomorrow, Miss Newman," he said. "Weather permitting."

She was through the trees in no time at all and on her way back across the meadow toward the lawns of Chalcote park. It must indeed be past teatime, she thought. If Jenny and Rosalie were back from the lake, they would wonder what on earth had happened to her.

Would she tell them? That she had walked and sat with a total stranger for well over an hour? That she had made an assignation to meet him again tomorrow? She did not believe she would. It would sound bad in the telling, yet there had been nothing bad about it at all. Quite the contrary. There could not be a more ordinary, pleasant gentleman in existence, or one with whom she could feel so very comfortable. Neither was there a gentleman with whom she had had an encounter less romantic. There had been no physical awareness at all.

If she told, Aunt Aggy would have ideas about coming along with her tomorrow as a chaperon. And then there would be the necessity for conversation among the three of them. It would not be a pleasant afternoon at all.

No, she would not tell. She was four-and-twenty years old. Quite old enough to do some things alone. Quite old enough to have some life of her own.

She would not tell. But she knew she would be looking forward to tomorrow afternoon with pleasure.

Chapter 2

Hartley Wade, Marquess of Carew, watched her go. He stood where he was, on his side of the stream, long after she had gone.

She was the most beautiful woman he had ever seen. By far the most beautiful. She was small and shapely and dainty and graceful. Her hair was honey-blond and worn in short curls. Her bonnet had not hidden its glory. Her eyes were the bluest blue, her lashes long and darker than her hair. Her face was lovely and smiling and animated and intelligent.

He smiled ruefully to himself. For all his seven-and-twenty years, he was reacting like a schoolboy to a rare glimpse of someone from the female world. He was in a fair way to being in love with her.

He turned about to make his way back up the hill through the trees. With the side of his right hand he rubbed at his upper thigh. He was going to suffer tonight from all the walking. Though perhaps not too much. He had not walked a great deal during the past few months, but he had ruthlessly exercised. He smiled anew at the remembered expression on Jackson's face when he had first walked into the famous pugilist's boxing saloon in London three years ago. When he had *limped* in, rather. Jackson was proud of him now and eager to show him off to some of his other patrons. But the marquess had only ever been there in private and had only ever worked with the master himself. He was no sideshow for a fair.

He arrived at the point close to the top of the hill where he had first seen her—Miss Samantha Newman. Yes, the tree definitely had to go. The view would be quite magnificent.

It had not struck him immediately that she had not realized who he was. Perhaps neither Thornhill nor his lady had described him to her. They were decent people. Perhaps they had not begun any description they might have given of him with the most obvious feature. Perhaps she did not know that the Marquess of Carew was a cripple. That was the label by which he was known, he was well aware, even if it was not strictly true. Had she heard that label, she would surely have realized who he was.

He had given her his name with some reluctance. But even that had meant nothing to her. *How do you do, Mr. Wade,* she had said politely. He had watched for the change in her manner, but it had not come.

The temptation had been overwhelming—the temptation not to enlighten her. And, of course, if she had been given no description of him and if his name meant nothing to her without his title, there was no reason why she should guess his identity—even though he had been roaming his own land. He was dressed for comfort in almost the oldest clothes he possessed. His valet had warned him just that morning that if his lordship insisted on wearing these boots one more time after today, he would send a public notice to all the newspapers that he was not responsible for his master's appearance.

But they were such comfortable boots, and such threats were not by any means new. Hargreaves had been with him, and threatening him, for eleven years.

The marquess continued on his way to the top of the hill and sat on the stone seat he had occupied with Miss Newman earlier. She had conversed with ease and had listened with what had seemed genuine interest. She had sat beside him for what must have been all of fifteen minutes in silence, a silence of remarkable comfort. She had not felt the necessity to speak to hold the silence at bay, nor had she felt the necessity of prompting him into speech.

She had said—what had been her exact words? He thought carefully. *I have enjoyed your company and been comfortable with you.* Her voice had held the ring of truth. Other women had uttered the first part of what she had said. None had ever said the rest. And none had ever spoken with sincerity.

He kept himself from company a great deal these days, though he was no hermit. He avoided female company whenever he could. It had become too demeaning, too hurtful, to see the instant spark of interest and acquisitiveness in female eyes as soon as he was identified and to be fawned over for the rest of that particular social event. His title was an impressive one, he supposed—he was the eighth marquess of his line. And, of course, there was this property in Yorkshire, and the one, almost equally large and prosperous, in Berkshire. He had more wealth than he would ever know what to do with.

He could have lived with the fawning, perhaps. Many gentlemen of his class had to. It was the way of the world. But there was also the disdain he sometimes surprised in female eyes at his unprepossessing appearance. And sometimes it was worse than disdain. Sometimes it was distaste or even disgust at his grotesque limp and his twisted hand. He rarely appeared outside his home now without a glove on at least his right hand.

Lord Byron's limp, of course, had only succeeded in making him more attractive to the ladies. But then the Marquess of Carew did not have either Lord Byron's beauty or his charisma.

He wondered how Samantha Newman would have reacted if he had given her his full name. Would he have seen that familiar gleam of avaricious interest? She had admitted that she was four-and-twenty years old. She was somewhat past the normal marrying age for a woman. Though he could not imagine the reason, even if she was dowryless. She was so very beautiful.

Beauty and the beast, he thought ruefully, resting his left hand flat on the stone seat beside him, where she had sat.

He had not seen disgust in her face. Only concern when she had thought that he had recently hurt himself, and then embarrassment when she had realized her faux pas.

But perhaps the disgust would have been there if she had known who he was and had seen him as someone whose favor she might court.

No. He closed his eyes and lifted his face to the lowering sun. He did not want to believe that of her. He had liked her. It was not just her looks, though his first sight of her had fairly robbed him of breath. He had *liked* her.

Ah, more than that.

He opened his eyes and got to his feet. It was time to go home. He would not after all go to the lake today to make his plans for improvement. Perhaps she would go there with him tomorrow and he could dream along with her and explain his ideas to her. If the weather held. The clouds gathering in the west did not look promising. He hoped the weather would hold. He looked forward to tomorrow more than he had looked forward to any tomorrow for a long time.

Perhaps by tomorrow she would have discovered his identity for herself. If she described him to Thornhill or his lady, they would tell her with whom she had spent an hour of the afternoon. Or perhaps she simply would not come. Perhaps the afternoon had not meant as much to her as it had to him, and she would not keep their appointment. Tomorrow, if she did come, he would tell her for himself who he was. He would take the risk of seeing her attitude change. But in the meantime he would instruct his servants not to spread the word that he had arrived home unexpectedly yesterday.

He hoped the weather would hold.

He hoped she would come.

Ah, yes. It was more than her beauty. And more than the fact that he had liked her.

He really had reverted to boyhood emotions. He was head over ears in love with her.

Beauty and the beast, indeed!

For two days it rained a steady drizzle beyond the windows of Chalcote. Even the men did not venture outside, though the Earl of Thornhill complained that there was estate business to be attended to.

The children were restless and even peevish, and their nurse came close to the end of her tether about how to entertain them. And so the earl, willingly abetted by Sir Albert Boyle, shocked her by taking them on his back and galloping on a cavalry charge all over the house—though she should be past shock by now, she admitted to the housekeeper belowstairs, having had five years of experience of his lordship's unconventional behavior as a father. Lady Boyle was shocked, too, and somewhat charmed, and joined with the rest of the household in a noisy romp of hide-and-seek in which only the kitchens and the outdoors were out-of-bounds. Even Lady Brill participated—though once, when everyone had searched for her for longer than half an hour and had concluded that she must have found that one perfect hiding place none of the rest of them had yet discovered, she was finally found to be stretched out on her own bed, fast asleep.

The game lasted, with brief intervals, for two days.

There were guests for dinner on the second day, neighbors who had visited or been visited several times during the past three months. There were cards and music and conversation after dinner. It was all very pleasant. It was just a pity, the countess said afterward, that the Marquess of Carew had not yet returned to Highmoor Abbey. It would be good to see a different face for a change.

"You would like him, Sam," she said. "He is a very pleasant gentleman, but he never seems to be in residence when you are here. We must plan more carefully next time."

"Samantha does not need to add to her court," the earl said firmly. "It is as large as an army battalion as it is. One more member might turn her head and make her conceited." He winked at his wife when he knew Samantha was looking at him.

It was on the tip of Samantha's tongue to mention the landscape gardener who was staying at Highmoor—Mr. Wade. He was a gentleman, after all. That had been very obvious from his conversation and manners. But perhaps he would be uncomfortable in such elevated company, and perhaps he did not have the clothes to enable him to dine with the likes of Gabriel and Albert. Besides . . . Oh, besides, she wanted to keep him as her own secret companion for the moment. She did not want to see everyone else being polite—though of course both Gabriel and Jenny would be genuinely courteous—to a gentleman who would so obviously be out of his milieu.

She enjoyed the two days. And she fretted at being confined to the house yet again. She was severely disappointed at being denied the treat of another walk at Highmoor with Mr. Wade. She had enjoyed his company so very much. It had been a great novelty, she had realized after returning to Chalcote and looking back on the hour she had spent with him, to be treated as a person with a mind. She was so accustomed to seeing nothing but admiration and open attraction in men's eyes. That was flattering, of course, but she often had the impression that she was seen only as a pretty face and not as a real person at all.

Mr. Wade had shown no attraction to her. He had merely enjoyed explaining his theories and ideas to her. And he had enjoyed, too, just being with her in lovely surroundings, she believed. Perhaps it was silly to feel so after merely one relatively short encounter, but she had the feeling that she and Mr. Wade could be friends. Companions. She had very few real friends, though she was fortunate enough to have hordes of friendly acquaintances. How had he phrased it? She thought carefully so that she might remember his exact words: . . . *a special companion, one with whom one can talk or be silent with equal comfort.*

She felt again that sense of discovery the words had brought when they were uttered. She did not want love as other women wanted it. Her one experience with love at the age of eighteen had been humiliating and excruciatingly painful. She did not want that feeling ever again. What she really wanted—and she had not realized it until he had put it into words for her—was a special companion.

Mr. Wade could be a special companion, she sensed. Perhaps it was ridiculous to think so when she had met him only once. Perhaps he had forgotten about her as soon as he turned back from the stream that afternoon. Perhaps he would not have kept their appointment even if it had not rained. And perhaps now she would never see him again. Perhaps his work at Highmoor was complete and he had left.

She would be sorry not to see him again.

On the third day the rain had stopped. All morning low clouds threatened more, but by the afternoon they were breaking up and the sun was shining through the gaps.

The earl, with his friend in tow, had ridden off early with the estate steward to sort out some problem with a distant tenant. But they were back soon after noon and announced that it was a perfect afternoon for a family ride, since a walk would only soak boots and hems.

"Rosie will appreciate the rest, will you not, my love?" Sir Albert said, smiling gently at his pregnant wife. "Emmy will be quite safe on the pony Gabe picked out for her when we first arrived, and Jane will ride up with me."

Lady Boyle had a terror of horses and seemed quite thankful that her delicate condition put her joining the riding party quite out of the question.

"You must insist that Michael keep his pony to a sedate walk, Gabriel," the countess said. "Or Emily will feel obliged to try to keep pace with him, and I shall have a heart seizure on the spot, and Rosalie will have one as soon as she hears of it."

The earl winked and grinned at her. "Mary will be up before me begging for a cavalry charge," he said.

His countess tutted. "Then I had better have her up before me," she said. "Sam, you must help me keep this madman in order."

"If you will not mind terribly," Samantha said, "I believe I will go walking."

"Ah, this madman has put terror into her," the earl said. "It is to be a cavalry charge without sabers, Samantha, my dear."

"Then it is to be a charge without purpose," she said, smiling at him. "*Will* you mind?"

"How could you possibly not want to ride with four squealing infants, a mad cavalryman, a scold, and only one normal gentleman?" he asked her. "Some people are very strange. Of course we do not mind, Samantha. You must do what gives you the greatest pleasure. That was why you were invited here."

"Oh, I am *not* a scold," the countess said indignantly. "And do stop winking at me, Gabriel, or I will believe you must have a speck of dust in your eye. Sam, your feet and your hem are gong to be *soaked*. But there, I will not scold. And do stop laughing, Gabriel. Sam, I have endured six years of this. Am I an angel or am I not?"

"I am," the earl said. "The angel Gabriel."

Samantha left them when her cousin was tutting again and then chuckling with Albert and Rosalie. She remembered how she and Jenny had called the Earl of Thornhill Lucifer when they first knew him, because of his dark satanic looks. When they learned his given name, it had been an amusing irony, though it had not seemed so amusing at the time. He really had seemed like Lucifer, deliberately bringing to an end Jenny's betrothal to Lionel.

Samantha shuddered. She rarely dredged up that name or

the person belonging to it out of her subconscious mind. The devil in angel's garb. The only man she had ever loved—or would ever love. That one sour experience had been more than enough for a lifetime.

She changed into one of her older dresses and pulled on her half boots, though she had hoped that with winter over she would not have to wear them again for a while. She drew on a cloak, since even with the intermittent sunshine it looked chilly outside, and tied the ribbons of a bonnet securely beneath her chin.

He would not be there, she thought as she left the house. Even if he was still at Highmoor, he would not think of keeping an appointment two days late. Besides, pleasant as the afternoon was—though definitely chilly and gusty—the grass underfoot was really quite wet.

He would not be there, but she would enjoy the walk anyway. And surely the stone bench inside the folly at the top of the hill would be dry and sheltered enough so that she could sit there enjoying the view and the solitude for a while. It was better than riding with the others, feeling her loneliness.

The word, verbalized in her mind, took her by surprise. She was not lonely. Never that. She was almost always in congenial company. Her life was as she wanted it to be. Why had she suddenly described herself as lonely?

She crossed the stepping-stones and strode up the hill, not stopping even once to catch her breath. The air was invigorating, she thought, even better than it had been three days ago. And the sky looked lovely, with white clouds scudding across the blue. She made for the top, trying not to expect to see him there, trying to convince herself that she wanted to be alone there so that she could enjoy the view without distraction.

She stopped when she was within sight of the folly. And felt a surging of happiness, which she did not stop to analyze. She smiled brightly and stepped forward.

He was getting to his feet and smiling with his eyes at her.

"What a climb," she said. "I may never recover my breath."

"Please do," he said. "I am not sure I would fancy having to carry a dead body back down such a steep slope."

Other gentlemen of her acquaintance would have rushed to her assistance, using the excuse to touch her, to take her by the hand, even perhaps to risk setting an arm about her waist. A brisk and quite harmless flirtation would have ensued. Mr. Wade merely motioned to the bench.

"Come and sit down," he said.

She laughed and walked toward him, a new spring in her step despite her breathlessness.

Her cheeks and even the tip of her nose were rosy from the chill and the wind. Her curls were somewhat disheveled beneath her bonnet. The hems of her green walking dress and the gray cloak over it were darkened with moisture to the depth of several inches. Her boots were wet and blades of grass clung to them.

She was even more beautiful than he remembered.

He had been trying to convince himself that she would not come and that he would not particularly mind if she did not. He really was busy with ideas for renovations that would begin as soon as spring was more advanced. He would be able to think and work without distraction if she did not come. He would not wait long, he had told himself when he first arrived at the top of the hill. Just ten minutes.

She came at the end of fifteen. He was somewhat alarmed to realize that he had never felt happier in his life.

"Better?" he asked after she had seated herself beside him. There was a fragrance about her that he had noticed last time. Violets? It was not overpowering. It was very subtle. It seemed to be the smell of her rather than of any perfume she wore.

"I believe so," she said, one hand over her heart. She

laughed again, a bright, totally happy sound. "I believe it is almost safe to say that I will survive."

"I am glad," he said. One of those curls would feel soft and silky wrapped about one of his fingers.

"Was not the rain wretched?" she said. "We played hide-and-seek for two days with the children and had to pretend for all of that time not to see them, even when they were perfectly visible behind sheer draperies or beneath desks."

"You were bored?" he asked, a quite improper image of her with an infant at her breast flashing unexpectedly into his mind.

"Not at all," she said. "It was a thoroughly enjoyable romp. I believe I am still a child at heart—an alarming thought. But I was disappointed about our walk. I thought you might not still be at Highmoor. I thought perhaps you would not think of coming today instead. I did not expect to see you here today, but I came anyway." She smiled at him. "Just in case."

She had really wanted to come. She had been disappointed by the rain. She had been anxious today—anxious that he would not come. But she had come anyway. Just in case.

He had planned this part of their meeting—if she came. He was going to turn to her and tell her he was very sorry but he had misled her last time. He had done so, he would say, because she had looked embarrassed to be caught trespassing and he had not wanted to distress her further. But in reality he was more than just Hartley Wade. He was the Marquess of Carew.

That was what he had planned. But she had wanted to meet him. She had come today on the chance that he would be there. She had wanted to spend the afternoon with him just as he was—a sort of cripple of nondescript appearance with not even some of his finery to improve his looks.

She had wanted to be with Hartley Wade, landscape gardener. And she looked pleased to be with him.

How would she react to the knowledge of his real identity? Did he want to find out?

He was enjoying being Hartley Wade. He had never enjoyed anything more in his life. He wanted to continue as he was—just for this afternoon. At the end of it, or next time if there was a next time, he would tell her the truth. But not now.

"I expect to be at Highmoor for a while yet," he said. "There are several plans to make and the marquess to consult when he returns home. And then the work to supervise if he gives his approval and wishes to begin immediately. And I was disappointed, too. And so I came today, as soon as it was not raining. Just in case you would be here also."

She smiled brightly at him. She had white and perfect teeth. Her mouth curved up invitingly at the corners. It was the most kissable mouth he had ever seen.

"Well," she said, "I am recovered, Mr. Wade. Are you going to show me the lake? Is it far? And more to the point, is it all downhill?"

"But uphill on the way back," he said. "No, not far." He got to his feet but did not offer his hand to assist her. He was afraid to touch her. Even if he kept her on his left-hand side, she would be more aware of his limp if she held to his arm. And she might be embarrassed or disgusted. "You will like it. It is the most secluded and the loveliest part of the estate."

"I wonder if the Marquess of Carew appreciates his home," she said. "He is away from it a great deal, is he not? If I were the owner of all this beauty, I am not sure I could bear to leave it."

But there was loneliness to contend with when one lived at home, a loneliness that even houseguests could not quite alleviate. It was when he was at home that he felt most keenly the absence of a woman from his life. And children. But he despaired of ever finding the woman who would love him for himself.

Not that he had ever loved any woman—though he had

been fond of the woman who had been his mistress for five years before her sudden death a year and a half ago, the only mistress he had ever employed. But his feelings for her had not had the depth of love.

He suspected that his feelings for Miss Samantha Newman could have such depth, though at the moment he was only very much in love with her.

"He appreciates it," he said, "else why would he be going to such great expense to make it more lovely?"

"Perhaps," she said, "to make of it an even greater showpiece. But that was unkind. Please forgive me. I do not even know the gentleman. But Jenny—my cousin, Lady Thornhill—says that he is a pleasant gentleman."

Bless the earl's lady. She had never been anything but kind and courteous to him, though she was one of this world's beautiful people.

"Here we are," he said. "Mind your step. The slope is rather steep. I would hate to see you hurtle downward and straight into the water."

"It might forever prejudice my opinion against the place," she said with a laugh.

But she was not laughing a few moments later. She stopped when they were still almost at the top of the slope, when the lake came into view, nestled between the hill on one side and trees on the other. She stood for a few moments, saying nothing.

"Oh," she said at last, her voice hushed. "It must be the loveliest place on earth."

That was the moment when he knew that he was not in love with her, like any schoolboy with any beautiful woman.

That was when he knew, without any doubt and despite such a short acquaintance, that he loved her.

Chapter 3

There was something almost magical about it. The lake at Chalcote was lovely, with its wide expanse of water and the boathouse and the grassy banks on which the family picnicked and played. But this was different. This was—enchanted.

Perhaps it was the rather steep hill, she thought, and the trees on the other side. They enclosed it, making it seem in a little world of its own. They made the water look deep and still.

"Shall we go down?" he asked. "It is even lovelier from the water's edge."

They descended sedately, though she could see that the slope leveled off before it reached the water so that there was a flat bank on which to stand or sit. She was glad that he did not offer either his hand or his arm. She had noticed that he had never done so. Most gentleman would have, making her feel frail and ladylike. But touching meant physical awareness. It made one immediately aware that one was of a different gender from one's companion.

She was glad that there was no such awareness with Mr. Wade. It would have spoiled what she thought was a budding friendship. She had never had a gentleman as a friend, she realized. Not really.

Yes, he was right, she thought when they were standing on the bank, looking across the water. "Peace," she said quietly. "Perfect peace. It makes one aware of—oh, of what?"

"The presence of God?" he suggested.

"Yes." She closed her eyes and breathed in the smell of water and damp vegetation. "Yes, there are places like that, are there not? Churches almost always. Sometimes other places. This place."

"I have always liked it wild," he said, "though I would like to give it a touch of—of human appreciation. Perhaps a chapel." He laughed softly. "But that would be an affectation. Certainly nothing suggesting human activity. I did think once of boats and a boathouse, but I dismissed the idea as soon as it came to me. What do you think?"

"No boats," she said.

"A bridge, perhaps," he said, pointing to the narrow end of the lake, where a waterfall down the hillside poured in its waters. "The idea keeps returning to me. But a bridge to nowhere is another affectation, is it not?"

"A stone bridge," she said, "with arches. Three, I think. Leading to a small pavilion or summerhouse."

"Yes." He was silent for a few moments. "Fully enclosed with glass windows on all six or eight sides. Where one can sit and be warm."

"And dry," she said. She laughed. "A rain house. The lake must look lovely in the rain, with mist on the hills and in the trees."

"A rain house," he said softly. "I like it."

"It could be wonderfully cozy and peaceful," she said. "I believe I would spend a great deal of time there if I lived here."

"A bridge and a rain house," he said. "That is what it will be. I have puzzled for years over exactly what should be done here, and you have helped me solve the problem."

"Perhaps," she said, "you should employ me as your assistant, Mr. Wade."

He turned his head to smile at her. He had one of the loveliest smiles she had ever seen. It went all the way back inside his eyes and drew an answering smile from her.

"Could I afford you?" he asked.

"Probably not," she said. "Will the Marquess of Carew think you are quite mad when you suggest a bridge and a *rain* house here?"

"Quite possibly," he said. "But he has great faith in my judgment. And when he sees the finished products, he will fall in love with them without further ado."

"I hope so," she said. "I would not want them to be neglected."

They stood side by side, looking about them, in perfect harmony, perfect peace.

"I could live here happily for the rest of my life," she said at last with a sigh. But she chuckled at the thought. "If I were just the hermit type."

"Wearing a sackcloth shirt," he said, "and taking your morning plunge into the lake."

"Ugh," she said, shivering, and they both laughed. But she sobered again. "I suppose I should be going back to Chalcote. I must have been here an hour or longer. The time has flown."

"Have you ever seen the inside of the abbey?" he asked.

She shook her head.

"Would you like to?" he asked. "Tomorrow? I would love to show it to you."

"It does not seem proper," she said, "to view a gentleman's home when he is not in residence." It would be even more improper if he were, she thought.

"I would show you only the public rooms," he said. "There are numerous visitors here during the summer. The housekeeper is authorized to show them the parts of the house that are not private—the most magnificent parts. I know them well enough to show them, too."

Highmoor Abbey had looked so very beautiful from a distance. She was very tempted. And his eyes were smiling at her.

"Tomorrow?" he asked.

"Oh." She felt suddenly like a child being denied a treat.

"We are going visiting tomorrow. I could not possibly be rude enough to absent myself."

"The day after?" he suggested.

"And the day after we are expecting visitors." She pulled a face and smiled apologetically at him. But she had a sudden idea. "Will you come too? I know that Gabriel and Jenny—the earl and countess, you know—would be delighted." And yet as soon as she said it, she felt sorry. Absurd as it seemed, she did not want to share her friend with her family.

"I think not," he said quietly. "I had better stay here and at least pretend to work. But thank you."

They smiled regretfully at each other. She had enjoyed these two afternoons with him so very much. She thought he might have spoiled her forever for the normal sort of flirtatious afternoons she sometimes spent with gentlemen out driving or at garden parties. Friendship was so much more comfortable.

"I could come the afternoon after that," she said hopefully. "Will you still be here?"

"Yes," he said. "I was not sure you wanted to. It would be a long walk for you. Do you ride?"

"Yes," she said. "Of course."

"Perhaps I could meet you," he said. "At the gatehouse to Highmoor? The same time as today?"

She nodded and smiled. "I must go now," she said. "You need not come with me. It is a long walk to the stream and back."

"But like last time," he said, "I must make myself personally responsible for seeing all trespassers cleared from Highmoor property."

They scrambled up the bank together and then up to the top of the hill and down the slope to the stream and the stepping-stones to Chalcote land, chatting easily on a variety of topics. She stopped and turned to him before crossing to the other side.

"Thank you, Mr. Wade," she said. "This has been so pleasant."

"And for me," he said. "I shall look forward to seeing you three days from now."

After crossing the stones, she turned to wave to him before the trees cut him from her view. He was a gentleman, she thought, a single gentleman. And for longer than an hour on two separate afternoons she had been alone with him in secluded countryside, where they had not seen even one other person. No one knew where she was. And this second time she had deliberately met him. It was almost like a tryst they had arranged. It was dreadfully improper, even for a woman of four-and-twenty. Aunt Aggy would have a fit of the vapors if she knew. Gabriel would frown and look like Lucifer again. Even Jenny would look reproachful.

Why had it not seemed improper at all? Just because there was no flirtation involved, no touching, no romance? Or was it because of his appearance? He was such a very ordinary looking man—except perhaps when he smiled with his eyes, or with his whole face. And so totally unfashionable. And then there was the twisted, gloved hand and the heavy limp. Perhaps it was his appearance. She tried to imagine him as a handsome, perfectly made man. Would she feel the impropriety then? She rather thought she would. She would be attracted to such a man.

She felt no attraction at all to Mr. Wade. Except as a friend. She smiled. Except as a special companion.

The days crawled by. His utter solitude was his own fault, of course. If he had only made known his return home, he would have had callers. Thornhill would have been among the first. And he would have called on his neighbors. He would have had invitations to dinner. He would have issued invitations. Oh, yes, it was entirely his own fault that he was so very solitary.

And all because of a little creature so beautiful from the

outside of her person right through to her soul that she was as unattainable as a star in a different galaxy. All because he was afraid for her to know who he was, lest he see a change in her, lest he see her humanness. He did not want her to look on him as the immensely wealthy and eligible Marquess of Carew. He wanted her to continue to see him as plain—very plain—Hartley Wade.

Every smile she gave Hartley Wade was a treasure to be stored up for future pleasure, because each smile was guileless and sincere as well as utterly beautiful. Every word she spoke to him had been committed carefully to memory. *It must be the loveliest place on earth . . . Perhaps you should employ me as your assistant . . . I could live here happily for the rest of my life . . . Will you come, too? . . . This has been so pleasant.*

He did not want her to know. He wanted the fantasy to continue—for one more afternoon. And so he imposed seclusion on himself, not leaving his land lest he be seen and word should spread. He walked and rode about the park for almost every daylight hour of the two interminable days, thinking about her, dreaming about her, calling himself every abusive name he could think of, from idiot on down.

He could not sleep from thinking of her, and when he did sleep he dreamed of her, dreams in which she was always just beyond the reach of his outstretched arms, and always smiling at him and telling him how pleasant this had been.

One evening, after he had dismissed his valet for the night, he stood in front of a pier glass, dressed only in his shirt and pantaloons, and looked at himself—something he rarely did, apart from careless glances.

He smiled ruefully at his image and then looked downward and closed his eyes. How imbecilic he was being. He set his right hand on his left and massaged his palm with his left thumb, pressing hard over stiff tendons, pushing his fingers straight one by one. She must be the most beautiful little creature ever to have lived. How could any man look at her and not want her and love her? She could choose any man she wanted. She could choose the most handsome man in England. She doubtless had a large court of admirers. The reason she was still unwed at the age of four-and-twenty must be that her choices were legion.

And he dared to want her himself?

He opened his eyes and forced himself to look at his image again. He watched his thin, twisted hand being massaged and exercised—but never brought back quite to full use.

And he dared to love her himself?

If she knew who he was, a demon in his brain told him, perhaps she would want him. Or his title. Or his property. Or his wealth.

No woman could ever want *him*. Though Dorothea had loved him, he remembered. Not at first. He had been merely a man who could afford to pay for her favors and set her up with the security of a prolonged relationship. But she had grown to love him. She had told him so and he had believed her. He would always be grateful to her, poor Dorothea. He had been fond of her.

But Dorothea had been rather plump and plain, ten years his senior, an aging courtesan even when he had first gone to her to lose his virginity.

No other woman could ever want him. Certainly not Miss Samantha Newman. The idea was laughable. He laughed softly, his eyes closed again.

But she had enjoyed their two afternoons together. She had enjoyed his company. And there was to be another. She was going to allow him to show her his greatest treasure, his home. And he was going to have the memory of her there, inside Highmoor Abbey, gazing admiringly at all the state rooms. He was sure she would admire them. And all the while, as unobtrusively as he could, he would admire *her* and commit to memory her every look and gesture and word.

Oh, yes, he was going to remain Mr. Hartley Wade for one more afternoon. He prayed for good weather. In the meanwhile, the days seemed endless and dreary, and the only way he could bring himself any peace was to walk to the lake and stand on the bank staring at the place where the three-arched bridge and the rain house—he smiled at her name for the pavilion—would stand when he had had them constructed later in the year.

But the morning of the appointed day finally came, and then the afternoon. And all his prayers had been answered. Not only was it not raining, but the sun was shining down from a cloudless sky. There was even heat in the air. He gave instructions at the house before he left. Until they saw Miss Newman and drew their own conclusions, his staff would think him mad—first forbidding them to spread word of his return and now forbidding them to use his title for the rest of the day.

He rode down the long, winding driveway toward the gatehouse, from where he would be still out of sight of anyone riding along the road. He tried to persuade himself that he would not be too disappointed if she did not come.

But he knew as soon as he saw her, a scant two minutes after his own arrival, that he would have been very disappointed indeed. Devastated.

She saw him almost immediately and raised a hand in greeting. At the same time, her beautiful face lit up with a happy smile. Yes, happy. She was happy to see him.

She was dressed in a very smart and fashionable riding habit of dark green velvet. She wore an absurd little matching riding hat perched on her blond curls, its paler green feather curling enticingly down over one ear and beneath her chin. His mind searched for a more superlative word than beautiful but could not find one.

"Have you ever known a more glorious spring day?" she called to him gaily when she was within earshot.

"No, never," he said truthfully, smiling at her.

Never. And there would never be another such.

He did not take her immediately to the house. He took her off the driveway and through old and widely spaced trees.

"It was a tangled, overgrown, ancient forest," he said,

"and quite impenetrable except to wild animals of the smaller variety. I had it cleared out so that it could become a deer park and so that it could be walked and ridden in. Of course"—he laughed—"the marquess then decided that there was to be no hunting on his land. The deer have an idyllic life here."

"Oh," she said, "I am so glad. Do you disapprove?" She hoped he did not. She hoped he did not enjoy blood sports. But almost all men did. They saw it as a slur on their manhood to admit otherwise. Her respect for the Marquess of Carew rose.

"No," he said. "I created the deer park only on the understanding that it be in the nature of a preserve. Look." He pointed with his whip. There were five or them, lovely and stately and quite unafraid, though they must have seen and heard the horses and humans no more than a hundred feet away.

"How can anyone want to shoot them?" she said, and he smiled at her with his eyes.

He took her all the way around the more open part of the park, with the abbey always visible. From the front it still looked as if it might be a cathedral. The other three sides were a strange mixture of architectural designs. Successive marquesses had obviously all made their mark on the building. And yet the result was curiously pleasing. Samantha could not think of a house—and she had seen many of England's most stately—that she admired more.

"Thank you," Mr. Wade said when she told him so.

"Have you had a hand in its design, then?" she asked him.

He looked at her blankly for a moment before laughing. "No," he said. "But I shall pass along your compliment to the marquess. I am merely anticipating his response and expressing it to you while you are able to hear it."

"How absurd you are," she said.

The park was quite unconventionally designed. There were no formal parterre gardens before the house but only a wide cobbled terrace and several large flowerpots, empty at this time of year. But there were flower beds and rock gardens, some of them already full of green shoots; one of them, in a more sheltered area, was overflowing with blooming crocuses and primroses. But there was nothing symmetrical about their design. Most of them were unexpected, in hollows that were hidden from the eye until one was almost on top of them. All of them took careful advantage of the contours of the land.

"It is strange," she said. "But I like it. Is it your work?"

"Not so much my *work,* to be fair to the gardeners," he said. "But my design. I suppose it is strange. To the human mind, anyway, which demands orderliness and symmetry. Nature makes no such demands. Had you noticed? That tree on the slope where we first met, for example. And sometimes I have to argue a point with nature. But not always. I like to work with nature rather than against it, so that everything in a park looks natural even if it is not so in fact."

"You must have spent a great deal of time here," she said. "The marquess must have a deep respect for your work." Again her respect for the master went up.

"He has no artistic sense himself," he said, a twinkle in his eye. "But he can recognize it and encourage it in others. I have designed several parks in other parts of England. But this is my favorite."

"Do you live close to here?" she asked. It seemed a shame for him to have spent so much time and creative energy dreaming up such beauty if he rarely had the chance to see it all.

"Not too far away," he said. "Shall we take the horses to the stable and go into the abbey?"

"Yes, please," she said. She hoped the interior would not be disappointing. But she desperately wanted to see it for herself, now that she had been so close. She worried a little about what the servants would think. Would they know who she was? Would they be scandalized to see her alone with their master's hired landscape gardener? But she was not going to allow servants to spoil her afternoon. The three-day delay had seemed endless. And she had felt so happy to see him again, waiting for her at the gatehouse. Her friend.

The hall robbed her of breath. It was two stories high and seemingly all carved stone pillars and great Gothic arches. It felt as though one were walking into a cathedral.

"The oldest and most magnificent part of the house," he said. "Apart from the tiled floor, which my gr—, which my employer's grandfather had put down, this is the entryway almost exactly as it was until the abbey was confiscated by Henry the Eighth."

"Oh!" was the most intelligent comment she could think to make.

A footman bowed to her after Mr. Wade had signaled to him, and took her hat and her whip and the outer jacket of her riding habit. He made a very stiff half-bow to Mr. Wade and, without a word, took his hat and whip. Samantha found herself biting her lower lip at the obvious slight. They must see him here as a servant, little better than themselves, though he was very obviously a gentleman. Servants could be far more discourteous than their betters. But Mr. Wade made no comment. Perhaps he had not noticed.

They spent all of an hour walking about the state rooms—the grand ballroom, the drawing room, the dining room, the reception hall, the bedchamber where King Charles the Second himself had once slept. She looked at Rembrandts and Van Dycks and one magnificent seascape by Mr. Reynolds. It was all more glorious than even she could have pictured.

"Imagine living here," she said to Mr. Wade when they were in the ballroom, stretching her arms wide and twirling twice about. "Imagine all this being your very own."

"Would you like it?" he asked.

"Perhaps not." She stopped twirling. "Surroundings are not everything, are they? There are other things more important." She laughed. "But that will not stop me from *imagining* living here."

"You should marry the Marquess of Carew," he said.

"Indeed." She laughed. "He is a single gentleman, is he not? How old is he? Is he young and handsome? Or is he old and doddering? But no matter. Bring him on and I will set about charming him witless."

"Would you?" He was smiling at her, his head to one side.

"The Marchioness of Carew," she said, waving an imaginary fan languidly before her face. "It has a definite ring to it, does it not? I do believe you should bow to me, sir."

"Do you?" He did not bow.

"I shall have you beheaded for insubordination," she said, raising her chin and looking along the length of her nose at him. "I shall have my husband, the marquess, order it. The marchioness. Of Highmoor Abbey in Yorkshire, you know." She waved a hand before his face for him to kiss.

He did not kiss it.

"I told you I am still a child at heart," she said, reverting to her normal self. "I would not try charming him even if he were the proverbial tall, dark, and handsome gentleman—like Gabriel. I would not exchange my freedom even for all this." She waved an arm about the ballroom without looking away from his face.

"Is your freedom so precious to you, then?" he asked.

"Yes," she said. "Have you wondered why I am unwed at my age? It is because I have decided never to marry."

"Ah," he said. There was a smile in his eyes, but very far back. Most people would not have even realized that it was there. "I think you must have been hurt badly."

She was jolted with surprise. Gentlemen were in the habit of telling her that she was the happiest, sunniest-natured lady of their acquaintance.

"Yes," she said. "A long time ago. It does not matter any longer."

"Except," he said, "that it has blighted your life."

"It has not," she said. "Oh, it has not. What a strange thing to say."

"Forgive me," he said, smiling more fully. "Come to my office and let me order tea. It is the marquess's office, of course, but I have appropriated it for my use while I am here and he is not."

Friends knew each other, she thought. He had seen something that no one else had ever seen. And he had perceived something about her that even she had not perceived—or not admitted, anyway. Had her life been blighted? Had she allowed *him* such power over her?

"Thank you," she said. "Tea would be nice."

Chapter 4

He was glad he had thought of offering her tea in his office rather than in the drawing room. He found the drawing room cold and impersonal unless he was entertaining a large gathering. His office, on the other hand, was where he spent most of his time indoors when he was out of his own apartments. It was a cozy room, not small really, but filled with his own personal treasures and never quite tidy since the maids had learned not to move books—especially ones that lay open.

He seated her in an ancient, comfortable chair to one side of the fire, which his servants always made up as soon as he stepped inside the house, and sat in its twin at the opposite side. His father had been going to have the chairs thrown out years ago, calling them a disgrace to so grand a place as Highmoor Abbey, but he had appropriated them for his study and he did not believe he would ever let them go.

Now he knew that he would not. And he knew that his study would become even more precious to him in the future, because the greatest treasure of his life had been there for tea one afternoon. She looked small and dainty in the chair. She looked comfortable.

He was glad she had made a joke of marrying the Marquess of Carew after some demon in him had made him suggest it as a possibility. But he was sorry that someone had broken her heart. She made light of it now and she always seemed cheerful enough, but he did not believe he had exaggerated in saying that it had blighted her life. Most ladies of her age would have been married long ago and have had children in the nursery by now. Especially ladies as lovely as she was. But there was no other lady as lovely as she. . . .

They talked about books after she had seen some of the titles of those lying on the small table beside her. And about music and opera and the theater. Their tastes were similar, though she had never studied Latin or Greek, as he had, and she had never read the plays she had seen performed. And she preferred a tenor voice to a soprano, unlike him, and a cello to a violin. Both of them preferred the pianoforte to either.

He had never known a woman easier to talk to. But then he had never known a lady who was unaware of his identity. He wondered if it made a difference. She had said in the ballroom that she would not set her cap at the Marquess of Carew even if she had the opportunity to do so. But if she did know that he was the marquess instead of just a gentleman so far down on his luck that he was forced to hire out his services as a landscape gardener—if she did know, would it make a difference? Would she be less comfortable with him? Would she feel the impropriety of their behavior more acutely? She seemed quite unaware of it now. And yet it was even more dreadfully improper for them to be indoors alone together thus than it had been for them to roam the park together.

"What happened?" she asked him quietly. He realized that they had been sitting through one of their silences, which never seemed awkward, and that he had absently fallen into one of his habits. He was massaging his right palm with his left thumb and straightening his fingers one by one. Her eyes were on his hands. "Was it an accident? Or were you born—" Her eyes flew to his face and she blushed. "I am so sorry. It is none of my business. Please forgive me."

It was a measure of the friendship that had grown be-

tween them, perhaps, that he could tell her, a virtual
stranger, that an unhappy love affair the details of which he
did not know had blighted her life, and that she could ask
him what had happened to leave his right hand and foot deformed. Good manners would have kept both of them silent
on such personal matters had they been merely acquaintances.

"It was an accident." He smiled at her as he told her the
lie he had been telling for most of his life. He had never told
the truth, even to his parents right after it had happened.
There was no point in telling the truth now. "I was six years
old. I was out riding my new pony with my cousin." His
cousin had been ten. "We had left the groom far behind. I
was showing off, showing how I could gallop to match the
pace of a cousin four years older than me, and showing how
I could jump a fence. But I did not clear it. I crashed very
heavily right down onto the fence, breaking bones and tear-
ing ligaments. By some miracle my pony escaped serious
harm. The physician told my father that both my leg and my
arm would have to be amputated, but fortunately for me my
mother had a totally genuine fit of the vapors."

He smiled at her grimace of horror.

"It was a long time ago," he said. "The physician did his
best to set the broken bones, but of course there was permanent damage. Both my father and I were told that I would
never be able to use either my right leg or my right arm
again. But I can be stubborn about some things."

"Courageous," she said. "Determined."

"Stubborn." He laughed. "My mother shrieked when she
first saw me limping about and swore that I would do myself dreadful harm. My father merely commented that I
would make myself the laughingstock."

"Poor little boy," she said, head to one side, blue eyes large
with sympathy. "Children should not have to suffer so."

"Suffering can make all the difference in a person's life,"
he said. "It can be a definite force for good. At the risk of
sounding conceited, I would have to say that I am reason-

ably happy with the person I have become. Perhaps I would not have liked the person I would have been without the accident." Perhaps he would have always been the sniveling, cringing, self-pitying coward he had been as a young child.

"I am sorry for my unmannerly curiosity," she said. "Please forgive me."

"There is nothing to forgive," he said. "Friends talk from the heart, do they not? I believe we have become friends. Have we?"

"Yes." She smiled slowly and warmly. "Yes, we have, Mr. Wade."

There was not even the glimmering of a sign in her eyes that they were anything more than that. Of course. How foolish of him even to have dreamed of such a thing, let alone to have hoped. But how unbelievably wonderful it was to see Miss Samantha Newman smiling so kindly at him and agreeing with him that they were friends.

"And this friend," he said, getting reluctantly to his feet, "had better see you on your way back to Chalcote before every constable in the county is called out to search for you. You did not tell Thornhill or his lady where you were going?"

"No." She flushed rather guiltily as she got up herself without his assistance. "They might have thought it improper. My aunt—Lady Brill—might have felt obliged to accompany me as chaperon. I suppose it *is* improper. I suppose I should have a chaperon. But it does not feel wrong, and I do not feel the need of a female protector. And if one cannot exercise a little personal judgment and enjoy a little freedom at such an advanced age as mine, one might as well be shut up inside a cage." She laughed lightly.

"I will ride with you as far as the gatehouse," he said, opening the door of the study for her to precede him from the room. "There is a folly overlooking the lake that I have not shown you yet. And farther back behind the house there is a stretch of rapids where the stream flows downhill. I have ideas for creating a more spectacular series of waterfalls there, but I do not want to spoil the natural beauty. I

would like to hear your opinion. Will you walk there with
me, perhaps three afternoons from today?"

She turned her head to smile at him as they left the house,
her jacket back on and her hat at an even jauntier angle than
before. "I would love to," she said, "and will studiously resist all attempts to organize any other entertainment for that
afternoon. I shall pray piously for good weather."

"The usual time at the top of the hill?" he asked.

"Yes." She laughed. "By the time I return to London for
the Season, I shall be the fittest dancer in any ballroom. I
shall smile in sympathy at the ladies and gentlemen wheezing all around me after the first set of country dances."

He wished he could dance. He had always wished it, perhaps because he knew that he never could. He avoided ballrooms. Although he spent almost as much time in London
during the year as most other gentlemen, he rarely accepted
any of his invitations to the round of social activities that
accompanied the Season. He was not very well known, especially by the ladies of the *ton,* despite his rank and fortune and eligible marital status.

"I wish I could be there to see it," he said. They had ridden
their horses out of the stable yard and turned in the direction
of the gatehouse, a mile or so distant. "This lawn stretches all
the way to the gatehouse. It is temptingly long and level, is it
not? Do you enjoy taking your horse to a gallop?"

She looked at him and down to his right leg. She opened
her mouth to ask if he was sure he ought to—he was certain
that was what she was about to say. But she bit her lip instead, and when her eyes came back up to his, there was
mischief dancing in them.

"I will race you," she said, and she was off before he
could recover from his surprise, her laughter almost a shriek.

He stayed half a length behind her, enjoying her excitement and her exuberance—and also her careful and excellent
horsemanship. Another episode to commit to memory, he
thought as he surged past her when they were only yards from
the gatehouse. He turned his head to laugh at her chagrin.

"Unfair," she said, her voice breathless. "Oh, unfair. Gabriel has given me a horse lame in all four legs."

"That is an insulting fib for which you can expect to fry," he said, looking over the splendid chestnut she rode. "The Earl of Thornhill keeps the best stables in these parts—or so I have heard. We did not agree on a wager."

"Oh," she said, pretending to the sullenness of defeat. "What do you suppose I owe you?"

"That is a delightful feather in your cap," he said. "Literally, I mean."

"My—" Her laughter was more of a giggle as she removed her hat. "I am not at all sure that it is detachable, and I would hate to have to give you the whole hat, sir. If there is anything more scandalous than riding about the countryside alone, it is doing so hatless. I would never live down the ignominy if someone were to see me. Ah, here it comes."

And she handed him the curled green feather that had been circling her head and nestling against her ear and beneath her chin.

"Thank you." He inclined his head and chuckled as she pinned the absurd hat back on her hair. "If anyone asks, you will have to say it blew away in the wind."

He raised a hand in farewell as she rode off. He then placed the feather carefully in his right hand before taking up the reins with his left once more and turning back in the direction of home.

He wondered what she would think if she knew that the prize she had just awarded him would be treasured more than any of the costliest of his possessions for the rest of his life.

It was a good thing that one person could not see into another's mind or heart, he thought. What a fool he would appear to her if she could see into his. And how horrified she would be.

Three days. How would he fill them? How would he stop himself from descending to the horribly immature measure of counting the hours?

* * *

The day finally came and the sun was shining. Still. It had
not stopped shining all through every day since the afternoon of her visit to Highmoor Abbey. The law of averages
said that it must rain soon, but she had hoped—foolishly,
she had even prayed—that it would not be today.

She did not know why she valued Mr. Wade's friendship
so dearly. He was a man of very ordinary appearance, and
she would guess that though he was a gentleman, he was
poor. But then she was not looking at him as a possible
suitor, so his appearance and his financial status were of no
concern to her at all. That was why she valued him so
much, she decided. She had always felt some physical attraction to all the gentlemen who made up her court—she
was beginning to describe them to herself by that term,
after hearing it from Gabriel so often. She could not have
encouraged them and flirted with them and held them always at arm's length if she had not.

She felt no attraction whatsoever to Mr. Wade. No revulsion, either, of course, despite the physical handicaps.
Just—oh, just the warmth of friendship. She could not remember the person, man or woman, whose company she
had more enjoyed and more yearned for when she was not
with him. Even Jenny, she thought disloyally, had never
been such a dear friend.

She hoped he would not have to go away soon. He had
spoken of planning waterfalls north of the house. He had
spoken of seeing the work at the lake started this year. Surely
he stayed to oversee his plans brought to fruition when he
was designing something new. Would he stay all summer?

But she would not be staying that long, she remembered
with a jolt. She would be going to London for the Season.
She always went to London for the Season. This would be
her seventh—she would wince at the number, perhaps, if
she were in search of a husband. Many young ladies considered it an unutterable humiliation to have to go back for a
second Season unattached. Jenny and Gabriel were not planning to go this year. They did not always go, being far hap-

pier in the country romping with their children. And Jenny had told her in an unguarded moment—and been mortally embarrassed afterward—that they were trying for another.

Perhaps, Samantha thought, she would stay at Chalcote this year, too. But she dismissed the thought immediately. Kind and hospitable as they both were, Jenny and Gabriel needed to have their home to themselves for at least a part of the year. And she and Aunt Aggy had already been here for three months. Too long. Soon—as soon as she had control of her fortune—Samantha was going to set up for herself somewhere so that she would have a home of her own in which to spend those slack months when there was nothing much happening anywhere but in country homes.

No, she could not stay at Chalcote. Soon she and Aunt Aggy must return to London. But she tried to put the thought from her mind. There would be another few weeks first. Another few chances to explore Highmoor land with Mr. Wade. If he wanted to explore them with her, of course. If he did not tire of their friendship.

She did not really understand what the attraction of the friendship was. She did not try to understand it. She was too busy enjoying it.

But it was not to last much longer after all. She was sitting alone at the breakfast table, staring into space. Gabriel and Albert had gone off riding about some business somewhere, and Jenny was in the nursery with Mary, who had fallen out of bed during the night and bumped her head and was still feeling the need of her mother's soothing words and arms.

Aunt Agatha came into the breakfast room, bringing with her the usual pile of letters from her friends in London. She kissed her niece, exchanged pleasantries with her, took toast and coffee, and settled to reading the latest news and gossip from town after Samantha had assured her that no, of course she did not mind if Aunt Agatha was unsociable for a few minutes.

"Oh, dear," her aunt said after three of those minutes had passed. "Oh, dear, oh, dear. Poor Sophie."

"Is Lady Sophia ill?" Samantha inquired politely.

"An oaf of a coachman ran her down when she was crossing the street," her aunt said, still frowning down at her letter. "He even had the nerve to curse her and to ride off without stopping. She was carried home with a broken leg."

"How nasty," Samantha said, concerned. "I do hope she is not in too much discomfort."

"She is," Lady Brill said. "But worse than that, she is languishing for lack of company, poor Sophie. You know how visiting and exchanging news is the breath of life to her, Samantha, dear."

"Yes." Samantha could not quite suppress a smile. Being confined to her own home with a broken leg must be fairly killing her aunt's closest friend.

But the smile was wiped away almost immediately. "I must go to her," Lady Brill said decisively. "Poor, dear Sophie. And almost no one in town yet to pay her calls. The least I can do, dearest—the very least—is go to sit with her in her hour of need."

Selfishly, the implications for Samantha herself were instantly apparent to her. But so were her obligations.

"When shall we leave?" she asked.

"Oh." Lady Brill looked at her and her frown became worried. "I will be dragging you away from dear Jennifer and Lord Thornhill weeks earlier than we expected. But you cannot stay here, can you, dear? There will be no one with whom to travel back to town next month for the Season. You certainly could not travel alone. Will you mind very, very much? Poor Sophie, you know."

Samantha leaned across the table to set a hand over her aunt's. She minded very much indeed, but for a reason that was quite foolish from any rational consideration. "Of course I will not mind," she said. "I think it very sweet of you to want to return to keep Lady Sophia company. And why should I mind being in town, even if the Season has not yet begun? There is always something to do there. Besides, I need a whole new wardrobe of clothes. I have simply nothing to wear that everyone has not already seen."

"That is very sweet of you, dear," Lady Brill said, looking relieved. "Very sweet indeed. And perhaps this will be the year when you will find the gentleman of your dreams. He will come along, mark my words, even though you keep insisting that you are not even in search of him. I have never heard such nonsense in my life."

Samantha smiled. "When do you want to leave?" she asked. *Please not today. Oh, please, not today.*

"Tomorrow morning?" her aunt asked apologetically. "As early as possible. Will that be too much of a rush for you, dear?"

The door opened at that moment and Lady Thornhill came in. She assured them that Mary, who was not normally a clinging infant, had thoroughly enjoyed her moment of tragedy but could no longer resist the urge to play with Emily and Jane. Michael had gone with the men.

"Oh," she said, looking genuinely dismayed when Lady Brill had given her news and told of their plans, "are we to lose you both so soon, then? I had counted on at least another two or three weeks."

And yet, Samantha thought as she made her way upstairs soon after to give her maid instructions to begin packing for the next day's journey, Jenny must feel some relief, too, to know that soon she was to have Gabriel and her children to herself again. Albert and Rosalie were to leave within the week.

In six years, Samantha had not envied her cousin's married state. She had only pitied her, even though she had always been well aware that Jenny's marriage had quickly developed from its disastrous beginning into a very deep love match. Today for the first time she felt—oh, not envy. No. Nor loneliness. Only—she could not put a word to what she felt.

But she did feel sorrow to know that this afternoon's meet-

ing with Mr. Wade was to be the last. It was very unlikely
that she would ever see him again, even though it seemed that
he had been to Highmoor several times. It would be just too
unrealistic to expect that any future visit of his there would
coincide with one of her own to Chalcote. And extremely unlikely that she would encounter him anywhere else.

This afternoon would be their final meeting, then. And
she would not even be able to suggest that they correspond,
despite the fact that they were friends. They were, after all,
a single gentleman and a single lady, who had no ties of
blood. They could not correspond. Some things were just
too improper to be seriously considered.

She left early for her meeting with him. Yet she hurried
toward her destination as if she were late. She hurried with
eager footsteps and a heavy heart. She did not want the
friendship to end. And she resented the fact that it must end
just because social convention frowned heavily on any relationship between a man and a woman that did not lead
them in due course to the altar.

It was very foolish.

She had no wish whatsoever to go to the altar with Mr.
Wade.

But she had every wish in the world to have him as a
friend.

She briefly wondered why.

She was very early at the meeting place. At least half an
hour early, she estimated, though she had no watch with
her. She was going to have a long wait. She did not want to
wait. This afternoon was too precious. Their last together.

But as she approached the temple at the top of the hill, he
stood up from the stone bench inside it and waited for her
to come up to him. He was as unfashionable and as shabby
as ever. He was smiling.

His smile warmed her more than the sun.

"You see?" she called gaily. "I have come all this distance and am hardly out of breath."

"My heartiest congratulations," he said.

Chapter 5

She was all in pink, except for her straw bonnet, and as pretty as the proverbial picture. She was flushed and bright-eyed, and it was pleasant for a moment to imagine that she was a woman hurrying to meet her lover—him.

Pleasant and absurd.

"Since you are not at all breathless," he said, "you will, of course, not need to rest here for a while. We will march onward to the rapids, shall we?"

"Ah," she said, laughing. "How ungentlemanly you are. You have called my bluff." She went past him and collapsed with exaggerated exhaustion onto the bench. "You are early."

"And so are you," he said. "Weather like this is not to be wasted, is it?" He sat down beside her, careful to leave a few inches of space between them.

"How long are you planning to be here at Highmoor?" she asked him. "Long? Or will you be leaving soon?"

She was beginning to feel the impropriety, he guessed. Perhaps she was finding it increasingly difficult to give reasonable excuses to her relatives for so many afternoon absences. She was hoping that he would leave soon so that she would not have to tell him their meetings must end. He felt infinitely sad.

"I will probably be staying for a while," he said. "But—"

"I am leaving tomorrow," she said hurriedly and breathlessly. Her face was turned toward the sky, but her eyes were tightly closed. "I have to return to London with my aunt. Her friend has been housebound by an accident; Aunt Aggy wants to be with her. We will be leaving early in the morning."

He felt panic coil inside him. "The Season will be beginning soon enough," he said. "I daresay you will be happy to be back in town."

She had opened her eyes and was looking down the hill and across the fields and meadows below.

"Yes," she said. "I have many friends there, and more will be arriving every week. And there is always something to do in town. Sir Albert and Lady Boyle will be leaving Chalcote within the week. Jenny and Gabriel will enjoy having their home to themselves again, though they would be far too polite to admit as much even to each other, I would think. Yes, it will be good to be back. I am looking forward to it."

He was memorizing her profile—long-lashed blue eyes, straight little nose, sweetly curving lips, soft skin with a becoming blush of color on her cheeks, shining blond curls beneath the brim of her bonnet, the very feminine though not voluptuous curve of her bosom.

He wondered if he was being hopelessly fanciful, hopelessly romantic, to believe that he would always remember her, always love her.

She turned her head and smiled at him, and it pleased him to imagine that there was a certain bleakness in her eyes. "And you will be able to work without interruption when I am gone," she said.

"Yes." He dared not think of how he was going to feel after she had gone.

"You really are no gentleman." Her smile deepened. "You are supposed to assure me that I have been no bother at all and that you will miss me when I am gone."

"You have been no bother at all," he said. "I will miss you when you are gone."

"And I will miss you," she said. If there had been any wistfulness in her expression, it vanished instantly. "I have never met a landscape gardener before. I did not realize there were such people. I thought one merely sallied outdoors with a spade and a trowel and some flower seeds and set about creating one's garden."

He laughed.

"I thought follies grew up out of the soil—quite accidentally in the most picturesque places," she said. "And in my naiveté, I thought that all lakes and waterfalls and views were created by nature. I did not know there were men who liked to follow in God's footsteps, correcting his mistakes."

He laughed again. "Is that what I am doing?" he asked her. "It sounds rather dangerous for my chances in the hereafter, does it not? Do you think God will be offended?"

She chuckled with him but failed to take her turn in the conversation. They were left, when the laughter ended, looking at each other, a mere few inches apart. For the first time there was an awkwardness between them, a need to fill the silence.

She filled it first. "Where are the rapids?" she asked.

He scrambled to his feet. "A good march away," he said. "I hope your shoes are comfortable." As well as dainty. She had abandoned her half boots today. Her unshod foot, he thought, would fit on the palm of his hand.

"If I get blisters," she said, "I will have a few days of carriage travel in which to nurse them. What a horrid thought. I hate lengthy carriage journeys. One feels at the end of them that every bone in one's body has been jostled into a different position. One is reluctant to peep into a looking glass for fear that one will be unrecognizable." She laughed gaily.

They laughed a great deal during the rest of the afternoon and talked mostly nonsense. They were comfortable and happy together. Oh, yes, and vastly uncomfortable, too, somewhere beneath the surface of their gaiety. It was always very difficult to live through the last event of a good interlude, he thought. One could not enjoy it. One was too aware of the need to enjoy it to the full because there would be no more.

The afternoon was an agony to him.

He could remember sitting at Dorothea's bedside when she was nearing the end—it had come unbelievably quickly. She had been conscious and able to listen and even to talk a little. It had been so hard to talk to her. There had always been the awareness—*these might be the very last words I will ever speak to her*. And she had been good to him. He had wanted to say something memorable—not that she would have long in which to remember.

She was the one who had said it—and he had remembered ever since. *I am so very fortunate*, she had whispered to him over and over again during what had turned out to be their last hour together. He thought she had meant that she was fortunate to die while she was still his mistress, before he tired of her. He had been humbled by her devotion. And so he had told her the big lie, and had never been sorry. *I love you, my sweet*, he had whispered back.

Partings were such wrenchingly dreadful things. He knew by her manner that Samantha did not look forward to this one, but for her, of course, it was a mere friendship that was ending. She would feel sorrow rather than agony. And so he had the extra burden during the afternoon of hiding his own excruciating pain. For three days he had counted the hours. Now he was counting minutes, not knowing exactly how many he had left.

She loved the rapids, with their bare, jutting rocks and the canopy of trees overhead and the sense—created by the sound of rushing water—of utter seclusion. The laughter and the bantering stopped for several minutes while she wandered slowly up and down the rocky bank and he gazed at her.

"Not a huge waterfall," she said to him at last. "It would be too much, too overpowering. It is wildness that is called for here rather than grandeur. But a series of smaller falls, yes. It would be an improvement—if this can be improved upon. Oh, it is lovely, Mr. Wade. How I envy the Marquess of Carew his home."

That had been his thought exactly—a series of falls

rather than one great one. Something to stand beside and stroll beside. Something to catch the light and shade at different angles.

"I am sorry," she said, looking at him with contrite eyes. "You are the landscaper. I was merely to approve or disapprove your ideas. Now tell me that you planned a huge waterfall and I shall squirm with embarrassment."

"Your mind must be attuned to mine," he said. "You suggested exactly what I had planned."

She set her head to one side in a characteristic gesture that he would always remember about her. It was something she did when she thought of something particularly important to her. "Yes, that is it," she said. "The reason we are friends. We think alike."

"But you do not like sopranos," he said.

"Yes, I do." She smiled. "But I prefer tenors."

They were back to the lightness and the laughter. And the sadness.

He considered asking her back to the house for tea. But they had spent too long on their walk. Besides, he had the feeling that being indoors with her, sipping on their tea, would be awkward this afternoon. He considered taking her to the folly above the lake he had mentioned to her at the house. But it was too late. And again, sitting in such a quiet, secluded spot, there would be awkwardness. He did not believe that this afternoon they would be able to sit through one of their companionable silences.

"It is time for me to go home," she said quietly, the lightness and laughter gone from her voice again.

"Yes," he said. "They will wonder where you are."

It was a long walk back to the stream. He had the impression that she wanted to stride along quickly. But she had to match her pace to his limp. He could have suggested that they part company before reaching it, as she had suggested on two previous occasions, but he did not do so. He could not let her go before he had to, agonizing as these final minutes were.

They walked in silence.

The sun was sparkling off the water of the stream. There were daffodil buds among the trees on the other side. He had not noticed before that they were almost ready to bloom.

She turned to him. "Thank you for these afternoons," she said with formal politeness. "They have been very pleasant."

"Thank *you*." He made her a half-bow. "I hope you have a safe journey. And a pleasurable Season."

"Thank you," she said. "I hope the Marquess of Carew will approve all the renovations you have planned."

She smiled at him.

He smiled at her.

"Well," she said briskly. "Good-bye, Mr. Wade."

"Good-bye, Miss Newman," he said. He thought that she was going to offer him her hand, but she did not. Perhaps she found the thought of touching his right hand distasteful—though he did not really believe it was that.

She turned and tripped lightly across the stepping-stones, holding her skirt high enough that he had a glimpse of her trim ankles above the dainty shoes. He waited for the final moment, schooled his features for it. He had his smile ready and his left hand ready.

She did not turn back. Within moments she was lost among the trees.

He was left feeling that he had been robbed of something infinitely precious. Something quite, quite irreplaceable. He was left feeling emptiness and panic and a pain deeper than any he had felt before, even if he included the year following his "accident" when he was six. This was not a physical pain and he did not know how it was to be healed. Or whether it could be healed.

He swallowed three times against a gurgling in his throat before turning to make his weary way back to Highmoor Abbey.

She had hugged and kissed the children and left them in the nursery with their nurse. She had hugged Rosalie, though Albert had warned her to be careful not to squash his new offspring and won for himself a look of gentle reproach from his blushing wife. She had shaken hands with him and with Gabriel and then turned both cheeks for the latter's kiss. He had held onto her hand and told her that she must come back at any time her court could spare her and for as long as she wished.

"You are as close as any sister to Jennifer, my dear," he said. "You must not neglect her out of any mistaken idea that you are imposing on our hospitality."

"Thank you," she whispered to him and squeezed his hand tightly.

She hated good-byes. *Hated* them.

And then, just outside the carriage, she watched as Jenny kissed Aunt Aggy and Gabriel handed the older lady inside. Then Samantha hugged Jenny herself.

"I have had a wonderful time here," she said. "Thank you so much for having me. I do wish you were coming to town for the Season. It is going to seem an age."

"I believe," her cousin whispered to her, "I do believe, Sam, that I have good reason for staying away from the bustle of town life this spring. Keep your fingers crossed for me."

"Are you whispering secrets, my love?" Gabriel asked, looking sternly at his wife. "Is she telling you how we seem about to increase the world's population, Samantha?"

They both blushed while he chuckled.

"Allow me," he said, offering Samantha his hand.

And then she was inside the carriage, sitting next to Aunt Aggy, who was dabbing a handkerchief to her eyes and trying her hardest not to snivel. Samantha patted her knee reassuringly.

They were on their way. They both leaned forward to wave. Jenny and Gabriel were standing together on the terrace, his arm about her waist. Albert and Rosalie were in the doorway, her arm linked through his. Sometimes, Samantha thought, it was hard to know why she distrusted love and marriage so much. But she saw far more marriages in which there was either mutual indifference or open hostility than unions like these two. And love, she knew from experience, was an extremely unpleasant emotion.

She sat back in her seat and closed her eyes. She drew a slow and deep breath. She hated partings, even those that were only temporary.

"There, that is done," her aunt said briskly, blowing her nose rather loudly and putting her handkerchief away inside her reticule. "I always feel fine once I have made my farewells and driven out of sight. I must say we had a very pleasant stay, dear. It is just a pity that there were so few eligible gentlemen for you to meet."

Aunt Agatha was of the undying opinion that Prince Charming himself was about to make an appearance in her niece's life to sweep her off her feet in true fairy-tale tradition.

"I enjoyed the week Francis was here," Samantha said. "He is always good company."

"And he adores you," Aunt Agatha said. "But I cannot like the idea of your marrying a gentleman who favors lavender coats, Samantha."

Samantha laughed.

"It is a great shame," her aunt said, "that the Marquess of Carew was not in residence—yet again. He is a single gentleman and by no means in his dotage, or so I have heard. I have never met him, which seems strange, really, does it not? I believe he must be somewhat reclusive. Though if that were true, one would expect him to live at home most of the time. Yet he certainly does not do that."

"Perhaps he is unbelievably handsome," Samantha said, "and if I but met him, I would fall wildly in love with him and he with me and we would be wed within the month." She always enjoyed teasing Aunt Aggy, who did not really have much of a sense of humor—mainly because she did not always recognize that she was being teased.

"Well, dear," she said, "I must confess that has been my hope ever since Jennifer married Lord Thornhill and we first came here and discovered that Chalcote marches right alongside Highmoor land. Maybe next time. Though it is altogether possible that before that you will have found the gentleman you dream of. The Season always brings some new faces to town."

They were passing the imposing stone gateposts leading to Highmoor land. Just beyond them, not quite in sight, was the gatehouse. And a mile or more beyond that, Highmoor Abbey. Behind it—a good way behind it—the trees and the stream and the rapids. And to the right of that, the hills and the lake and then the stream again, forming the border between Chalcote and Highmoor.

There was an ache in Samantha's chest that had been there since the afternoon before. It puzzled her. It was not that she did not know its cause. She did. But the ache, the sense of grief, seemed far in excess of the circumstances.

They had been wonderful afternoons—all four of them. Unconventional, carefree afternoons with a companion whose mind was in tune with her own. Not a handsome or in any way attractive companion—not physically, at least. Nothing that would help explain the depression she was feeling at the knowledge that she would never see him again, that they would never again spend such an afternoon together.

She had not even been able to turn back yesterday after crossing the stream to wave to him, as she had done on the other three afternoons. Stupidly, she had been afraid that she was about to cry.

She wished now that she could go back and wave. Have one last look at him.

She leaned forward suddenly and peered through the window. A hedgerow hid it from sight almost immediately. But she had not been mistaken. For the merest moment she had been able to see the abbey in the distance.

She was surprised and utterly mortified a moment later to hear a great hiccup of an inelegant sob and to realize that it had come from her. She bit her upper lip hard enough to draw blood, but she could not stop the terrible ache in her throat or the tears that spilled over onto her cheeks.

She hoped that Aunt Aggy had fallen asleep. But it was much too soon for that.

"Oh, my poor dear," her aunt said, patting her back as Samantha had patted her knee a few minutes earlier. "You and Jennifer are so close that it is a joy to see. Though I feel for you now when you are driving away from her. And all because I wanted to give dear Sophie some of my company. You will feel better once we have stopped for luncheon and put some distance between us and Chalcote."

"Yes," Samantha said. "I know I will, Aunt Agatha. I am just being foolish."

She felt very guilty.

Life quickly became less solitary. He let word seep out that he was at home. There were callers—several of them. Thornhill was first, as he had expected, riding over from Chalcote with his friend, Sir Albert Boyle. They were pleasant company, the two of them. Thornhill and the marquess were in the way of being friends now, though there had been too many years between them when they were growing up for them to have been boyhood chums.

He was invited to Chalcote the following evening for dinner and enjoyed the company of his amiable, kind-hearted hosts and their friends. He was amused to see the terror die out of the eyes of the extremely shy Lady Boyle almost as soon as she had been presented to him and realized that he was not an imposing or a forbidding figure, despite the grandeur of his title. He set himself to putting her even more at her ease and found the subject that loosened her tongue and relaxed her tension. Before the evening was over, he felt that he knew her children as well as anyone, though he had not set eyes on them. He guessed that the third, which she was carrying quite visibly despite the discreetly loose folds of her gown, would be no burden to her.

"What a pity it is that you did not arrive home two days

sooner, my lord," Thornhill's lady said. "My aunt and my cousin have just returned to London after a three-month stay. I would have so liked for you to have met them."

"Miss Newman is in possession of both youth and beauty," Thornhill said, amusement in his voice. "I believe my wife has matchmaking tendencies, Carew."

"Oh, you wretch!" his lady said in dismay. "I have no such leanings, my lord. I merely thought it would have been pleasant for them to have met you and for you to have met them. Oh, do stop grinning at me, Gabriel. I do believe I am *blushing*."

The marquess had always liked them as a couple. Courteous and well-bred as they undoubtedly were, there were frequent glimpses of the informality and deep affection of their personal relationship.

"What Gabe means," Sir Albert said, "is that Jennifer is very close to her cousin and would love nothing better than to have her established permanently on an adjoining estate."

"Oh," the countess said, outraged, "this is the outside of enough. This is infamous. Now I *know* I am blushing. What will you think of us, my lord?"

He laughed. "I am wishing," he said, "that I might have had a look at this paragon. But, alas, it seems that I am too late. It is the story of my life. Lady Boyle, do you find that your children thrive on Yorkshire air? We Yorkshiremen have thought of bottling it and sending it south at a profit, you know."

The conversation turned into different channels.

And there were other callers, other invitations. The Ogdens had a niece staying with them and clearly had hopes when he came to dinner and was presented to her. But there was such naked horror in her face when he moved into the room and when his gloved right hand became visible to her that he did not embarrass her by engaging her in conversation during the evening more than strict courtesy dictated, much to the disappointment of his hosts.

The solitariness largely disappeared. It might have vanished completely had he wished. There were invitations for all sorts of daytime activities with his peers, as well as to the more formal evening entertainments. But he had always liked to keep to himself much of the time.

He spent most of his days, when there was no rain and sometimes even when there was, tramping about his park. He wandered many times to the lake, trying to let the peace of the place seep into his mind. But he kept looking at the spot where the bridge would be erected and a pavilion built beyond it. And he kept hearing her voice calling it a rain house. He walked out to the rapids and tried to become a part of the utter seclusion of the scene. But he could see her wandering the bank and telling him that there should be a series of waterfalls there rather than one grand one. And he kept seeing her head tip to one side as she told him that that was why they were friends—because they thought alike.

He sat on the stone bench at the top of the hill and set his hand on the seat beside him. But it was so very empty. And so very cold. And solitariness there became naked loneliness.

He wandered down to the stream and the stepping-stones across to Thornhill's land. He looked across at the blooming daffodils and imagined her disappearing among the trees in her pink dress and spencer and her straw bonnet. But she did not look back. He had smiles to give her and a hand with which to acknowledge her.

But she did not look back.

He sat beside the fire in his study, gazing at the empty chair at the other side. The very empty chair. And he could hear her asking what had happened—had it been an accident, or had he been born this way? But he could not bring her back to tell her the truth, instead of the lie he had always told. Not that he would tell the truth even if she were sitting there now. . . .

He found he could no longer work in his study. He had to take his books upstairs with him. He found that it had not been such a good idea to bring her into the house after all. She haunted it.

He rarely drank, except for a social drink with guests or a host. He could not remember a time when he had been drunk. But he got thoroughly foxed one night, sitting in his study with a decanter of brandy, staring at the empty chair, becoming more bedeviled with self-pity with each mouthful.

Beauty and the beast. The only way he might stand even a remote chance with her was to reveal his identity and hope that it would lure her into an interest for him that went beyond friendship. But then he would despise her—and himself for setting out such lures and taking advantage of them.

Beauty and the beast. She was more lovely than any woman he had seen or dreamed of. It was a beauty that went beyond the merely physical. There was sunshine in her and warmth and intelligence and laughter.

He did not realize he was drunk until he got to his feet to go up to bed and found himself on his hands and knees, the room spinning wildly about him. He did not know the effects of drunkenness until he was lying on his bed—somehow he had called his valet and that astonished individual had helped him upstairs and undressed him—and found himself in imminent danger of spinning off into space. He clung to the outer edges of the mattress with both hands—even his right. Then he disgraced himself utterly by not making it to the close stool in time before retching up all his insides.

It was late the following day—very late—when he made his decision.

He usually stayed away from London during the height of the Season. This year would be an exception. He was going to London. He was going to see her again even if she did not see him. He did not know why he had not thought of it before. Why not torture himself further? The pain surely could not be any worse anyway. And the Season was about to begin. She had been gone for a whole month.

Yes, he thought, happy now that his life had turned in a definite direction—even if it turned out, as it very likely would, that it was a disastrous direction.

Yes, he was going to London.

Chapter 6

She was enjoying spring in town. She always did. Life took on its familiar routine and became busier every week, as more and more of her friends and acquaintances arrived from the country for the new session of Parliament and for the Season.

There were visits to modistes and extended sessions for fittings and viewings of fashion plates and the choosing of fabrics. There were shopping trips for slippers and fans and gloves and bonnets and a dozen and one other things. There were visits to the library and the galleries and walks in the parks and drives. There were calls to be paid and received.

There was her court to receive—she often enjoyed a private smile over Gabriel's description of her admirers. Lord Francis Kneller, the first to call, informed her that after her seventh Season—she had been rash enough to give him the number—a young lady became officially known as a spinster and had to retire to a country cottage with a trunkful of large white mobcaps.

"You had better avoid the ignominy, Samantha," he said languidly, fingering a jeweled snuffbox but deciding against opening it, "and marry me."

"The choice is between a trunkful of mobcaps and you with your lavender and pink evening clothes, Francis?" she said, tapping her cheek thoughtfully with one finger. "What a shockingly difficult choice. I shall think seriously upon the matter during the Season and give you my answer later. Shall I?"

"The choice will be easier," he said, "once you have seen my new turquoise coat. Satin, you know, with a silver waistcoat and turquoise embroidery. Together, they will bowl you right off your feet."

She laughed and tapped him affectionately on the arm. She wondered how he would react if she accepted his proposal. He would be deeply shocked. Probably horrified. He played the game with her because he knew it was safe. She doubted that Francis would ever marry, unless it was for dynastic reasons. He was too indolent and too frivolous.

"This I can hardly wait to see," she said.

The others all came, too, one by one, as they returned to town. Mr. Wishart came for tea, bringing a large bouquet of spring flowers with him. Mr. Carruthers escorted her to the library and appeared surprised when she took home with her the texts of two plays instead of novels. In Mr. Carruthers's experience ladies read only novels. Sir Robin Talbot took her to the National Gallery and they had a very pleasant afternoon conversing about art. Mr. Nicholson took her driving in the park and made her a marriage offer—again. She refused him—again. He was perhaps the only one of her suitors who seriously wished to marry her, she believed, and yet he always cheerfully accepted defeat. Perhaps he did not really want very badly to marry her. Surely if he did he would have to retire with something of a broken heart after she had refused him so many times.

It was all very pleasant. She was glad to be in London, glad to be busy again, glad to be back in her familiar world. And of course soon the Season would be in full swing, and there would be scarcely a moment in which to wonder if one was happy or sad, enthusiastic or bored, exuberant or exhausted. There would be more invitations to choose among than there were hours in the day.

It was only very occasionally that she literally stopped in her tracks and frowned at a fleeting feeling. She could never quite get her mind around it. It was not a pleasant feeling. It was rather as if the bottom fell out of her stomach—or out of her world—and she was about to fall in after it. And yet she always jolted back to reality before it could happen and before she could even understand what had caused the feeling.

Sometimes if she was walking early in the park, or if she was down by the Serpentine, she would see children tripping along in front of their parents or nurses and the feeling would be there. Was it that she missed Michael and Mary and even Rosalie Boyle's girls? Perhaps. She was fond of them. She did not want children of her own, of course. She did not want that emotional tie. Or sometimes the park was more deserted than usual, and she felt almost as if she were in the country. With a hill and a lake and rapids close by. She was missing Chalcote? Yes, of course she was. It was a beautiful estate, and it was owned by Gabriel and Jenny, two of the dearest people in her life.

Sometimes there were not even clues that strong. Sometimes she was laughing with her friends over some nonsense—she rarely talked seriously with her friends, especially the gentlemen. Or sometimes she was shopping, involved in the purchase of some quite unnecessary frivolity. Or sometimes she just remembered Francis's joke about the seven years and what awaited her afterward.

She never knew what brought on the feeling. It always came quite without warning and disappeared so soon afterward that any person who happened to be with her at the time did not even notice that anything had happened.

She thought sometimes of Highmoor and Mr. Wade. Not often. For some reason she did not stop to analyze, she did not like to remember those afternoons. Doing so depressed her. They had been very pleasant and he had been very pleasant and there was an end to the matter. Those afternoons would never be repeated, and she would never see him again. It did not matter. It was a brief, unimportant episode from her past that should be pleasant to remember but was not. Perhaps later. Perhaps at some other time.

She wished—absurdly, she still wished—that she could

go back and change just one moment out of those meetings. She wished she had turned back to wave at the end. If her final memory of him was of seeing him standing at the other side of the stream, his hand raised, his face lit by his lovely smile, perhaps she could put the whole memory away. Perhaps she would not feel slightly distressed every time she remembered.

It seemed that warm friendship was not for her any more than love was. That made her a very—shallow person, did it not?

Lady Rochester's ball was recognized, by all agreement, as the main opening event of the Season. It was bound to be an impossible squeeze and therefore an unqualified success. Samantha looked forward to it. There was always an excitement about beginning the social whirl yet again. And perhaps there would be someone new. . . . Not that she needed new beaux. It was just that sometimes interest flagged. She felt instantly contrite. Some young ladies of *ton* would give half their fortunes for even one or two of the gentlemen who paid court to Samantha Newman.

Hyde Park was becoming crowded during the afternoons for what was known as the fashionable hour. And the unusually fine weather that they were being graced with was bringing everyone out in force. Perhaps the biggest crowd of all turned out on the afternoon of the day before the Rochester ball. Samantha rode up beside Mr. Nicholson in his new curricle, twirling a confection of a new parasol above her head, smiling gaily and with genuine enjoyment at the people about her. It was a good thing they had not come with serious intentions for a drive, she thought. The press of vehicles and horses about them on the paths was thick, and the intention of most riders was to observe and converse rather than to exercise their horses.

She spoke with friends and acquaintances to whom they could draw close and waved to others who were too far distant.

"How very pleasant this is," she commented to Mr. Nicholson during a brief respite, while one group of acquaintances drew away and another was still approaching. "I am so happy that the Season is starting again."

"My only complaint," he said, "is that I have to share you with the whole world, Miss Newman."

"But I could think of no more congenial companion with whom to make the drive to and from the park, sir," she said. She laughed gaily from sheer exuberance and gave her parasol an exceptionally enthusiastic twirl.

It was at that precise moment that her eyes met those of a gentleman some distance farther on in the crowd and she froze. Utterly. To ice. She forgot to breathe.

The most handsome man in the world, Jenny had once called him. And she had agreed, though she had called him cold. His hair was more blond than her own—almost silver-blond. His eyes were as blue as her own, but a paler shade. His features and his physique were perfect. A Greek God. The angel Gabriel, she and Jenny had called him before they had known that the *other* man—the one they had called his counterpart, Lucifer—had been christened Gabriel. A strange, coincidental irony.

Her eyes met his now across the milling crowd of humanity. He was as beautiful and as dazzling as ever, though she had not set eyes on him in six years. He had been out of the country, banished by his father.

Her eyes met his and held. He looked back appreciatively and touched the brim of his hat with his riding whip.

". . . trying to rival the sun and succeeding quite admirably. Beautiful ladies ought not to be allowed to wear yellow." It was the languid voice of Lord Francis Kneller, who was leaning from his horse's back and draping an arm along the side of the curricle. "I am going to challenge Nicholson to pistols at dawn for luring you into his curricle while the rest of us male mortals must ride alone."

He had disappeared in the crowd. Breath shuddered back

into her. "Nonsense, Francis," she said without her usual spirit, unable to think of anything witty to say in return.

He sat upright again and grinned at her. "Crawled out at the wrong side of the bed this morning, did you, pet?" he asked. *"Nonsense, Francis."* He imitated her sharp tone.

"I say," Lord Hawthorne, his young cousin, exclaimed. He was a young gentleman who had hovered in the outer circle of Samantha's court all last Season, though he must be two or three years her junior. "Frank just pointed out Rushford to me—the notorious Rushford. Did anyone know that he was back?"

Samantha swallowed convulsively. Of course. She had heard that his father had died. But she always thought of Lionel—when she could not stop herself from thinking about him—as Viscount Kersey. He was the Earl of Rushford now, and had been for a couple of years.

"He appeared last week," Mr. Nicholson said. "One would not have thought he would have the nerve. I suppose he is to be admired for having the courage to appear here again after such a shocking scandal. But it must have been years ago."

Six. It had been six years ago.

"I hear he is being received," Lord Hawthorne said. "And I hear he has appeared at White's." There was faint envy in his voice. Lord Hawthorne was still waiting for his entrée to the hallowed halls of the most prestigious gentlemen's club in London.

"The ladies will be intrigued," Mr. Nicholson said. "They always are intrigued by the very gentlemen they should spurn. And, of course, he always was a handsome devil. Oh, do beg pardon, Miss Newman. Did you ever meet the Earl of Rushford? He was Viscount Kersey until a year or so ago."

Samantha was feeling somewhat dizzy. She had always wondered—with a fascinated sort of dread—how it would feel to see him again. She had hoped that the shame surrounding his departure from England would keep him away for the rest of his life. But he was back. And she had seen him again. She felt—dizzy.

"It was Miss Newman's cousin—the present Lady Thornhill—who was at the heart of the scandal," Lord Francis said quietly, without any of the usual bored cynicism in his voice. "I am sure Miss Newman will not wish to be reminded of the gentleman, Ted. Do you suppose that the flowers in Miss Tweedsmuir's bonnet have denuded someone's whole garden? Or do they come from a very large garden, perhaps, and have merely emptied out a corner of it. They must weigh half a ton."

"It is a very modish bonnet, Francis," Samantha said, twirling her parasol again, "and doubtless the envy of half the ladies in the park. She is, after all, drawing a great deal of attention her way, and what more could any lady ask for?" She was deeply grateful for the deliberate change of topic.

"It is a blatant ploy," he said, all ennui again, "to have people look at the bonnet and not at the face beneath it. It is a pity she cannot wear it into ballrooms."

"Francis," Samantha said sharply, "you are wickedly unkind."

"Not to you, my sweet," he said, "except to object to your yellow gown, which makes the sunshine look dim—especially when one looks at the face and figure of the lady inside the gown."

He heaped several more lavish compliments on her during the next minute or so, while Lord Hawthorne looked on in envy and Mr. Nicholson looked impatient to move off. And then they were indeed moving forward, until Lady Penniford and Lord Danton stopped in their barouche to ask Samantha how her aunt and her aunt's friend did.

Samantha no longer looked about her to any distance. She was afraid to look. It took all the effort of her training and experience to keep smiling and conversing, to give Mr. Nicholson and everyone to whom they talked no inkling of the seething upheaval that was churning inside her.

She was home half an hour later, though it seemed ten times as long as that. She ran lightly upstairs, was relieved to find the drawing room empty, was even more relieved to receive no answer to her tap on the door of her aunt's sitting room, and rushed on to her own rooms. Aunt Aggy must still be with Lady Sophia, who was making the most of her invalid state now that there were plenty of friends in town to visit her and sit with her.

Samantha kicked off her slippers in her dressing room and tossed her bonnet in the direction of the nearest chair. She peeled off her gloves and sent them flying after the bonnet. Then she hurried into her bedchamber and threw herself facedown across her bed.

He was back. She clutched fistfuls of the bedcover in both hands and held tight. She had seen him again. And he had seen her. And had acknowledged her. He had not been at all aghast. He had looked at her *appreciatively*. She had seen enough admiration in men's eyes to have recognized it in his.

How dared he.

After what had happened.

He had been Jenny's betrothed. Jenny had been besotted with him, ecstatic to be officially betrothed to him after five years of loving him and having an unofficial understanding with him. Samantha had not particularly liked him. She had always thought that there was a coldness behind the undeniably handsome exterior. Until he had solicited her hand for a set at one ball, that was, and led her outside and down into the garden, presumably because he was upset that Jenny had just spent half an hour with Lord Thornhill. And he had kissed her.

She had been eighteen years old. It had been her first kiss. He had been the most handsome man of her experience. It had been an impossibly tempting combination. She had tumbled into love with him. And had been pained by it, and by his tragic claim to love her while he was bound to marry Jenny, and by guilt because Jenny had loved him so dearly and had been so very happy with her dreams of a future with him. He had suggested that *she* try to do something to end the betrothal, since honor forbade him to do so.

She had been so very naive. She had suppressed her uneasiness, her feeling that it was not very honorable to suggest that the woman he claimed to love do something to end his betrothal to her cousin and closest friend. She had been hopelessly in love, though at least she had not consented to do that for him. He had been forced to do it another way, forging an incriminating letter from Gabriel to Jenny and having the letter read publicly to a whole ballroomful of members of the *ton*. He had brought terrible ruin on Jenny and had forced Gabriel to rush her into a marriage that neither of them wanted—at the time.

Even then, poor, naive girl that she was—though she had not known then of the forgery—Samantha had believed that he would come to claim her. She had maneuvered a brief meeting with him in the hallway outside yet another ballroom—and he had laughed at her and assured her that she must have misunderstood what had been merely gallantry on his part. He had dared to look at her with amused sympathy.

That was the last time she had seen him—until this afternoon. His father had discovered the truth and had forced him to make it publicly known, so that Jenny's reputation might be restored. And then his father had banished him.

She had hated him from that day to this. Hated him for the terrible thing he had done to Jenny, hated him for ruining her own first Season and for toying with the fragile emotions of an innocent and naive young girl. She had hated him for humiliating her so. And she had hated him as a genuinely evil man.

And yet she knew that there was a thin line between hatred and love. For six years she had hated him and feared—deeply feared—that perhaps she still loved him. For six years she had hoped fiercely that her feelings would never be put to the test, that he would never come home to England, that she would never see him again. For six years she had distrusted love, though she had seen signs about her that it could bring happiness. Jenny and Gabriel loved each other and were happy. Rosalie and Albert loved and were happy. But love for her was something to be dreaded, something to be avoided at all costs.

Now she had seen him again, shining and beautiful like an angel, even though she knew that he had the heart of the devil. And her own heart had turned over inside her. She would see him again, she supposed. It was highly probable. And from the way he had looked at her, without withdrawing his eyes hastily and in some confusion, it seemed altogether possible that he would not avoid a direct meeting. They might meet again. He might speak to her.

She was terribly afraid. Afraid of the evil. Afraid that somehow he still had power over her.

She thought fleetingly of returning to Chalcote. Gabriel had said she might go there whenever she wished. Perhaps, she thought . . . perhaps Mr. Wade would still be at Highmoor. But she knew she would not go. Could not go. If he was back in England, this thing must be faced sooner or later. Better sooner than later. Perhaps it would not be as bad as she expected. Perhaps, if she could once meet him face to face, she would find that, after all, he was just a gentleman she did not like.

Perhaps if she stayed she could be freed at last.

She knew it was a forlorn hope.

It had been worth coming, he convinced himself, despite the fact that he had left Highmoor just at the time of year he usually enjoyed being there most of all. He liked to be there when the fields were being sown on his farms. He liked working alongside his laborers. They had stopped looking at him askance, first because he was an aristocrat and was not expected to soil his hands with real dirt, and second because he was a cripple. They had accepted the fact that he was somewhat eccentric.

And he liked to supervise the work of preparing the park for its summer splendor. This year, more than most others, he had had plans for major renovations that would have taken all summer to effect.

Perhaps next year.

It was time he spent a few months of the spring in London, doing his duty as a member of the House of Lords. And it was pleasant to see faces he had not seen in years—male faces, almost exclusively—and to renew old acquaintances. He even ventured to White's two or three times, though he had never been one to spend his days at a club. It was going to be good to have the chance to enjoy concerts and plays in plenty. It was good to spend some time at Jackson's again to hone his skills, though it was more difficult to schedule times alone with the pugilist himself. And he was able to do some fencing again. He had tried it almost ten years ago now, out of sheer obstinacy, after his father had observed that that was one skill at least that he must never think of mastering. Balance on one's feet was of paramount importance to the exercise, as was skill with one's hands. He was naturally right-handed and had never achieved anything more than an awkward competency with his left. His handwriting looked from a distance like the scrawl of a spider.

But he had persisted and sometimes won bouts against less experienced swordsmen. Never against the best, of course, though he had once surprised one of them with an undeniable hit. But he was able to give even the best of them a run for their money.

It was something he enjoyed. Any conquest against his handicaps was a personal triumph.

No, it had not been a waste of his time to come to town. He did not call upon Samantha, however, though he considered doing so each day of his first week in town. Why not send in his card, after all, and pay a courtesy call on her? He even had cards made that omitted his title. But he never did call.

He saw her once on Bond Street, quite by accident. She was on the arm of a very tall, rather thin, very fashionably dressed gentleman. They were both laughing and looking very merry. The Marquess of Carew ducked into the doorway of a bootmaker's shop and found that his heart was hammering against his ribs and his mind was contemplating murder. She did not see him.

He went home, feeling very foolish.

He caught sight of her another day, coming out of the library with another gentleman, more handsome though not quite as fashionable as the first. Again she was smiling and looking as if she held the sunshine inside herself and was allowing some of it to spill over. Again he managed to duck out of sight before she saw him.

He considered going back home on the evening of that day. But he had made the long journey only days before, and the Season had not even started yet. He could not be so cowardly.

His arrival in town had been noted. A small but steady trickle of invitations had begun to arrive. He had been invited to Lady Rochester's ball. Friends had told him that it was expected to be the first great squeeze of the Season. Would not everyone be surprised and even shocked if he were to turn up at a *ball*! Though he knew of many gentlemen and even a few ladies who attended balls without ever intending to dance at them. There were always rooms for cards and rooms for sitting and gossiping or for eating and drinking.

She would almost certainly be at the ball.

If it was a great squeeze, it would be possible for him to go there and see her without being seen. He would be able to see her dressed in all the finery of a *ton* ball. He would be able to watch her dance. Without himself being seen.

But he dismissed the thought. Those other two times, though he had hidden from sight, had been accidental encounters. He had not planned to see her. If he went to the ball deliberately to see her and hide from her, he would be in the nature of a spy, a peeping Tom, a stalker. It was not a pleasant notion.

No, if he went to the ball . . . *if*? Was he seriously considering it, then? If he went, it must be with the intention of letting her see him, of greeting her, of letting her know who he was. It would be better than calling on her at Lady Brill's house. It would be a briefer meeting—he could not, after all, ask her to dance and ensure that he would have her to himself for half an hour. It would be a more public meeting. It would be ideal.

And she should know who he was. Perhaps she had already forgotten him, but he felt guilty for having deceived her.

If she knew who he was and if he continued to appear at some of the *ton* events of the Season, perhaps they could continue their friendship. Perhaps occasionally he could call on her, take her for a drive, invite her to sit in his box at the theater with him.

Perhaps life need not be as bleak as he had thought for the last month and a half that it must be.

But would it be enough—even assuming she would be willing to continue the acquaintance? Would it not be better to have nothing of her than to have an occasional and casual friendship?

And what if his earlier fears were confirmed? What if she showed another type of interest in him once she knew his real identity? But it was a fear unworthy of him. It was not something she would do. He must trust his good opinion of her.

How would he be able to stand seeing her sparkle at other, more handsome gentlemen? How would he cope with the jealousy?

He would cope because he was a mature man, he thought, and because his eyes were open to reality. He would cope because he must.

Yes, he decided finally just the evening before the Rochester ball, when a couple of friends asked him teasingly if he had accepted his invitation. Yes, he was going to go. He was going to see her. And he was going to let her see him.

"Yes, of course," he said to a grinning Lord Gerson and an interested Duke of Bridgwater. "I would not miss it for worlds."

Lord Gerson slapped the duke on the back and roared with laughter. "This I must see," he said. "All the mamas with eligible hopefuls will fall off their chairs, Carew."

"Now this is fascinating," his grace said, raising his quizzing glass and having the gall to peer through it at the marquess. "One might almost imagine that there was one particular eligible hopeful, Hart, my dear chap."

"This is rich." Lord Gerson launched into renewed guffaws of mirth.

"I shall call here with my carriage?" his grace suggested. "We must go together, the three of us. Moral support and all that."

"Yes," the marquess said, quelling the ridiculous, schoolboyish panic. "Yes, do that, Bridge, will you?"

Chapter 7

A squeeze it was indeed. They knew as soon as they approached Hanover Square that Lady Rochester's ball must already be pronounced an unqualified success. They could not even get onto the square with the carriage, but must sit and wait a full twenty minutes while it crawled forward behind a long line of others. An equally long line soon formed behind them.

"Louisa will be very gratified," Lady Brill said, uttering probably the understatement of the evening. Lady Rochester would be more than ecstatic.

There was a special excitement about arriving at a *ton* ball that never quite faded, even at the beginning of a seventh year, Samantha found. Even the tedious wait merely built the feeling of anticipation, that breathless, heart-pounding notion that tonight might be the beginning of the rest of one's life, that something might happen during the coming hours to change the course of one's life.

It almost never happened that way, of course. One saw the same faces, conversed with the same people, danced the same dances every time. But the feeling never quite went away.

Every window of the mansion appeared to be brightly lit. A carpet had been rolled out, down the shallow stone steps and across the pavement, so that those alighting from their carriages might have the illusion of never having had to step outdoors. There were smartly liveried footmen everywhere, discreetly busy. And so much finery and priceless jewelry displayed on so many elegant and not-so-elegant persons of *ton* that one immediately lost any pretensions to personal conceit.

Samantha smiled and stepped out of the carriage. She was in her own milieu and felt thoroughly at home in it. But she could not help remembering her very first ball during her first Season. There had been so much excitement, so much anxiety, so much hope. So much innocence. She would not go back, she thought now, even if she could. There were crowds of people in the hall, talking rather too loudly and laughing rather too heartily. And there was a solid line of people on the stairs, waiting to ascend and pass along the receiving line into the ballroom. There were numerous young girls in the crowd, dressed in the uniform of virginal white gown and white accessories. The most extravagant jewelry any of them wore was a string of pearls. They looked everything she had once been—the poor girls.

"We do not need to go to the ladies' withdrawing room," Lady Brill said after looking over her charge—if the term still applied to a lady of four-and-twenty. "You look quite as handsome as you have ever looked, my dear. I do not know how you do it. I like the colors."

Samantha did too. The silver lace overdress sparkled in the light of candles and gave a smoky hue to the dark green silk gown beneath it. Apart from three ruffles at the hem, her low-necked, short-sleeved gown was unadorned. She had learned from experience that beautiful fabrics and skilled workmanship ought to be left to speak for themselves. She always avoided plumes in her hair, too, though they were very fashionable and Aunt Aggy had told her that she needed the height they would lend her. But she preferred the simplicity of a few flowers in her hair or a ribbon threaded through her curls. Tonight it was a silver ribbon. And silver gloves and slippers. And a fan that by happy chance matched the green of her gown.

"You ought not to have been issued an invitation, Samantha," a familiar, rather bored voice said from behind her shoulder. "Lady Rochester should have more wisdom. You will outshine every other lady present and ruin the evening for every last one of them."

She smiled in amusement as she turned. "Oh," she said appreciatively, "you were quite right, Francis. The turquoise is quite, quite splendid. I am impressed."

He made her an elegant bow. "And would you marry a man who wears turquoise?" he asked, causing a large dowager to turn her head, adorned with six nodding purple plumes, sharply in his direction.

"Definitely not," Samantha said. "I should be afraid of being outshone, Francis. Besides, you might always backslide into pink or lavender, and I should feel cheated. Are you going to offer us your arms and keep us company on the stairs?"

"How could I resist making myself the envy of every male in the house by having the two loveliest ladies to escort?" he asked, offering one arm to Samantha and the other to Lady Brill.

Samantha laughed gaily. Lady Brill tutted and took the offered arm.

Another fifteen minutes passed before they finally stepped into the ballroom. It was the usual scene. The floor itself was empty, in anticipation of the dancing. Crowds lined all four walls, talking and gossiping and laughing. Several people, mostly in couples, promenaded about, looking for acquaintances or merely hoping to be seen and admired. The members of the orchestra were tuning their instruments. The floral decorations, all in varying shades of pink, were hardly noticeable in comparison with the gorgeous clothes and jewels of the gathered guests.

Samantha was soon in conversation with two of her lady friends and a gathering army of gentlemen acquaintances. Hers was the usual court, though Mr. Bains brought with him a neighbor from the country, a tall gentleman who was handsome even without the distinguishing feature of bright red hair. He bowed to all three ladies, but somehow maneuvered matters that he was soon in conversation with Samantha and signing her card for a quadrille later in the evening.

Perhaps the Season would have something new to offer, she thought. A new beau. Did she need a new beau? She never knew quite what to do with the old ones, beyond teasing them and flirting with them and making it quite clear to all of them that it was just a game they played, that she was not in the business of seeking a husband. She never had any wish to lead a man on only to dash his honest and sincere hopes.

She was a little apprehensive tonight. Well, perhaps more than a little. She was afraid that Lionel, Lord Rushford, would be there. But surely not. Somehow he had found the impudence—or the courage, depending how one looked upon it—to return to London and even to ride in Hyde Park during the fashionable hour. But those things he was free to do. There had never been any criminal charges against him, after all. No one could forbid him to live and move about in England. His father was dead now and no longer held the purse strings. But surely he would not receive any invitations to *ton* events. . . .

I hear he is being received.

She could hear Lord Hawthorne saying those words. But surely not by most people, and surely in no very public manner.

Even if he had been invited and even if he had accepted, he would surely keep his distance from her. He would not wish for the embarrassment of a reacquaintance. He had not approached her in the park yesterday, after all. Even though he had looked his fill.

She need not feel apprehensive, she had been telling herself all day. But she was. It was a great relief to glance all about the ballroom and see beyond any doubt that he was not there. There was no possibility that she could have missed him if he had been there. He was so very blond and so very beautiful. One could not miss Lionel even in the largest crowd.

She danced the opening set of country dances with Sir Robin Talbot. He was a skilled, graceful dancer. She always enjoyed being partnered by him. It was an energetic dance. She was breathless and felt flushed at the end of it. Briefly she remembered her boast that after all the walking and hill climbing at Highmoor she would be fitter than anyone else in a London ballroom. But she pushed the thought aside again before she could even smile over it. It brought on one of those feelings of falling into a deep depression.

She fanned herself as she talked with a crowd of acquaintances between sets. She was laughing at poor Lord Hawthorne, whom Francis was teasing because he had just danced with a particularly pretty young lady who was making her debut this year. Lord Hawthorne was blushing behind his exaggeratedly high starched collar points and assuring his cousin that indeed he did not have intentions of offering for the chit tomorrow morning. How absurd!

"Though she is uncommonly pretty, Frank," he added, causing a fresh burst of laughter from the group.

Someone touched Samantha lightly on her gloved arm. Even as she turned with a smile to greet the new arrival, she felt Francis's hand close protectively about her other elbow and heard him utter a muffled oath.

"It *is*," a startlingly familiar voice said. "I could scarce believe that after so many years you could be even more lovely than you were as a girl."

She had the sensation of falling into his pale blue eyes as they gazed into hers with open appreciation. There was almost no other sensation at all. Other sounds and sights around her receded, and with them all awareness of where she was. There were only his eyes. Only him.

"Rushford," a voice said in coldly courteous acknowledgment from a long way away. "A famous squeeze, is it not? This is my set, I believe, Samantha."

Lionel.

He inclined his head to her without removing his eyes from hers. "Samantha," he said. "How are you?"

She heard someone speak. A female voice, quite cool, quite in possession of itself. "I am quite well, I thank you, my lord."

"I saw you in the park yesterday," he said. "I could not believe it was you. But now I can see that indeed it was. And is."

"Samantha?" It was Francis's voice, unusually curt. "The sets are forming."

"You are engaged to dance with Miss Crowther," she heard herself say.

"Devil take it," Francis said, and then apologized to the ladies for his language and released her arm to stride away.

"Dare I hope," Lionel, Lord Rushford asked, "that you have this set free, Samantha? Will you honor me by dancing it with me?"

"Thank you," she said. Even though she was still looking into his eyes and the world was still in recession, her mind somehow told her that she had not indeed promised the set to anyone, though one of her court was bound to lead her out. She never had to miss any dances at any ball.

She had placed her hand in his and stepped away from the group before the world came jolting back. A world that seemed focused all on her. Or on him, rather, she supposed. It had been a very public humiliation, though she had not been there to see it. His father, who had read publicly the letter Gabriel was supposed to have written to Jenny while she was betrothed to Lionel, had made his son read an equally public confession and apology before leaving for the Continent.

He was the focus now of fascinated stares and of an excited buzz of conversation. And she had agreed to dance with him. It was a waltz. Of all the dances it might have been, it was a waltz. She wondered how many people would remember that it had been her cousin who had been at the heart of the scandal with him. Yet she was according him the public courtesy of dancing with him.

"You are more lovely than you were," he said as he set one hand against the back of her waist and clasped her hand with his. "Far more lovely, Samantha. You are a woman now. I cannot take my eyes off you."

She could feel his hands on her. She could feel his body heat, though they touched nowhere else. She felt surrounded by him. Suddenly she felt suffocated by him. She smiled from sheer instinct.

"Thank you," she said curtly. She tried to look about her, to detach herself from the aura of his powerful presence, but everywhere about her she met curious eyes. She stopped looking.

"I came home," he said. "I had to come."

"I daresay one would become homesick after being out of the country for a number of years," she said. "It is only natural."

"I was homesick," he said softly, tightening his hand almost imperceptibly against her back. "But for people more than places. For one particular person, whom I treated unpardonably because I would not have her share my disgrace. For one person I have never forgotten for a single day, Samantha."

She looked into his eyes in shock, forgetting for one moment to smile. His silver-blond hair seemed thicker and shinier than ever. For the first time she noticed that he was dressed in pale blue and silver and white and looked like a prince from a fairy tale. But his words and their obvious meaning had jolted her finally out of the spell his sudden appearance had cast on her. She felt a welcoming fury build inside her as she smiled again.

"How gratified that person will be, my lord," she said, "if she is able to forgive you and if she has not long forgotten you."

His eyes became almost warm. "Ah," he said, and the word was almost a caress. "Yes. You have grown up indeed, Samantha. I had hoped for it. You are angry and unforgiving and I am glad of it. You should not forgive me easily."

"Or ever?" She made her eyes sparkle.

He smiled back, something Lionel had rarely done in those weeks when she had seen him frequently in his capacity as Jenny's betrothed. Treacherously, she felt a lurching of desire deep in her womb. And an equal recoiling in horror. Could he really believe her naive enough to become entangled in his web again? When she knew how cruel and callous and self-serving he was?

Had he set himself that challenge?

And was there any possibility at all that he would win?

She grew cold with terror.

They danced in silence after that—for twenty interminable minutes. He waltzed superbly, never missing a step, never allowing her to collide with any other dancer, never slowing their progress about the perimeter of the ballroom or missing the sweep of a full twirl. His hand was firm and steady in hers. His shoulder was firmly muscled. His cologne was subtle and faultlessly masculine. She could remember his kiss—her first—openmouthed, skilled, persuasive. He was the only man she had ever kissed who had used his tongue as well as his lips. A practiced seducer. Was it any wonder that she had fallen hard for him and had her heart quite shattered by his ultimate rejection? She had been a mere girl, inexperienced and naive.

No longer.

She danced and smiled. And tried to think of her beaux and her friends and of Jenny and the much-wanted third child she and Gabriel were now definitely expecting and of Lady Sophia, whose leg was miraculously healing now that the Season was beginning and there was much to be seen and done beyond the confines of her own home. She tried to think of Highmoor and the view from the hill to the abbey, spoiled only by the presence of a single tree on the slope. She thought of Mr. Wade and pushed the image away again, or she tried to.

And she felt Lionel's magnificence and his attractiveness. She knew she hated him and despised him—despised him anew since their brief conversation at the beginning of the waltz. But she also wondered in fascination and dread how his kiss would feel now that she had had more experience herself. And how his body would feel against her own slightly more knowledgeable one—though only slightly. She was still woefully ignorant for a woman of her age. She wondered . . . No, no she did not. She did not wonder that at all. She was not given to lascivious thoughts.

She wondered if the waltz would ever end.

It did. But by the end of it she felt breathless and bruised and bewildered and unhappy. Desperately unhappy. Unhappy to the point of tears. He returned her to her group— Aunt Aggy was away in the card room, the necessity for close chaperonage long in the past—and bowed over her hand before thanking her for the honor and taking his leave of her.

Francis was looking uncommonly belligerent but showed his good breeding by resisting talking about what he clearly wanted to talk about. Francis, of course, had been a close friend of Gabriel's at the time of the catastrophe. It was only later that he had become one of her beaux—though only because she was safe to flirt with and propose marriage to occasionally, she knew.

"The Earl of Rushford?" Helena Cox said, her eyes as wide as the proverbial saucers. "I have heard all about him. And you *danced* with him, Sam? I do not care what they say of him." She giggled. "He is *gorgeous*."

Mr. Wishart coughed and Helena giggled again. "Oh, and you too, sir," she said. "Of course."

"Gorgeous Wishart," Sir Robin said. "It sounds altogether more distinguished than mere George Wishart, does it not? We must let it be generally known that George has officially changed his name."

"You asked for it, Gorgeous," Francis said in a falsetto voice when Mr. Wishart protested hotly.

She could stand it no longer. There was no air left in the ballroom, and what little there was was hot and perfumed and nauseating. There was no space in which to move. And the noise was deafening. She would faint—or worse, vomit—if she stood where she was for a moment longer.

"Excuse me," she said hastily and turned to hurry away. She wormed her way through the crowds, occasionally having a brief path cleared by someone who saw her coming, once or twice having to stop for a moment to return the greeting of an acquaintance. The doors seemed a mile away.

She reached them eventually and hurried out into the comparative coolness and emptiness of the landing beyond. And was forced to stop when someone stepped into her path and did not move out of it. She looked up into his face, not very far above her own.

Never, never in her whole life had she felt such a rush of pure happiness.

Lord Gerson and the Duke of Bridgwater were greeted with refined enthusiasm by Lady Rochester, who had stayed on with her husband at the entrance to the ballroom to greet latecomers. She smiled with bland courtesy at the Marquess of Carew until his name was mentioned. Then her eyes widened and filled with interest.

"The elusive marquess," she said. "Welcome." But she made the mistake of extending her hand to him instead of merely curtsying. She glanced down in hasty, quickly veiled shock at the thin, gloved, hooked hand that shook her own. He did not see how she reacted to his limp as he followed his friends into the ballroom.

He felt shy, a rather ridiculous emotion for a man of seven-and-twenty to feel. And awkward and conspicuous. His friends wanted to promenade about the edge of the ball-room to find out whom they knew, to examine the new faces—young and female, of course—of the Season. But he wanted to stand still. He wanted only to look about him to see if she was there. He was no longer sure that he wished to make himself known to her. If she was there, he would not hide from her, he thought. But if she did not see him, then he would be content merely to watch her. *If* she was there. He hated the thought that he might have put himself through this torture for nothing.

His friends stayed with him for a while, the duke teasing him about being as skittish as the freshest female recruit from the schoolroom, Gerson finding every remark hilarious.

"Is she here?" his grace asked, making free with his quizzing glass as he gazed about at the milling masses.

"She?" the marquess said. He had not yet had the time or the courage to make a thorough examination of the room.

"I hope she is worthy of this devotion of yours," the duke said. "Pretty, is she, Hart? Young? Supple? Mouthwatering? And panting to become a marchioness?"

"This is rich," Lord Gerson said. "You must point her out to us, Carew. You really must."

But his grace's elegant sweep of the room with his glass halted abruptly and he pursed his lips. He whistled softly. "Look at that," he said quietly. "Pretty, young, supple, did I say? And mouthwatering? And bedworthy, too. Deliciously bedworthy. Not a day over eighteen, if my eyes do not deceive me."

"Muir's chit," Lord Gerson said, following the direction of his friend's quizzing glass. "Maybe only half a day over, Bridge. With a dowry to lend her beauty even if she were not already overendowed."

"You know him?" his grace asked. "Present me, Gerson, there's a good chap. I have to have a closer look. And feel, if it is only the girl's hand. What would you wager that her card is already overflowing?"

Lord Gerson laughed heartily, and the two of them began to make their slow way toward the pretty young lady in white who was making a pathetic attempt to appear fashionably bored with all that was proceeding about her. The marquess smiled in sympathy for the girl.

But Bridge was going to have to wait for his introduction. The next set was about to begin and a handsome young fresh-faced lad was talking to the girl. But not leading her out. Of course, the marquess thought as soon as the music began. It was a waltz. She would not be allowed to dance it, since it was obvious she had only just made her come out and she must have permission from one of the patronesses of Almack's before she could dance the scandalous waltz. Perhaps later in the Season, if she was fortunate. Perhaps not until next year.

He had never seen the waltz performed, though he had heard of it. It had sounded to him like a marvelously romantic dance, each couple a unit unto itself, the man and his partner dancing face to face through the whole of it, able to look at each other and converse with each other for the full half hour.

And indeed it looked as wonderful as it had sounded. He watched for a few moments, enviously.

He had been aware during the five minutes or so he had been inside the ballroom that he had almost deliberately avoided looking about him for Samantha. He was not quite sure why. Was it because he was afraid she would not be there? Or because he was afraid she would?

In the event, he did not have to search for her. She waltzed into his line of vision. His heart lurched. She shimmered in a delightfully simple gown that looked both green and silver from this distance. She waltzed with grace and beauty. She smiled with pleasure.

His eyes followed her with love and with longing for several moments before he spared a glance for her partner. But when he did so, his eyes became riveted.

And his blood ran cold.

Chapter 8

He had lied so consistently and so often about the events of that morning when he was six years old that sometimes—not often, it was true—he almost forgot himself that it was a lie.

That his accident had been no accident at all.

He had been a disappointment to his father. Born five years after his father and mother's marriage, it had seemed that he was probably to be the only child of the union. And while his father might have been glad that he had at least begotten a son, he had deplored the weakness of that son. He had been a small and sickly child, the darling of his mother, overprotected and coddled. A sniveling coward, his father had called him contemptuously on one occasion—it was when at the age of five he had gone running home crying because some village boys had chanted names at him and he had thought they were going to attack him.

Sometimes his father was not even glad about his gender. For had he not been his father's heir, then his father's nephew would have been heir to at least part of his property and fortune. And his father adored his nephew, his sister's son, four years Hartley's senior. Lionel, Viscount Kersey, he had been then. A handsome, charming, fearless boy, who had basked in his uncle's favor and had taunted his cousin—except in the hearing of his aunt.

Hartley had adored him and feared him, had ached for his visits to Highmoor and then longed for his departures.

Sometimes Lionel had deliberately tried—usually successfully—to make him cry, pushing him painfully against doorways with a surreptitiously jabbed elbow, jumping out at him from dark corners at night, spilling his milk at table when his nurse was not looking—he had been endlessly inventive.

One thing Hartley had been good at was riding. Even his father had grudgingly admitted that he had a good seat and a firm hand on the reins. He had loved galloping his pony over permitted stretches of land and jumping over specially constructed fences—ones that would collapse easily if he did not clear them.

Vanity and the need to impress Lionel had made him rash one morning. Lionel had dared him to gallop with him across a forbidden meadow, one with ground that was too uneven and that had too many rabbit holes to be on the permitted route. He had accepted the dare, and they had left behind the startled groom who always rode with them. Before the man could catch up, they had been across the field and approaching a low, solid gate. Quite jumpable. Even so, he would not have jumped it if Lionel had not shouted a challenge. But Lionel had shouted and he had jumped.

He would have cleared the obstacle without any trouble at all—even in his need to impress, he had not been *that* rash. But Lionel had chosen to jump it at the same moment. He had been laughing. And one arm had shot out, its hand balled into a fist, and struck Hartley on the hip.

He had been midway through his jump. He had crashed down right onto the gate, smashing both it and himself in his fall. By some miracle his horse had cleared the gate and landed safely on the other side. By another miracle—though it did not seem a miracle for many months afterward—he himself had lived.

He had been conscious when the groom galloped up, his face contorted with terror, and then galloped off again to fetch help. Lionel had knelt over him, his face ashen, telling him over and over again that it had been an accident and he had better not forget it or make up stories that would shift the blame to someone else. That it was Hartley who had suggested both the gallop and the jump. Lionel had come after him to try to stop him.

During the few minutes of blessedly numbing shock before the weeks and months of truly hellish pain had set in, he had assured Lionel that he would never tell. Never, never, never. Even in those moments there had been the necessity to appear noble in his cousin's eyes.

"There is nothing to tell, you bleeding little worm," Lionel had hissed at him. For some reason those words had remained indelibly etched on his brain ever since.

And he never had told.

There were precious few good effects of what had happened that day. One of them was that he had stopped worshiping or even liking Lionel. Another was that he developed an iron will, a strong determination to conquer his disabilities. Although his mother lived for another four years after his accident, he never allowed her after that day to coddle him, to protect him. He knew almost from the start, despite what the physician told his father in his hearing, that he would walk again, that he would use his right arm and hand again, that he would learn to compensate for their stiffness by using his left hand, that he would make of his body the fittest, strongest instrument it could possibly be.

And he had learned to like himself, to accept himself for what he was. He was human, of course. It was not that he never envied other men or longed to be what he was not. But he did not allow envy or bitterness to gnaw away at him. He lived with reality.

Lionel had been ten years old. A mere child. Hartley forgave him when he was well past that age himself and looked back. He never liked him, but he forgave him and accepted him as his basically cold, selfish cousin.

But dislike had intensified into something much stronger again. His father had been ill. The physician had thought for a while that he would not recover. Lionel had come. There had always been a strong bond between uncle and nephew.

And he had begun an affair with the Countess of Thorn-hill—the former countess, young stepmother of the present earl. Hartley, young and romantic, had adored her from afar for several years. She was very beautiful and very kind and not many years his senior. But he would not have presumed to treat her or even to think of her with disrespect.

Lionel had become her lover and had regaled his cousin's unwilling ears with lurid, graphic descriptions of exactly what he did to her and what she did to show her ap-preciation—and her love. It had been a great joke to Lionel that she claimed to love him.

Hartley had thought he was making it all up—until the countess disappeared with the present earl and the story be-came too strong to be entirely disbelieved that they had run away to the Continent together because she was with child by her own stepson. Hartley disbelieved the one part of that story, of course. The child was Lionel's—Lionel himself had disappeared in fright some weeks before the countess left with Gabriel.

She was living now in Switzerland with her daughter and her second husband. He believed there were a few more children from that second marriage. Once, on the only oc-casion he had asked the present Thornhill about her, he had been told that she was happy. He was glad of that. He had liked her. And of course it was understandable that she had fallen for Lionel's charms. He was undoubtedly one of the handsomest men in England. She had been years younger than her husband, and the late earl had always been sickly. When older and wiser, the Marquess of Carew realized that it was probable the two of them had never had a regular marital relationship. She must have been lonely.

His dislike of Lionel had grown into something resem-bling hatred. Certainly he despised him heartily. And he had heard a garbled version of how Lionel had locked horns with the present Thornhill after the latter returned from Switzerland, leaving his stepmother behind. Somehow Lionel had tricked Thornhill into marrying his lady. She had been betrothed to Lionel himself at the time. But the marquess could not believe that Lionel had won any great victory there. Thornhill's lady was well rid of the blackguard, and there could be little doubt that her marriage to Thornhill was now a love match, however it had started.

He would have been happy if he could have avoided all contact with Lionel, now the Earl of Rushford, for the rest of his life.

Samantha Newman was waltzing with Lionel.

The Marquess of Carew's blood ran cold.

His one hand was splayed against her delicately arched back while the other held hers. Her left hand was on his shoulder.

Suddenly the waltz seemed the most obscenely intimate dance ever invented.

They were beautiful together. Quite spectacularly, heart-stoppingly beautiful.

The devil and his prey.

The marquess had not even heard that Lionel was back in England. Yet there he was, obviously using his considerable charm—and succeeding. She was smiling and not looking about her as many of the other dancers were. She seemed totally absorbed in her partner, though she was not talking to him or he to her. An ominous sign. Were they well acquainted, then? So well acquainted that they did not even feel the need to make conversation?

His heart sank like lead within him. He could remember being with her himself in companionable silence.

And now she was with Lionel.

Instinct told him to get out of there. Out of the ballroom and out of the Rochester mansion. To go back to his town house. Back to Highmoor. To forget about her. He must forget about her. He had been foolish to come after her like a lovesick puppy.

But he could not move. Even though his attention was focused on the waltzing couple, he was not unaware of the curious glances he was receiving from some people close to him and of some nudging elbows and murmuring voices. He did not want to walk away—limp away—in their sight. Besides, he had the foolish notion that she might need him. He could not leave her alone with Lionel—alone with him and a few hundred other people, he thought in self-mockery.

But he could not leave her alone. Perhaps she did not know about Lionel—though she was Lady Thornhill's cousin. Perhaps she was being charmed. Perhaps she would be the next to disappear to Switzerland. His left hand balled into a fist at his side.

And so he remained where he was, watching her, watching *him,* torturing himself with the possibility that they were an item, a couple, that perhaps at the age of thirty-one and with the weight of an earl's title on his shoulders, Lionel was at last in search of a bride. And what lovelier bride could he choose than Samantha Newman?

It was an interminable half hour. Half an hour of excruciating torture. When the music came to an end, he watched Lionel escort her to a group of young people—the marquess recognized only Lord Francis Kneller, whom he had met a few times at Chalcote. He was a friend of Thornhill's, a pleasant if somewhat dandified fellow. Lionel bowed over her hand and took his leave of her.

Perhaps after all, then, it was not as bad as he had feared. Perhaps they were merely distant acquaintances who had shared a dance. That was what a ball was for, after all.

But he felt no wish to stay longer. He did not want to see her dance with any other gentleman. He did not wish for her to see him. He looked about for his two friends, but they were both deep in conversation—Bridge with Muir while Muir's pretty daughter hovered close by—at the far side of the ballroom. He would leave without them. He would walk home. It was no great distance.

But when he reached the doorway, he could not resist one last look back. She was no longer with the group. His searching eyes found her making her way rather slowly through the crowd toward the door, smiling, exchanging greetings with several people as she passed. She was coming in his direction, though he did not believe she had seen him.

He took several steps back so that he was no longer in the ballroom but was on the landing beyond. He was about to turn to flee as fast as he could down the stairs before she reached the doors herself and saw him. But he stopped. What would be the harm in greeting her himself, in seeing recognition in her eyes, in being the recipient of her smile once more? One last time. Tomorrow he would start on his return journey to Yorkshire. He should never have left.

He stopped and waited for her.

She came through the doors in a rush. She looked a little bewildered, dazzled perhaps by the dancing and the crowds. She had not seen him, though she was only feet away from him. He stepped into her path. For a moment he thought she was going to move around him without even looking at him, but she did look.

And stopped in her tracks.

And her face lit up with such bright and total delight that all else about him faded into oblivion.

"Mr. Wade!" Her voice was all astonishment and warm welcome. "How wonderful. Oh, how *happy* I am to see you." She stretched out both hands to him.

He took them, noticed fleetingly that she did not flinch at all from the touch of his right hand in its silk glove, and found himself grinning foolishly back at her.

"Hello, Miss Newman," he said.

She could scarcely believe the evidence of her own eyes. What was he doing here? Did he know someone who had somehow wangled him an invitation? He was smartly though conservatively dressed in brown and dull gold and white. But it did not matter how the miracle had happened. What was important was that it had. If there was anyone she could have hoped would be waiting for her beyond the ballroom doors, it would have been he.

She did not stop to ponder that strange thought.

"What are you *doing* here?" she asked. But she did not wait for his answer. "I never dreamed . . . You are the last person . . . Oh, but this is so *wonderful*. I am so happy to see you again."

She had been distraught over the encounter with Lionel. All that pent-up emotion now came bursting out of her as happiness in seeing her dearest friend, when she had thought never to see him again. And just at the moment when she most needed him.

"It is so hot in here and so stuffy and so crowded," she said. "Come outside for a moment? Come and stroll with me." She had never felt a greater need to get away from the gathered *ton*.

"It will be my pleasure," he said, offering her his left arm and favoring her with that dear smile of the eyes that always warmed her right down to her toes.

Despite the miles they had walked together at Highmoor, this was the first time, she realized, that she had taken his arm. She was far more aware than she had been at Highmoor of his heavy limp and rather slow progress. They had to descend the stairs to reach the door to the garden. He steadied himself against the banister with the outside of his right wrist.

He was drawing some attention. Curious eyes looked at him and then looked hastily away again. A few gentlemen nodded to him in recognition. One of them, she noticed, then proceeded to whisper into his wife's ear.

She had her right arm linked through his. She rested her left hand on his arm, too, feeling a tender sort of protectiveness toward him. Maybe he was a nobody in the eyes of the *ton* and many people would feel that he had no business being here, but he was her dear friend. Let any of them just try to say something to him. They would have her to contend with.

The garden had been lit for the occasion with colored lanterns strung in the trees and lamps lit on the terrace. It was a small garden, but it had been cleverly landscaped to look larger and deceptively secluded. It was hard to believe that they were in the middle of the largest and busiest city in England. Perhaps in all the world, for all she knew.

She had a sudden thought and laughed softly. "Did you landscape this garden, by any chance?" she asked.

"I did, actually." He laughed too. "It was several years ago, one of my first projects. I drew up the plans for the old baron, the present Rochester's father. He completed the work only just before his death."

She laughed again. "I might have known," she said. "And so that is how you came by your invitation. But you did not tell me you were planning to come to London. How unkind of you! Were you hoping that I would not see you and never know? And I thought we were friends."

She spoke lightly, but there was a heavy feeling deep inside, a fear that perhaps that was exactly it.

"I did not know I was coming here until very recently," he said. "And I did hope to see you. I came tonight with the intention of saying hello to you and discovering if you remembered me or not."

"Did you?" She was strangely touched that he would take time away from whatever job had brought him here just to say hello to her. And even if he had landscaped this garden, he had still been only an employee of a man now dead. It must not have been easy to wangle an invitation to this ball. He was a gentleman, but that fact alone did not ensure him entrée to *ton* events. "Of course I remember you. Those afternoons were among the loveliest I have ever spent."

They were, too. If she cast her mind back over all the picnics and excursions and Venetian breakfasts and garden parties she had ever attended, none of them had left her with such warm memories as those four afternoons spent at Highmoor.

There were not many people in the garden. It was not a cold evening, but neither was it warm. It felt wonderfully refreshing to Samantha. She breathed in fresh air and closed her eyes. And stopped walking. They were beneath the low boughs of a beech tree.

"I could almost imagine that we were back in the country," she said. "I was never more reluctant to come back to town than I was this spring."

"The early springtime was unusually lovely at Highmoor this year," he said.

She felt a wave of intense nostalgia for those afternoons. She thought of seeing Lionel in the park yesterday and of the dread his appreciative look had aroused in her—a dread that he would try to renew their acquaintance, a dread that she would somehow respond. And she thought of waltzing with him just a short while ago and of his impudent, seductive words. And of the desire and horror she had felt. She felt them again now, both coiled and throbbing deep in her womb.

"I have missed you so much," she heard herself say in a thin, distressed voice. She felt instant embarrassment—and the need for arms to hold her.

She was never sure afterward whether he had felt her need and responded to it or whether she had moved to satisfy her own need. But his arms were there where she wanted and needed them. They were about her and holding her comfortingly against his surprisingly strong and well-muscled body. His left arm was tight about her waist.

She rested her cheek against his shoulder as her arms wrapped themselves about his waist, and she breathed in the smell of—what? Not cologne. Soap. A comforting, clean smell. She felt sheltered, comforted. Wonderfully comforted. She fit against him much more cozily than she did against any of the beaux she had allowed to embrace her. She was usually so much smaller than the gentlemen who escorted her.

Another thing she was never sure of afterward. Did he nudge his shoulder in order to get her to raise her head? Or did she raise it for herself? In all truth she thought it must have been the latter. But however it was, neither loosened their hold on the other, and so they looked into each other's eyes with no more than a few inches separating them. His gray eyes looked kindly and seriously back into hers.

"Kiss me." It was a whisper, but in an unmistakably feminine voice. That at least was quite embarrassingly clear in her memory afterward.

His kiss surprised her. Most men of her experience kissed with closed lips, only the pressure against her own denoting their ardor. Those few who had dared to part their lips had done so with lascivious intent and had all been swiftly put in their places—all except Lionel.

Mr. Wade kissed with parted lips. She felt the warmth and moisture of his mouth against her own. But he kissed gently, softly, almost tenderly. He kissed wonderfully. She kissed him back in the same way and felt relaxation and a healing sort of peace seep back into her body and into her soul.

He was very dear to her, she thought. A very dear friend. Not that they should be kissing—especially with mouths rather than lips. Friends did not kiss, not like this anyway. But she had needed his arms and even his mouth to take away the rawness of the injury Lionel had inflicted on her. And he had felt her need and was giving her comfort in the way she needed it.

That was what friends were for.

She turned her head when the kiss was over and nestled her cheek against his shoulder. His right arm was lightly about her. His left hand was gently massaging the back of her head. Her hair was going to be disheveled, she thought, without caring in the least.

She sighed with contentment. "Oh, I do love you so very, very much," she said. And froze. Had she really said those exact words? But she could hear the echo of them as clearly as if they were still being spoken. How mortifying in the extreme. He would think she had windmills in her head.

She whipped her head up and dropped her arms from about his waist. Whatever was she doing, clinging to him and kissing him and telling him she loved him, just as if he were her lover?

She looked at him in confusion. "I am so sorry," she said. "I did not mean . . . Whatever will you think . . ."

But he set one finger against her lips and pressed. His eyes were smiling. He shook his head. "You need not be embarrassed," he said, his voice so gentle and so sane that she relaxed instantly. That was another good thing about friends. One could utter any idiocy and they would understand. "I think I had better take you back inside."

Her eyes widened. "Oh, dear," she said. "I have promised this set. It must have started already. How unspeakably ill-mannered of me."

But she turned to him when they were indoors and at the top of the staircase again. She could both see and hear that the set had indeed begun. It would be impossible now to join it. The next set was free. She must sit with Mr. Hancock through what remained of this and ask if she might grant him the next set instead.

"Will I see you later?" she asked. "I have a few sets free after supper."

"I must leave," he said. "I have another engagement."

"Oh." She was disappointed. She wanted to ask him when she would see him again, but she had been inexcusably forward in her behavior to him more than once already this evening. She did not ask the question and he did not volunteer the information. "Good night, then. Thank you. Thank you for . . ." For holding her? And kissing her? "I am glad you came."

"So am I," he said. "Good night."

He waited until she had turned away. She hurried back into the ballroom to find and make her apologies to Mr. Hancock. She felt better, she thought, except that she did not know when or even if she would ever see him again.

The wonder of it struck her. Had he really been here? Had she walked with him and talked with him and been comforted by his arms and his kiss?

There was a certain panic in the thought that she might never see him again.

The first person she saw when she returned to the ball-room was Lionel, Earl of Rushford. He was looking at her with appreciative and lustful eyes across the width of the ballroom.

She wished she had gone with Mr. Wade. Anywhere with him.

She was afraid again.

Chapter 9

It was a long walk home, especially for one who did not walk easily. It was a chilly evening. And a dark one, for a gentleman walking the streets of London unaccompanied and unarmed.

He did not think of any of it. He hardly even noticed his surroundings. He entered his town house, handed his cloak, hat, and gloves to the butler, climbed the stairs to his room, dismissed his valet, and stretched out fully clothed on his bed. He stared upward at the silk-lined canopy.

He could not quite believe that it had happened. All the way home he had avoided thinking about it or reliving any of it. He was afraid now to think of it. He was afraid to pinch himself, lest he wake up and find that it had all been a dream.

But he could not stop the memories.

Her face lighting up with unmistakable joy at seeing him.

Her assurance, undeniably genuine, that she was so very happy to see him.

Her suggestion that they walk outdoors together for a while, though it had turned out later that she had promised the coming set to another man. She had totally forgotten it in her happiness at seeing him.

The way both her hands had rested on his arm as they went downstairs and outside into the garden.

The nostalgia with which she had talked of those afternoons at Highmoor.

He tried to stop thinking. Surely if he really thought

about them, the next memories would crumble away and he would realize that they had been a fabrication of his imagination. A foolish fabrication. They could not possibly have happened in reality.

But thought could not always be stopped at will. And there they were—real memories of what had really happened.

She had stepped into his arms and set her own about his waist and her head against his shoulder.

God. Oh, God, it had really happened. He could feel her again. He could feel her warm, soft curves all along the length of his body. He could feel her arms tight about him. He could feel her curls soft and tickly against his cheek. He could smell her hair and that elusive violet smell he had noticed at Highmoor.

And then—ah, God, then.

She had lifted her head and gazed with soft warmth and *love*—even then he had thought it was love and had not believed the evidence of his own senses—into his eyes.

Kiss me. He shut his eyes very tightly, listening to her soft whisper again. Yearning—there had been yearning in her voice. And in her eyes.

And so he had kissed her. And she had kissed him back with warm and parted lips. She had kissed him with gentleness and tenderness. His mind had not found those words at the time, but his body and his heart had felt them.

She had missed him. She had said that, earlier, before the kiss.

He did not want to think beyond the kiss. It had happened, he knew. But it was too much. Too great a gift. Too far beyond belief and acceptance.

I do love you so very, very much.

No, no. She could not have meant it quite that way. What she had meant was that she felt an affection for him. He must not read too much into her words. Perhaps that was why he had laid a finger against her lips when she had been embarrassed at blurting out so stark a truth and had tried to explain. Perhaps he was afraid that it was not the truth.

I do love you so very, very much.

Friends—a man and a woman—did not talk thus to each other. Only lovers. Even Dorothea had not said that to him until close to the end.

No, he would not believe it too deeply. She was unbelievably beautiful and—perfect. He had seen her with three different men since his arrival in London, all handsome and young and fashionable. How could she have meant what she had said to him tonight? The idea was absurd.

"She loves me." He whispered the words into the candlelit darkness and felt foolish, even though there was no one to hear except him.

"She loves me," he said aloud and more firmly. He felt even more foolish. "Very, very much."

Was he going to set out on his return to Yorkshire tomorrow? Or was he going to try to see her again? How? By haunting fashionable areas during the daytime in the hope of catching a glimpse of her? By attending some other evening function in the hope of having a few words with her?

By calling on her? She was living at Lady Brill's. He knew that.

Dared he call on her? Would it not be an occasion of amusement to Lady Brill and others—and even perhaps to Samantha—if he went calling on her? But why should he not? He was the Marquess of Carew; for the first time he realized that he had not after all told her of that fact this evening. And she had been glad to see him tonight. More than glad.

I love you so very, very much.

He closed his eyes tightly again. He had to believe it. It had not been just the words themselves. Everything in that whole incredible encounter had led up to those words and confirmed them as true.

The miracle had happened.

She loved him.

They had not let it be known that they would be at home to visitors. Their plan was to spend the afternoon visiting. Their intention was to take Lady Sophia with them—her first outing since her accident. Samantha was supposed to drive in the park later with Lord Francis, but it was raining. He had sent a note to ask if she wished to join the world of the ducks, in which case he would don his oilskins and accompany her, or if she would prefer to honor him with her company on the morrow, weather permitting. She wrote back that she had checked but had discovered that she did not have webbed feet and that, yes, she would be delighted to drive out with him tomorrow.

And then a note had arrived from Lady Sophia, who considered that wet weather was not good for a recently broken limb, and would Agatha and Miss Newman humor her with a visit later in the afternoon? She was going to have a rest after luncheon, another adverse effect of the wet weather, it seemed.

And so they had an unexpectedly free half an afternoon and settled in Lady Brill's sitting room with their embroidery to have a cozy chat about last night's ball. Samantha allowed her aunt to do most of the talking. She preferred not to think about last night's ball. She could hardly believe that she had behaved with such dreadful forwardness toward Mr. Wade, who was, when all was said and done, practically a stranger. And she felt depressed about the fact that it was likely to be their only meeting in town. They would hardly move in the same circles there. And she did not want to think about Lionel and the strange, repellent attraction she had felt for him.

She had dreamed about him during the night. A horrible, shocking dream. He had been on the bed with her, looming over her, his body braced on his two arms on either side of her head. He had been looking at her with burning eyes and moistened lips. He had been telling her, his voice soft and persuasive, that of course she wanted him and it was silly to fight the feeling.

You are a woman now. I cannot take my eyes off you.

There had been that feeling in her womb again, and she had known that she was about to give in, to admit defeat. She *did* want him. There—close to her womb. But then she had felt nauseated with a revulsion at least equal to the desire and had pushed at his chest, desperate for air.

His right arm had collapsed and he had tumbled down on top of her. And had turned into Mr. Wade.

You need not be embarrassed, he had said, his voice gentle.

She had sobbed with relief and wrapped her arms tightly about him and relaxed and gone back to sleep.

She had woken with a pillow hugged tightly to her.

It was not a dream she enjoyed remembering.

Fortunately Aunt Aggy appeared not to have heard that Lionel was at the ball. She sighed after they had been sitting for almost an hour. "I suppose that soon we had better get ready to go," she said. "There is something about a rainy day that makes one wish to stay indoors, is there not, dear? But poor, dear Sophie will be lonely if I do not go to see her."

But there was a tap on the door at that moment, and Aunt Agatha's butler came in with a card on a silver tray.

"Did you not say we were not receiving this afternoon?" she asked him.

"I did, ma'am," he said. "But the gentleman wished me to ask if you would make an exception in his case."

Aunt Agatha picked up the card and glanced at it. Her eyebrows shot up and then drew together.

"You will never believe this, Samantha," she said. "The gall of the man. I had no idea he was back in England. And he is calling on us?"

Lionel. Samantha's stomach performed a somersault.

"The Earl of Rushford," Lady Brill said scornfully. "You

may tell him we are not at home." She looked fiercely at her butler. "You may tell him we do not plan to be at home for the rest of the Season."

"He danced with me last evening," Samantha said quietly.

Her aunt turned her fierce gaze on her, and the butler paused in the doorway.

"He took me by surprise," Samantha said. "And he was very civil. It would have seemed ill-mannered . . ." She folded her embroidery without conscious thought and set it beside her on the chair. "I danced with him."

"Gracious," her aunt said. "After the scandal of six years ago, Samantha? After he disgraced dear Jennifer with such deliberate malice? Her own father whipped her as a result!"

Samantha bit her lip. She hated the memory of listening outside Uncle Gerald's study door with Aunt Aggy and hearing his command to Jenny to bend over his desk and then the first two whistling strokes of his cane.

"Very well," her aunt said after a pause, "we will be *civil* to him, Samantha. Show him up." She looked at her butler again. "After all, it was six years ago. A man can sometimes learn wisdom in six years."

It was hard to believe that she had not fought against his admission, especially when Aunt Aggy herself had been reluctant to admit him. But she knew why. Of course she knew. Why keep denying it to herself? Why keep pretending?

She had never forgotten him. She had never stopped being fascinated by him. She had known last night that there was still something that drew her to him. She had known then that her life seemed destined for ugliness, not beauty, for pain, not happiness.

The only question that remained was whether she was going to continue to fight. What was the alternative to fighting? Oh, dear God, what was it?

And then he was in the room, filling it with his good looks and his charm and his charisma. He was bowing over Aunt Aggy's hand and assuring her that she was in remarkable good looks and that he would cherish the honor she had done him by admitting him on an afternoon when she was not officially receiving.

He was dressed in a coat of dark green superfine, Weston's finest, with buff pantaloons and sparkling Hessians. His linen was crisply white. He was even more breathtakingly handsome now than he had been six years ago, if that were possible.

And then he was turning to Samantha and bowing elegantly and gazing at her with burning eyes—oh, dear God, she had seen his eyes like that in her dream—and thanking her for the honor she had paid him in dancing a set with him last evening.

"I came, Miss Newman, ma'am," he said, including them both in his bow, "to make a more private and certainly more sincere apology for my part in the events of six years ago that caused such distress to your family."

"Well." Samantha noticed that her aunt melted without further ado. "Well, that is most civil of you, my lord, I am sure. I was just remarking to Samantha that a man can sometimes learn wisdom in six years."

"Thank you, ma'am," he said. "I believe I have."

Lady Brill ordered tea and they sat for twenty minutes, engaged in an amiable conversation, during which he told them about his travels and asked after the health and happiness of Lady Thornhill.

"I have always wished her happy," he said. "I was young and fearful, as most young men are, of matrimony. But I never wished her harm and have been deeply ashamed of the distress I caused her." He looked at Samantha, his eyes warmly contrite.

He had never wished her harm? And yet he had maliciously caused that letter to be written and to be read aloud, a letter suggesting that Jenny and Lord Thornhill were lovers and intended to continue as lovers. If Gabriel had not married her, Jenny would have lived out her life in deep disgrace. Oh, yes, it would be a sin to try to forget—Uncle

Gerald had caned her after that letter was read to the *ton*. And Lionel had never wished her harm? He had not even had the excuse of youth. He had been five-and-twenty at the time.

And he had pretended a passion for her, Samantha, in the hope that she would tell Jenny and Jenny would end their betrothal. And then, when the betrothal was ended anyway, he had laughed at her and told her that she must have misunderstood what was only gallantry.

Had he changed so much in six years? Was it possible? Or was he still the snake he had been then? But even more suave.

How could she even fear that she still loved him? But if it was not love, what was it that bound her to him despite the horror she felt at being so bound?

"You are very quiet, Miss Newman," he said at last, bringing her attention back to the conversation. "Do you find me impossible to forgive? I could hardly blame you if you do."

Good manners dictated that she give him the answer he wanted. But she felt again the fury that had rescued her the evening before. He was playing with them, manipulating them. For what reason, she did not know. Perhaps for simple amusement.

Or perhaps he was sincere.

"Perhaps not impossible, my lord," she said carefully.

He got to his feet. "It is time I took my leave," he said, bowing to them again. He looked at Samantha. "I shall study to win your forgiveness before the Season is out, Miss Newman."

It had been *Samantha* the evening before, when Aunt Aggy had not been within hearing distance, she remembered. She nodded her head curtly.

"Would you do me the honor of walking to the door with me?" he asked.

Samantha's eyes flew to her aunt. But Lady Brill merely raised her eyebrows and shrugged almost imperceptibly.

Samantha was no girl, and he had not asked for a private visit with her, after all.

She preceded him from the room but took his offered arm to walk downstairs. Although it was higher above her own, it was not so very different from Mr. Wade's arm, she thought. It did not feel any stronger or any more firmly muscled despite the overall splendor of his physique.

"I know how difficult you find it to forgive me," he said quietly. "You have more to forgive me for than Lady Brill, and more than she knows of. But I will win your trust."

Perhaps he was sincere. How did one know if a man was sincere? She had not known this man for six years. It was a long time.

"I loved you even then," he said. "But it was hopeless. You too would have been ruined in the scandal, and I would have died sooner than ruin you. I still would. I never forgot you. I came home because I could no longer live without . . . Well, I do not want to sound like a bad melodrama."

But he did. How did one know if a man was sincere? Perhaps the way he remembered—or distorted—the past was a key. He had *not* loved her. And the scandal had not yet touched him when he had spurned her. If he would have died rather than ruin her, would he not have died rather than viciously humiliate and hurt her?

She did not know what his game was. But game it was.

"I came home, you know," he said, "because it is time I took a countess. And I wanted an English countess. An English rose—one more beautiful than any other." He took her hand from his arm and raised it to his lips without removing his eyes from hers. "Will you drive with me in the park tomorrow afternoon?"

"I have a prior appointment," she said.

"Tell me the man's name," he said, "so that I may slap a glove in his face." His eyes were burning into hers again.

He *was* still a snake. This was too polished a performance to be real. And not a pleasant performance.

"He is a man I like and admire," she said. "I would drive with him any day he asked, my lord. He is also a man I trust."

He sighed and released her hand. "And you do not trust me," he said. "I cannot blame you. But that will change. My honor on it."

She almost laughed and asked him the obvious question—*What honor?* But she could feel no amusement, and she did not want to prolong their conversation.

He made her an elegant bow and took his leave.

Aunt Aggy was still in her sitting room.

"Well," she said when Samantha returned there. "I have never seen such a transformation in my life. He has become a thoroughly amiable young man."

"Are you sure, Aunt?" Samantha asked her. "It was not all artifice? He was not laughing at us?"

"But to what purpose?" Her aunt's eyebrows shot up again. "It must have been extremely difficult, Samantha, for him to come here and say what he did. I honor his courage."

"He wanted me to drive with him tomorrow," Samantha said. "I was very glad that I am to drive with Francis."

"I believe," Lady Brill said, smiling archly, "he is smitten with you, Samantha. And it would hardly be surprising. You are as lovely now as when you made your come out. Lovelier. You have a self-assurance now that is quite becoming."

Samantha did not feel self-assured. Not any longer. Not now that he had come back.

"He was very complimentary," she said. "But I could not think him sincere, Aunt."

Lady Brill clucked her tongue. "I begin to despair of ever persuading you to step up to the altar with a presentable gentleman," she said. "But we must not stand here arguing. Poor Sophie will be despairing of our coming."

"Will you mind a great deal if I stay at home?" Samantha asked. She smiled. "The two of you can have a more comfortable coze if I am not there, anyway."

"What utter nonsense," her aunt said, but she made no attempt to persuade Samantha to accompany her after all.

It was a relief to be alone again, Samantha thought, retiring to her own room and sitting down at her escritoire to write a letter to Jenny. But no matter how many times she dipped her quill pen in the inkwell, she could not make a start on the letter beyond writing "My dear Jenny."

What would Jenny and Gabriel say if they were in town this year and knew what had happened in the last two days? She could almost imagine their horror. Imagining it helped. It helped her see that renewing an acquaintance with Lionel just would not do. They would not be fooled, as Aunt Aggy had been fooled, into thinking that he truly regretted the past. If he did regret it, surely he would pay her the courtesy of remaining out of her life.

She was four-and-twenty years old, she reminded herself. She prided herself on her maturity and her worldly wisdom. After six years of being "out," she believed she knew a great deal about human nature in general and about gentlemen in particular. For several years she had felt very much in charge of her own life and emotions.

Was she to revert now to the naiveté of her eighteen-year-old self? She had been able to excuse her own gullibility then because she had known no better. She had been in search of love and marriage and had known nothing about either. Would she ever be able to excuse herself for making the same mistake now?

What if he was sincere? But even if he was, it would be unpardonable to have anything to do with him. What would Jenny and Gabriel think?

She found herself drawing geometric patterns with her pen below the "My dear Jenny" on the page.

He was going to remain in London for the Season. Of that she had little doubt. And he was going to pursue her for that time. For what reason she did not know. Perhaps— there was a slim chance—he was sincere. Or perhaps it merely amused him to discover whether he could do to her again what he had done six years ago.

She was not sure she would be able to endure it.

Part of her was still foolishly fascinated by him, as she had admitted to herself before her visit. Part of her had never been able to let him go and get on with her life. She had thought she had done so. But if she had, why had she never been able to love any other man? Why had she never been able to marry?

He had a hold on her emotions that she neither welcomed nor understood. She could only admit it.

She set her pen down when there was a tap on her door.

"Come in," she called.

It was the butler again, bearing another card on his tray. Surely he had not come back, she thought. Surely he had not waited until Aunt Aggy left and then returned. She would not put such subterfuge past him. But she certainly would not receive him. The very idea!

She looked down at the card and then picked it up and closed her eyes as she brought her hand unconsciously to her lips.

"Where is he?" she asked.

"I put him in the salon downstairs, miss," the butler said. "He said only if it was not too much trouble to you."

Samantha got to her feet. She was smiling.

"It is no trouble at all," she said, and she brushed past him in the doorway and went running lightly down the stairs. She did not wait for him to come after her to open the door to the salon. She opened it herself and rushed inside with quite undignified eagerness. Her smile had widened.

"You came," she said, closing the door behind her and leaning back against it. "I wanted so badly last evening to ask when I would see you again, but it seemed presumptuous, and I had said and done so much else that was presumptuous before we said good night. I hope I did not give you a great disgust of me."

His eyes glowed as he smiled at her and she felt her first real happiness of the day.

"I came," he said.

Chapter 10

He had almost talked himself out of coming. In the gloomy light of a rainy day the events of last evening had seemed unreal. But the only alternative to coming was to go home, back to Highmoor, and know that he would never see her again. It was an alternative he could not contemplate.

All the way here his stomach had been tied in knots. He had tried to think of excuses for giving his coachman instructions to take a different direction. It was rather late in the afternoon. She would doubtless be from home. She would have other visitors. He should have written asking permission to call. But he had come, and his coachman had knocked on the door, and he had handed his card to Lady Brill's butler and asked if it might be taken to Miss Newman and if he might see her—but only if it was no trouble to her to see him.

The butler had looked with well-bred condescension on a babbling Mr. Hartley Wade.

He had paced the small salon with its heavy, rather old-fashioned furniture, wondering if it was too late to escape, hoping that she would send back some excuse not to see him.

And yet the moment the door burst open again and she hurried inside, closed the door and leaned back against it, and delivered her opening speech far faster and more breathlessly than she usually spoke, his nervousness and uncertainty fled. She was smiling. Her eyes were shining. And he listened to the words she spoke.

The miracle really had happened.

"I came," he said.

She laughed. "But you have avoided admitting that I gave you a disgust of me," she said. "I am so ashamed. If I had told Aunt Aggy how I behaved last night, she would have had a fit of the vapors. Do please forgive me."

"I wish you would not apologize," he said. "I was not disgusted." She looked delightfully pretty in sprigged muslin, he thought. She looked like a girl. Though perhaps that was no great compliment. She had all the allure and fascination of a woman.

"You are kind." Her smile softened. "As always. I am sorry my aunt is from home. But I will ring for tea here if you do not feel it would be too improper a tête-à-tête. We did not care about that at Highmoor, though, did we?"

"I'll not stay long," he said, quelling the temptation to be drawn into a mere social half hour, chatting about inconsequential matters. "Please don't bother with tea."

"Oh." She looked disappointed.

"I came to ask you something," he said. "I suppose I should lead up to it by gradual degrees, but I do not know how. I would rather just ask and hear your reply."

"I am intrigued," she said. She was still leaning back against the door, he noticed, her hands behind her, probably holding the door handle. "But I do hope the question is not that I will drive in the park with you tomorrow afternoon. If so, you will be the third to ask and I accepted the first. But I will be sorry if that is what you want. Perhaps—"

"I wondered," he said, "if you would marry me."

Her smile disappeared and she stared at him mutely, her eyes huge, her lips slightly parted.

It had been a disastrous way to ask. Baldly abrupt. Totally lacking in grace or courtliness. He wished he could withdraw the words and try again.

"I could try it on one knee," he said, smiling, "but I am afraid you might have to help haul me back to my feet again."

She did not smile. "What?" she said, her voice and her face bewildered.

He swallowed. It was too soon. He should have spent some time courting her first. Or perhaps he had been totally mistaken. But it was too late to retreat now.

"I would like to marry you," he said. "If you wish to marry me, that is. I know I am not much—" No, he must not apologize for his lack of stature and looks, for his deformed hand and foot. He was as he was. And she had told him she loved him. He had believed her.

Her eyes had focused on him again. "Don't belittle yourself," she said quietly, having obviously completed his sentence for herself. "You are wonderful just the way you are. Far more wonderful than any other man of my acquaintance."

They stared at each other, their eyes roaming each other's face, no real awkwardness between them.

"I thought never to marry," she said. "I have not given it serious consideration for a long time."

"Someone hurt you," he said gently. It hurt him to know that another man had hurt her—obviously very badly. "But life is not all pain. I would never hurt you. You would be quite safe with me." They were not the romantic words he had dreamed of saying and had tried to rehearse, but they were the words needed by the moment.

"I know I would," she said softly. "I always feel wonderfully safe and—and happy when I am with you. Do you with me? I—"

"Yes," he said. "Always."

She set her head back against the door and looked at him. "I would not have dreamed of feeling this tempted," she said.

"But only tempted?" He felt as if he were holding his breath. "Would you like time to consider?"

"Yes," she said. And then very quickly, she changed her mind. "No. I do not need time. Time only confuses the mind. I will marry you."

Despite his hopes and his dreams and even his expectations, he was stunned. He stared at her, not sure that he had heard right. But she was coming toward him, and she reached out both her hands when she was close.

"Thank you," she said, and there were tears shining in her eyes. "Oh, thank you."

He took her hands in his, not even conscious for once of the deformity of his right. He laughed, his voice breathless with relief.

"I muddled it horribly," he said. "I am so sorry. I have never done this before."

"I hope," she said, "since it has so embarrassed you, that you will not have to do it ever again. I will be a good wife to you, I promise. Oh, I do promise that. I shall make you—contented."

He rather thought that she would make him delirious, as she was making him now. He looked at her, so exquisitely pretty and dainty and warmhearted, and could not for the moment believe that she was his. His love. His betrothed. She was going to be his wife, the mother of his children.

"You already have," he said. "And I promise to see to it that you never regret the decision you have made today."

Two tears spilled over and trickled down her cheeks. She bit her lip and laughed. "Oh, dear," she said. "Is this really happening? I feared I would never see you again after last evening."

For answer he leaned forward and kissed her swiftly on both cheeks, brushing away the salt tears with his lips. "Is there anyone I must ask?" he said. "Even just for courtesy's sake? You do not still have a guardian, do you?"

"My uncle has control of my fortune until my next birthday," she said. "Viscount Nordal, Jenny's father. But it will be released to me immediately on my marriage. It is quite a respectable fortune. Perhaps you are marrying me for my money." She laughed lightly and breathlessly.

That was when he remembered. Oh, yes, he really had

made a mess of things. He had done everything quite the wrong way around.

She laughed again. "It was a bad joke," she said. "It was a *joke*. But very tasteless. I know you could never be mercenary. Forgive me."

He squeezed her right hand with his left.

"I will call on your uncle," he said. "And I will see about having the banns started. Next Sunday? Am I rushing you? I am almost ready to suggest a special license, but I want you to have a *wedding*. I want the whole world to see you as a bride. Just as soon as the banns can be read. Would you prefer to wait a while? Until summer, perhaps?"

"No." She shook her head slowly. "No, let's not wait. I want to be your wife—now, as soon as possible. I want to be with you. If you wish to reconsider the special license . . ."

But he shook his head, dizzying as the thought was of having her as his wife within the next couple of days. No, he would rather wait. He wanted to show her off to the whole *ton*. He wanted a wedding to remember. At St. George's, in Hanover Square.

"No," he said. "We must do this properly."

"Yes, sir." Her smile became almost impish. "I will practice wifely obedience, you see."

He laughed. "You will not find me a hard taskmaster," he said. "I must take my leave." He let go of her hands regretfully. "Your aunt's servants will be scandalized if I stay longer."

"Yes, sir," she said meekly. "When will I see you again? You must meet my aunt. Will you come tomorrow afternoon?"

"Yes." He had crossed the room to the door. He looked back, his hand on the handle. No, he could not leave like this. It would be unpardonable. He had put it off long enough. Too long. And even that was an understatement.

"There is something I have not told you," he said quietly.

"You are a convicted murderer," she said. "You have

had six wives and have murdered them all. Worse even than Henry the Eighth." She smiled merrily. "What have you not told me?"

He licked dry lips. "When I gave you my name at Highmoor," he said, "I thought you would recognize it and fill in what was missing. When you did not, I was tempted by the novelty of being just an itinerant landscape gardener. It seemed harmless at the time. I did not know that the day would come soon when I would want to ask you to marry me."

She merely stared at him. He thought her face had paled.

"Hartley Wade is not my complete name," he said. He swallowed. "I am Carew."

Her face was drained of every vestige of color. "The *Marquess* of Carew?" she said in an unnaturally high-pitched voice after the silence had stretched.

He nodded.

She opened her mouth more than once to speak. "You lied to me," she said at last.

"No," he said quickly. "I merely withheld the full truth. Though *merely* is a damning word, I must admit. And I suppose I did lie. We talked about me a few times in the third person, did we not? I pretended that he was someone other than myself."

"Why?" The word was whispered. She had closed her eyes very tightly, as if to shut off what was happening.

"You were there on the hill," he said, "so unexpected and so—pretty and so flustered at being caught trespassing. I expected to see you become stiff and formal and even more embarrassed when I gave you my name. Instead, you did not make the connection. And I was tempted. You would not understand, perhaps, the barrier my title puts between me and new acquaintances. I wanted to talk with you. I wanted you to admire my home and my park. I did not want to see that barrier go up."

"Oh," she said. She had looked at him while he spoke, but now her eyes closed again. "The things I said in the ballroom at Highmoor. In *your* ballroom." She spread her hands over her face.

He would have smiled at the memory, but he was too tense with fear.

"Does it make a difference?" he asked. "Will you wish to withdraw your acceptance of my offer? I am deeply sorry. Once one has deceived another, it is incredibly difficult to find the courage to undeceive her. But that is no excuse. Does it make a difference?"

He waited tensely for his world to end.

"I will not be just plain Mrs. Hartley Wade, then, will I?" she said.

"No." He did not dare hope. "You would be the Marchioness of Carew."

"Grand," she said. "Very grand. And Highmoor will be my home."

"Yes." *Will*, she had said, not *would*.

She laughed unexpectedly against her hands. "Perhaps I am marrying you for *your* money," she said. "Have you thought of that?"

"You did not know of it," he said. "But I know you well enough to trust that my title and wealth would have done nothing to sway you. I will always cherish the memory of your accepting me when you thought me an impoverished landscape gardener. Will you now accept me, knowing that I am the almost indecently wealthy Marquess of Carew?"

She sighed and lowered her hands before looking at him rather wanly. "Yes," she said. "How could I possibly resist the lure of Highmoor? *Have* you ever done any landscaping?"

He nodded. "Except in that one particular," he said, "I have always spoken the truth to you."

"Well," she said. "You will come tomorrow, *my lord*?" She smiled rather uncertainly at him.

"I would be honored," he said, "if you will call me Hartley. And if you will see me no differently than you ever have. Yes, I will come tomorrow."

They exchanged a look that was not quite a smile, and he

let himself out of the room. He took his cloak and hat from the butler, who must have been hovering in the hall all the time, and allowed the man to open the outer door for him.

A few moments later he was in his carriage on the way home, the rain beating against the windows. It was done, he thought, setting his head back against the squabs and closing his eyes. And she had accepted him—both as Mr. Wade and as the Marquess of Carew. She had accepted him.

She was going to be his wife.

I love you so very, very much.

They had not spoken of love this afternoon. He supposed he should have made that declaration a part of his marriage offer. He had been very gauche. But the words had not needed to be spoken. They were only words, after all. They loved each other. It had been there in every look and word they had exchanged. She had been willing to marry him just for himself. She had said yes, believing that he had nothing but himself to offer. Not that he had deliberately put her to the test. But he would always be able to remember that.

And soon—within a month—she would be his by both civil and church law. She would be his wife. He would be able to make love to her as well as loving her.

God. Ah, God. Happiness sometimes felt almost like agony.

"*What?*" Lord Francis Kneller almost fell off the seat of his high-perch phaeton and jerked on the ribbons sufficiently to cause one of his horses to snort and jerk its head and threaten mutiny. He skillfully brought it under control.

"I am going to marry the Marquess of Carew," she repeated. "Exactly four weeks from today. I do not believe I will be able to drive out with you like this again, Francis. But I do thank you for your friendship during the past five years."

"Friendship?" He glanced at her incredulously before giving the road leading to the park his attention again. "*Friendship*, Samantha? Good God, woman, I *love* you."

She gazed at him in shock.

"Francis," she said, "what a dreadful bouncer."

"Sorry," he muttered. "No, it was no lie, but it ought not to have been said. But Carew, Samantha. *Carew*? He is a crip—Oh, dash it. I am sorry—again."

"He is not," she said. "He had an accident. He manages very well. And he never complains."

"Where did you meet him?" he asked. She noticed that he had taken his phaeton past the gates into the park. "At Chalcote, I suppose. That bloody Gabe—sorry! I'll draw his cork when I see him next. And I suppose you were dazzled by his title and his fortune and Highmoor—dratted splendid place. I cannot think of any other reason why you would be marrying him. Good God, Samantha, you could do a thousand times better than him."

"Please take me home," she said quietly.

He drew a deep breath and blew it out through puffed cheeks. "Your trouble, Samantha," he said, "is that you are blind in one eye and keep the other firmly closed. You do not realize, do you, that all of us, all your blood—your *blessed* court, are head over boots for you. And you do not care the snap of two fingers for any of us. But Carew! I—words fail me. Yes, home it is." He turned a corner sharply enough to arouse shouts of protest and some profanities from other drivers. "You do not have to demand it again. Carew! Good Lord."

"I care for him," she said quietly.

"The man is the next thing to a recluse," he said. "He has nothing to recommend him to someone like you."

"And you do?" she asked him. "Francis, you never said—"

"Because I knew—or thought—you did not want to hear it," he said. "I wanted to try to trick you into caring for me. I thought perhaps time would do it. The devil and his pitchfork! How long have you known him?"

"Since the day you left Chalcote," she said. "I walked onto Highmoor property and he was there."

He swore. And did not even apologize afterward.

"Francis." She set a hand lightly on his arm, but he flinched and jerked away from her. "I am sorry. But I do care for him, you know. I care very much."

"He must be worth at least fifty thousand a year," he said. "At least! I suppose I would care very much, too, Samantha, if I was a woman."

She said no more and they proceeded in silence—a distressed silence on her part, an angry, frustrated one on his.

"Francis," she said as they drew nearer to Lady Brill's, "I do not want to lose your friendship."

"It never was friendship," he said.

"Yes, it was," she said. "It was always—fun. I always enjoyed your teasing insults. I always enjoyed matching wits with you. I thought that was all. I had no idea I would—hurt you by marrying someone else."

"I thought it was going to be Rushford, if anyone," he said, his jaw tightening. "I thought I saw a spark there, Samantha. More than a spark. I am glad at least it is not him. I would have fought dirty if he had tried anything, and if you had not had the sense to send him packing."

"No," she said. "There was nothing there, Francis. He merely took me by surprise and I danced with him. But there was nothing. I care for the Marquess of Carew. I am going to marry him. I am going to give him contentment. He is going to keep me safe."

"This would make a riveting romance, Samantha," he said. "I'll wager my hat you will make him contented. And from what is he to keep you safe, pray? Wolves like myself?"

"No," she said. "It was just a manner of speaking. He is going to—to keep me safe, that is all. We are to be wed at St. George's. It is what he wants. I was going to invite you. But perhaps you would rather I did not. I have written to Jenny and Gabriel, but I do not know if they will come. Jenny is—well, she is in delicate health again."

"Is she?" he said. "I thought Gabe was contented with two."

"I am hoping they will come," she said. "Will you if I invite you?"

"Carew would just adore seeing all your court in attendance at his wedding," he said.

"My friends," she said. "You are all my friends, Francis. Don't distress me with that other nonsense. It is nonsense, you know. We are all just friends."

"Someone should give you a looking glass for a gift some time, Samantha," he said. "Though that would not be quite sufficient, either. It is not just looks with you. Can Carew see beyond your looks? I'll bloody kill him if—"

"Francis." She spoke sharply to him. "That is enough. I have heard enough such words from you to last a lifetime. I will hear your apology, if you please."

He grinned for the first time. "Spoken like a true marchioness," he said. "When you are considerably older, your ladyship, you will have to invest in a jeweled lorgnette. You will wither everyone you turn it on. It would help, of course, if your nose was longer. Perhaps it will grow in time. I am sorry. I have been a perfect bounder over this whole thing, I must confess. You should have given me some sort of warning, Samantha. If you had written a note, I could have blackened both my valet's eyes and broken his nose and smashed all his remaining teeth, and by the time I saw you I would have been perfectly civil and amiable. My apologies. Forgive me?"

"Of course," she said. "But, Francis, you did not mean all that nonsense, did you? Not really. You were just trying to tease me into feeling rotten, you idiot, and you succeeded."

"Well, then," he said lightly, "my day is made, Samantha. You really care for him, then? I'll have to see for myself at your wedding."

"You will come?" She turned her head to smile brightly at him. "Oh, thank you, Francis. I am going to be very happy, you know. I am going to be very—"

"—safe," he said. "Yes, I know. The pinnacle of any maiden's dreams. To marry and live—safely ever after. Do you want to go back to the park? For once there would be something truly spectacular to announce there."

"No," she said. "Hartley is to announce our betrothal in tomorrow's papers. I would not say anything before then. Only to you, because you are my friend and I was engaged to drive out with you."

"Hartley," he said quietly. "*Do* you want to go back to the park?"

"I think I would rather not, if you do not mind very much, Francis," she said.

They were at Lady Brill's already. He descended nimbly from the high seat and lifted her to the ground. He kept his hands at her waist for a brief moment.

"I hope he keeps you very—safe, Samantha," he said. "And I hope you will be very happy, too. He is a lucky devil."

"Thank you," she said, smiling at him. "Thank you, Francis."

He waited until she had been admitted to the house by the butler, who appeared surprised to see her return so soon. Then he climbed back to his seat and drove away.

His valet had better not look sideways or any other ways at him for an hour or two after he returned home, he thought, or those two black eyes and that broken nose and those smashed teeth might well become a reality.

Carew! He had met the man at Chalcote the year before last and again last year. A pleasant enough fellow, quiet and unassuming. But he appeared to have nothing beyond his title and fortune to recommend him to any woman, least of all to someone of Samantha's beauty and charm. And yet she was the last person he would have expected to succumb to such temptation.

Lord Francis Kneller swore under his breath. And then, realizing that he no longer had an audience that might demand an apology, he swore more vehemently and marginally more satisfyingly.

Chapter 11

He finished his toast and sipped on his second cup of coffee. He was almost reluctant to get up from the breakfast table in order to dress for the outdoors before the Duke of Bridgwater arrived. He had promised to accompany his friend to Tattersall's. Bridge was in search of a pair of grays grand enough to complement his new curricle.

The Marquess of Carew looked down yet again at the *Morning Post* open on the table beside him. He set his left hand on it and touched the announcement with two fingers. He smiled. Now at last it was real to him. They were betrothed. The whole fashionable world would know it this morning.

Everyone would assume that it was a loveless match, that she was marrying him for his position and fortune, that he was marrying her for her beauty.

Only he and she would know. It was enough. It was a delicious secret, in fact. It did not matter what the world thought. He would take her home to Highmoor soon after the wedding and live with her there for the rest of their lives, with only the occasional visit elsewhere. She loved Highmoor already. They would raise their children there. It did not matter if no one else ever realized that they loved.

Viscount Nordal had been first surprised and then gratified. The girl had been difficult, he had explained, talking about Samantha as if she were still fresh from the schoolroom. She had refused more marriage offers than enough.

But of course she would have to have windmills in her head to have refused the Marquess of Carew.

The marquess had smiled secretly at the assumption that she could have had only one reason for accepting his offer.

Lady Brill, too, had looked surprised when she first saw him. She knew, of course, that he had proposed marriage to her niece and had been accepted. She had been very civil to him during tea while Samantha had been quiet, looking with an endearing mixture of eagerness and anxiety from him to her aunt. He believed that Lady Brill had liked him by the time he rose to take his leave.

He wondered if Samantha had told her aunt that she was marrying him because she loved him. But it did not matter.

He took a few more sips of his coffee, his eyes still on the newspaper. He could hear the knocker banging against the outer door. Bridge was early. But then he heard voices outside the breakfast room, one of them raised confidently.

"No, no," the voice said. "No need to announce me. I shall announce myself."

It was a voice the marquess had not heard for a number of years, but there was no mistaking it. He pursed his lips and took one last rueful look down at the *Post*.

Lionel, Earl of Rushford, opened the door himself and sauntered inside, glancing about him as he did so. He was looking as if he had just stepped out of Weston's. He was immaculately dressed in the best tradition of Beau Brummell, with nothing overstated. Nothing that Lionel might wear needed overstatement, of course. He looked as if his splendid body had been poured into his clothes.

The marquess did not rise.

"Good morning, Lionel," he said. "Come and join me for breakfast." He gestured toward an empty chair.

"You have made changes," his cousin said.

"Yes, as you see." He had not admired his father's preference for heavy draperies and ponderous furniture. He had made extensive changes both here and at Highmoor. His eye for beauty as a landscape gardener sometimes extended indoors, too.

"Uncle would turn over in his grave," Lionel said. He was at the sideboard, helping himself to something from each of the hot plates. The words were not spoken with any apparent rancor, but they did not need to be. Even after all these years, the marquess recognized the tone. He was his uncle's favorite, the words had suggested, more favored than the son his uncle had been ashamed of.

The suggestion could no longer hurt. Any pain he might have felt had been swallowed up in a far greater pain when he was six years old. But because he had never responded to taunts since then, he guessed that Lionel still thought he had the power to wound.

"You do not seem particularly surprised to see me," Lionel said, seating himself at the table—but not on the chair the marquess had indicated—and tucking into his breakfast.

"I saw you at the Rochester ball," the marquess said.

"But did not come near even to exchange civilities?" Lionel said. "Were you too busy tripping the light fantastic, Hart? That must have been a sight for sore eyes."

"You were dancing with Miss Newman," the marquess said.

"Ah." Lionel set down his knife and fork. "Yes, that. The reason I came. I understand congratulations are in order."

The marquess inclined his head.

"Samantha is exquisitely lovely," Lionel said. "Enough to set any male mouth to watering. You are a fortunate man, Hart."

It was not lost upon the marquess that his betrothed had been referred to by the name that even he had not used aloud yet. Perhaps deliberately so? Yes, probably.

"I am well aware of my good fortune, Lionel," he said. "Thank you."

" 'My face is my fortune, sir, she said.' " Lionel sang through the whole verse of the old song before chuckling. "But no longer, eh, Hart? Now she will exchange it for a far greater fortune. Yes, you are a lucky man indeed. Not that I am suggesting, of course, that she is marrying you for that alone. I am sure your—person offers other inducements. I do believe you have fine eyes."

He spoke with the greatest good nature. Anyone listening would have laughed with him and taken his words for light teasing. The Marquess of Carew was not deceived.

Or ruffled.

"I thank you for your congratulations, Lionel," he said, smiling. "You will, of course, come to the wedding?"

"I would not miss it for worlds," his cousin said. "I am almost your only remaining relative, am I not? In the absence of your mother and my uncle, I must be there myself. It will be affecting to watch you—walk up the aisle with the lovely Samantha."

He was a master at the art of innuendo, the marquess thought. A mere pause between words could speak volumes with Lionel.

"Thank you," he said. "I shall look forward to seeing you there."

"Doubtless you will be taking her back to Highmoor as soon as the wedding breakfast has been consumed," Lionel said. "I would if I were you, Hart. Incarcerate her there. You would not want her running around town once she is married, would you? You know what is said of married ladies. And every man wants to be quite sure of the paternity of at least his firstborn son, after all."

The fingers of the marquess's left hand curled about his napkin. He lifted it to his lips when he saw that Lionel had noted the action.

"A joke, of course," Lionel said, chuckling. "She has a spotless reputation and will doubtless be true to you. What woman would not?" He pushed his chair away and got to his feet, even though his plate was still half-full. "I can see that you are finished, Hart. You doubtless have plans for the morning. I will not keep you. I just felt compelled to come to assure you of a cousin's good wishes."

"Thank you." The marquess stayed where he was. "That was good of you, Lionel. You can show yourself out?"

He stayed where he was for a few minutes after his cousin had left. He smiled again at the announcement still spread on the table beside his plate. Lionel did not know, of course, that it was impossible to put doubts in his mind this morning. Not that he would have allowed himself to be goaded, anyway.

But there was annoyance nevertheless. Perhaps more than annoyance, if he was perfectly honest with himself. Fury. No, fury was an uncontrolled emotion, and his was quite under control. A steely anger, then.

Samantha. Lionel had deliberately called her by her given name to suggest a familiarity with her. He had suggested that she was capable of being unfaithful to him after marriage. He had suggested that she would be capable of conceiving another man's child and passing it off as his own.

He did not mind the insult such slurs cast upon himself and his ability to attract and to please and to control a wife. Lionel's opinion meant less than nothing to him. But he had better not try such insinuations on anyone else.

Let him breathe one breath of an insult on Samantha and there would be trouble. Lionel might yet learn a thing or two about letting the proverbial sleeping dog lie. This dog might not prove to be such an abject weakling as he doubtless thought.

Samantha was his. His possession after their marriage, though he did not believe he would ever be able to think of her in quite such terms. She was his by virtue of the facts that she loved him and he loved her and they were to be married. She was his.

He would protect what was his own.

She felt safe. And cheerful and at peace with herself. She knew she had done the right thing, despite the reactions of other people.

"I was more gratified than I can say," Uncle Gerald had said when he called at Lady Brill's, "to learn that you could be so wise, Samantha. Carew is worth seventy thousand a year, you know, and has made very generous provision indeed for you and any children of the marriage in the event that he should predecease you. The first boy, of course, will inherit."

It did not matter to her that half the members of the *ton*, or maybe a great deal more than half, would believe that she was marrying Hartley for his position and wealth. It was enough that she knew she was marrying him for friendship and safety. Because she liked him more than any other man she had known.

"You could have knocked me down with a feather," Aunt Aggy said after Hartley's afternoon call. "He is not at all the type of young man one would have expected you to choose. And I know, of course, that his title and his fortune did not weigh with you at all. I am happy to have this proof that you have acquired the wisdom to see beyond outer appearances to the man within. He is a very pleasant young man, dear. And I know you would not marry for anything less than love. I believe you have done very well for yourself."

She did not correct her aunt. What she and Hartley had was better than love. Far better. There would be none of the deceptive highs and shattering lows of love in their relationship. Only friendship and gentleness and kindness and—oh, and safety. She clung to the word and the idea more than to any other.

She wondered if it would be a normal marriage. She could not imagine anything more than friendship between them. It seemed almost embarrassing to think of more—until she remembered the kiss they had shared at the Rochester ball. That had been a wonderful kiss, warm and comforting. Perhaps the marriage bed would be like that, too. And she wanted the marriage bed, she realized, even though she had put marriage from her mind years ago and had never felt any great craving for what she would miss as a spinster.

There was no reason to believe that he had been suggesting a mere platonic relationship. He was a marquess—it was still difficult to adjust her mind to that reality—and would want an heir.

She wanted children. Now that she had made the quite unexpected and impulsive decision to marry—so that she would feel safe from the raw emotions that had threatened her with Lionel's return—she wanted all that marriage could offer her. Except love. Love terrified her. She was deeply thankful that Mr. Wade—Hartley—was just her friend. And soon to be her husband. The man who would initiate her in his own quiet way into the secrets of the marriage bed. Despite her age and her worldly wisdom, she knew only the essential fact of what would happen there.

She wanted it—with him. Without any extreme of emotion. With just—affection. There was affection between them, she believed.

Her "court" surprised her. None as much as Francis, it was true—she had been dreadfully upset over his quite uncharacteristic reaction to her announcement, until she met him at a soirée two evenings later and he was his old self, right down to the notorious lavender coat and to the indolent, teasing manner as he asked her if he had succeeded in squeezing a tear from her eye during the afternoon they had not gone to the park.

"Pray do not disappoint me by telling me that I did not succeed with my superior acting skills, Samantha," he said. "You deserved a little punishment for your defection, after all. Now whom am I expected to flirt with without running the danger of finding myself caught in parson's mousetrap?"

She was enormously relieved to learn that it had all been an act. At least, she chose to believe that it had been. She did not like to think that she really had hurt him.

A few of her former beaux quietly disappeared. Some of

them expressed disappointment, with varying degrees of intensity. One or two of them were hearty in their congratulations.

All of them believed the worst of her motives for betrothing herself to the Marquess of Carew. She did not care. But she did try to look at him through the eyes of the *ton*, many of whose members either had never seen him before he started to escort her to some evening entertainments or else were virtual strangers to him.

She saw a gentleman of little more than average height and of only average build—though she knew from the one occasion when her body had rested along the length of his that there was strength in his muscles. She saw a man who had no great claim to good looks, though there was nothing ugly about his face. And of course, she saw a man whose right arm was usually held stiffly to his side, the hand, always gloved, curled inward against his hip. And a man whose permanent limp jarred his whole body when he walked.

She could hardly blame people for the conclusions they must have drawn about her motives for marrying him. But she did not care. She could no longer see him as other people saw him unless she deliberately tried—she was not sure that she had ever seen him as others saw him. To her he was Hartley Wade, more recently the Marquess of Carew, her dear friend. Her savior—the word did not seem too extravagant.

He had saved her from herself.

She saw Lionel twice when she was with Hartley, once at the theater and once at a private concert, but neither time did he approach them, to her great relief. She did not still love him, she had decided. Of course she did not. She had more sense than that. It was just the eternal pull of the human will to what was undeniably attractive and evil.

Hartley had saved her from that. She had settled for friendship and contentment. And Lionel would have no further interest in whatever game he had been playing with her now that she was betrothed to another man.

She was safe.

But she attended a ball with her aunt one evening, two weeks after her betrothal. It was an invitation she had accepted long ago and felt obliged to honor. Besides, she loved to dance, and Hartley had urged her not to stop dancing because of him.

This time Lionel did not keep his distance. He approached her before the opening set began—her court was somewhat thinner about her than it had always been—and signed his name in her card next to the first waltz.

He did not speak for the first few minutes after their set began. He merely danced with her and gazed at her, a half smile on his lips. She could not tell if it was mocking or wistful.

"You did not believe me, did you?" he asked her at last, his voice low, intimate, although they were surrounded by dancers.

She looked up into his pale blue eyes.

"You did not trust me," he said. "You thought I would break your heart again, as I did six years ago."

When he looked and spoke like this, it was difficult not to forget all else except him and the feelings she had once had for him.

"I should not say anything more, should I?" he said. "It would be the honorable thing for me to step back in silence now that you are betrothed to someone else."

"Yes," she managed to whisper.

"You knew," he said, "that I was going to ask you to be my countess. Because I love you. Because I have always loved you."

Why was he doing it if he was not sincere? What could he hope to gain now? She looked into his eyes and saw nothing but sincerity and sadness.

It would be the honorable thing for me to step back in silence . . .

Why was he not doing the honorable thing? If he loved her, as he said he did, why was he trying to cause her distress? Francis, after his first outburst when she had taken him totally by surprise, had gone out of his way to release her from the burden of believing that she had hurt him. He had acted honorably, like the gentleman he was—despite a tendency toward dandyism, even foppishness.

But what if Lionel really loved her? What if he had really intended to offer for her? She might have been his wife. Lionel's instead of Hartley's. She felt the now almost familiar stabbing of desire in her womb.

But she would still be better off as Hartley's wife.

"Someone else asked me," she said. "And I accepted him. Because I wanted to."

"Because you love him?" He moved his head a little closer to hers. His eyes dropped to her lips. "Can you say those words, Samantha? *Because I love the Marquess of Carew.*"

"My feelings for my betrothed are none of your concern, my lord," she said.

"And for me?" he said. "Can you tell me in all honesty, Samantha, that you do not love me?"

"The question is impertinent," she said.

"You cannot, can you?" His eyes pleaded with her.

She clamped her lips together.

The encounter upset her for several days. But she was within two weeks of her wedding. She set her mind on it and the preparations that were being made for it. She longed for it.

Jenny and Gabriel were not coming. Samantha was both disappointed and relieved when she had her cousin's letter. She hated to think of their not being at her wedding, but she had dreaded, too, that if they came they would encounter Lionel somewhere in London.

Jenny herself was very disappointed. But Gabriel was always unwilling for her to travel during the early—and the late—months of her pregnancies, she explained. He was always terrified that she would miscarry and ruin her own health as well as losing their child. But he was disappointed, too.

"He says he is vastly impressed by your good sense, Sam," Jenny wrote. "And by that he does not mean your sense in marrying a man even wealthier than himself, I hasten to add. He means your sense in choosing a man of Lord Carew's kindness and good nature.

"I would choose stronger words myself. How naughty of you to have met him at Highmoor before you left for London and not to have told us. For shame! And I was so chagrined when he arrived home apparently the day after you left. I had great matchmaking hopes for the two of you, though I would never admit as much to Gabriel. He would crow with triumph and never let me forget it.

"Sam, how very *romantic*. I sigh with vicarious bliss. Clandestine meetings in Highmoor Park, the heartrending separation, and the heartsick lover going after you to claim your hand. And they were married and lived happily ever after—sigh! You see what being in an 'interesting condition' does to me? Oh, I *wish* we could be there at your wedding. I like him enormously, Sam, and of course I *love* you. And we are to be neighbors. I become delirious."

She had continued with strict instructions for Samantha to use her newfound influence—"all new husbands wrap very comfortably about one's little finger, Sam"—to persuade Lord Carew to bring her home immediately following the wedding night.

"And do not—I repeat, *do not*—listen with more than half an ear to the lecture Aunt Aggy will give you the night before your wedding," she had written in conclusion. "She will have you quaking in your slippers, Sam, with admonitions about duty and pain and discomfort and enduring for a mere few minutes each night and all the advantages accruing from marriage that quite offset such an unpalatable duty. Performing that particular duty is beautiful and wonderful and utterly pleasurable, Sam—I speak from personal experience, though I blush even as I write—when one loves the man concerned. So enjoy, my dear, your wedding night and every night following it—my blush deepens."

Even Jenny did not know their real reason for marrying. But it did not matter. Love had worked for her and Gabriel. But happy love was a rare commodity. Samantha was happier to settle for something else.

She waited for her wedding day with longing and a thinly veiled impatience. Once she was married, everything would finally be settled in her life. She could proceed to live contentedly ever after.

Sometimes it felt as if the day would never come.

Chapter 12

St. George's, Hanover Square—the fashionable church in which to wed. The first day of June—the fashionable time to marry. The weather was kind. More than kind—there was not a cloud in the sky, and the morning was hot without being oppressively so. The church was filled with modishly dressed members of the *ton*.

If he had ever had a dream of the beginning of wedded bliss, the Marquess of Carew thought as he waited rather nervously at the front of the church with an unusually solemn Duke of Bridgwater, then this was it. There was a great deal to be said for the quiet intimacy of a private ceremony, with only family and very close friends in attendance, but it was not what he wanted for himself.

He wanted the whole world to see their happiness. He wanted the whole world to know what a lucky fellow he was. He had never dreamed of winning for himself such a sweet and beautiful bride, and one, moreover, who had chosen him entirely for himself. He had never expected to find a bride who would love him. And although he had dreamed of loving a woman, he had never really expected to feel that love so powerfully and to have it returned.

To be marrying the woman he loved and the woman who loved him, especially when she happened to be the most beautiful woman in all England—oh, yes, it was an occasion to be celebrated with his peers and hers.

Brides were always late. There were some who would say that it was ill-bred for them to arrive early, or even on time. It showed an overeagerness, something a lady must never show for anyone or anything.

Samantha was on time. If he had been able to smile at that particular moment, the marquess would have smiled. If she was overeager, then his happiness could only be more complete. But he could not smile. At first he was so nervous that he was afraid when he got to his feet his legs would not hold him up. And then he saw her.

He was aware only that she was so beautiful his breath caught in his throat. He did not really see the delicate pink muslin high-waisted dress, as simply and elegantly styled as most of her clothes, or the flowers woven into her blond curls, or the simple posy of flowers she carried in one hand. He did not notice Viscount Nordal, on whose arm she walked down the aisle of the church toward him.

He saw only Samantha. His bride.

She was looking pale and rather frightened. She looked neither to left nor to right at the gathered congregation, though everyone, perhaps without exception, was looking at her. She was looking—at him. And he recognized the slight curving of her lips as an attempt at a smile. He smiled back, though he was not sure that his face responded to his will. He hoped she would know from his eyes that he was smiling at her, encouraging her, welcoming her.

And then they were there beside him and he knew, almost as if he had not yet realized it, that this was their wedding day, that in a matter of minutes they would be married. Irrevocably. For life. Lady Brill, he noticed, was already sniveling in the front pew.

"Dearly beloved, we are gathered . . ."

The familiar words. The familiar ceremony. So very familiar. And yet new and wonderful. Because this time the words were being spoken and the ceremony was being performed for them—for him and his own dearly beloved.

Such a very short ceremony, he thought, promising to love and to cherish and to keep her through all the vicissitudes of life, listening to her promise to love, honor, and obey him—though he would never, ever demand obedience of his love against her will. So short and yet so momentous.

In those few minutes and with very few words, two lives were being changed forever. Two lives were being interwoven, being made one. Man and wife. One body, one soul.

Bridge's hand, as he passed him the ring, was slightly unsteady, he noticed. His own was no longer so. He slid the ring onto her finger. The visual symbol of the endlessness of their union and their love.

"With this ring I thee wed . . ."

And with my body I thee worship, he said with his heart and his eyes as well as with his lips. *My beloved.*

And it was over. Almost before his mind had begun to comprehend that this was it, the most important event of his life. It was over.

"—I now pronounce you man and wife together . . ."

She was still pale. Her eyes, luminous and trusting, gazed into his.

He kissed her, very lightly, very briefly, on the lips. And while the congregation murmured with what sounded like a collective sigh, he smiled at her. His facial muscles obeyed his will this time. He smiled at his bride, his wife.

And she smiled back.

Sometimes happiness could be almost an agony, he had discovered on the day she had accepted his offer. But sometimes it could be such a welling of pure joy that it seemed impossible that one human frame could contain it without exploding into a million fragments.

There was the register to sign. And then the organ was pealing out a glorious anthem as he set his bride's right arm on his left and took her back along the aisle she had descended such a short while ago with her uncle. She was smiling, he saw, looking across at her, and there was color in her cheeks again. He smiled about him at the gathered *ton*, only a few of whom he knew well, but most of whom he had met within the past month. There was Lady Brill, with red-rimmed eyes and watery smile. And Gerson, grinning and winking. And Lionel, with an unfathomable expression.

They were outside on the pavement, the sounds of the organ suddenly faint behind them, a small crowd of the curious standing at a little distance from the waiting carriages. Soon the congregation would spill outside and there would be a damnable crush. He reached across with his stiff right hand and set it lightly on top of hers.

"Samantha Wade, Marchioness of Carew," he said. He wanted to be the first—after the rector—to say it aloud. "You look more beautiful than there are words to describe you."

"Oh, I do sound very grand." She laughed breathlessly. "And you look splendidly handsome, Hartley."

She was looking through the eyes of love, he thought fondly.

Their one moment of near privacy was at an end.

The ballroom at Carew House, Stanhope Gate, was large. Even so, it appeared crowded, with tables set up along its whole length and the cream of the *ton* seated for the wedding breakfast. Samantha, sitting beside her husband, still felt numb, as she had done since waking up from a fitful sleep. It was hard to grasp that it was over, that it was done. She was married. Hartley was her husband.

All yesterday she had been sick with indecision. Literally sick. She had vomited three separate times and had noticed her aunt's look of startled speculation. But the vomiting had been caused entirely by nerves and last-minute doubts. Was it right to marry just for convenience—for *safety*? What if, after all, life had love to offer her? It would be too late to discover that it did after tomorrow.

She had told Aunt Aggy only about the nerves. She had had to say *something* after her aunt had asked her straight out if it was possible she was increasing.

"Because if you had been," Aunt Aggy had said with a sigh after she had been assured that it was no such thing—

she had sounded almost disappointed, "I would not have to proceed to instruct you on what you must expect of your wedding night. I have no wish to add to your fears, dear, but it is as well to be prepared."

She had proceeded with the lecture Jenny had warned about. Samantha had blushed at the graphic and quite dispassionate description of the physical process—some of it she had not known before. But part of her mind had been elsewhere, unwillingly turning over her doubts once more.

Lionel had danced with her twice in the past two weeks. Each time he had been pale and restrained and serious and, of course, impossibly handsome. He had made no further reference to her betrothal. In fact, he had spoken very little—with his voice. His blue eyes had spoken volumes. And somehow she had found it difficult during those sets— waltzes, of course—to stop herself from looking into his eyes.

He had behaved honorably for the past two weeks. As honorably as Francis and Jeremy and Sir Robin and all the rest of her gentlemen friends. She would have preferred it if he had been more obviously snakelike.

She had begun to doubt again. To doubt her own judgment of him. Six years was a long time. He had spent those years traveling abroad. He had aged during those years from five-and-twenty to one-and-thirty. From young manhood to maturity.

What if he had been sincere all the time? He had told her that he had wanted her as his countess. She might have known with him again the heights of romantic love.

And perhaps the depths, too. Perhaps he was not sincere. And even if he had really wanted to marry her and had done so, would he have remained faithful to her for the rest of their lives? Would she have known again the misery that was the exact antithesis of the joy of love?

She was doing the right thing. The sort of affection she and Hartley felt for each other—she did not believe she was using too strong a word—would remain constant. He would

always be kind and gentle with her. They would always be
friends. She need never fear that he would be unfaithful.
And she—she would devote herself to him once they were
married. She would hope that there would be a child
soon—surely he meant for it to be a normal marriage. She
would be safe.

But the doubts had started again and had continued all
day and on through the night—a constant cycle of fear and
panic and reassurance and good sense.

And now it was all over. Now she could let the doubts
rest. It was too late now to doubt. They were married. The
wedding ceremony had affected her far more deeply than
she had expected. It had seemed up until she had seen him
this morning, looking smart and even handsome in a new
blue coat with gray breeches and very white linen, that it
was a practical and sensible alliance they were contracting.
But in the event it had turned out to be—a marriage. He
was not just a friend she had decided to live with for the
rest of her life. He was her husband.

She shivered with the finality of it.

He touched her hand with light fingertips and leaned toward her. "You have eaten very little," he said.

She smiled at him. "Would it not amaze everyone if the
bride ate heartily?" she asked.

She loved the way his eyes smiled. She could almost fall
in love with that smile, she thought, startled.

"Tomorrow," he said. "Tomorrow you will be able to eat
again."

She felt herself blushing. And yet she did not dread the
coming night, despite Aunt Aggy's warnings and her new
realization that there was more than the mere penetration of
her body to be expected. But she did not dread it. She was
only a little embarrassed at the thought of doing it with a
friend rather than with a lover.

They had been greeted by a dizzying number of people
outside the church, almost all of whom had kissed her
cheeks and squeezed her hand and pumped Hartley's

hand—he had offered his left, she noticed—and kissed him, too, if they happened to be female. But even so, she had not seen everyone. And even now, she had been sitting and eating—or not eating—in such a daze that she had not looked at each separate guest. There were a few—friends of Hartley's—that she did not even know or knew only very vaguely by sight.

He had presented her to Lord Gerson, one of his particular friends, a couple of weeks ago at an afternoon fête. She smiled at the man now and he winked at her. He seemed to find the marriage of his friend a huge joke. In fact, he had remarked to her at that fête that he had never seen Hartley in town during the Season before and had known that there must be a woman behind his appearance this time.

"And, by Jove, everything is as clear as daylight to me now that I have clapped eyes on you, Miss Newman," he had said. "Carew is a lucky dog."

There was Lord Hawthorne toward the back of the ballroom, not far from Francis. Francis was looking quite eye-catching in a lemon-yellow coat with pale turquoise waistcoat. It looked as if he were flirting with the ladies on either side of him. He was certainly doing a great deal of smiling and laughing.

Had he been serious? Probably not. He seemed to have recovered very nicely. She hoped he had not been serious. She was fond of him.

And there was—oh, dear God. Dear God! Had he been there all the time? He was seated in the middle of the ballroom, looking so startlingly conspicuous that she could not believe he had not suddenly appeared there from nowhere. Had he been at the church? What was he doing here? He had certainly not been on her guest list. And not on Hartley's, either, though he had told her that he had issued some verbal invitations and not bothered to add them to his written list. But Hartley could not have invited *him*.

Her eyes met his and he looked steadily and gravely at her before she snatched her eyes away. She had not noticed how hot the room had become, how heavy the air was with a hundred different perfumes. She breathed slowly through her mouth, determined not to pant.

There were speeches and toasts and applause and laughter. Hartley got up to speak and she smiled and touched his arm, aware that he was saying something complimentary about her and something about his own good fortune.

He was very sweet. Did he not realize that she was the fortunate one? She felt a sudden wave of gladness—that it was all over and doubts were at rest, that she was safe at last. With a man she trusted and liked.

Those who had not greeted them personally outside the church did so after the breakfast. Guests milled about the ballroom while servants discreetly tried to clear the tables. Guests wandered into the hall and the drawing room and out onto the terrace and into the garden. Samantha was separated from her husband, who was dragged off to the drawing room by someone she scarcely knew to meet an elderly dowager who had known his grandfather. Samantha was led into the garden by several of her lady friends, two of whom linked arms with her.

There she received the homage of her court—she could almost hear Gabriel's voice describing the scene thus and smiled, though she suddenly missed him and Jenny dreadfully.

Francis told her that they were all going to go into deep mourning the next day and into a permanent decline after that. But she tapped him sharply on the arm and reminded him that his behavior at table earlier had hardly been that of a man planning to pine away from unrequited love.

He grinned at her and squeezed both her hands and kissed both her cheeks. Sir Robin followed suit and then Jeremy Nicholson and several others.

She must go and find Hartley, she thought. It felt wrong to be without him.

"Oh, dear," she said suddenly, as her eyes blurred and tears spilled over onto her cheeks. Talking thus with all her old friends and suitors, she had realized anew that her life had changed irrevocably today, that she was a bride and a wife. And that the thought was a pleasing one. "Oh, dear, how foolish I am."

"You see, Samantha?" Sir Robin said. "You are grieving along with us. But for which one of us in particular? That is the intriguing question." He smiled kindly at her while Francis handed her a large linen handkerchief.

She dabbed at her eyes with it and then clutched it in her hand. Francis had turned away, his attention called by one of the ladies who had sat beside him at breakfast.

"Something old and something new," a quiet voice said into her ear, and she spun around, effectively cutting herself off from the small group that still lingered about her. "The pearls are the ones you had as a girl. Your mother's, at a guess. The dress is new and very lovely."

"Thank you," she said, smiling uncertainly at Lionel. She did not like to ask him what he did there. She feared he must have brazened his way in without an invitation. But why?

"Something borrowed," he said, one long, well-manicured finger flicking at the handkerchief she held clutched in one hand. "But nothing blue, Samantha?"

"I did not think of it," she said, gazing into his blue eyes. They looked sad.

"I did," he said. "I brought you a wedding gift. A family heirloom. It has always been very precious to me. I wanted to give it to you on the occasion of your wedding." The shadow of a frown crossed his brow for one moment, but he smiled as he reached into a pocket and brought out a small box. He did not hand it to her but opened it and showed her the contents. His eyes looked into her face the whole while.

She breathed in deeply. The sapphire stone of the brooch was surrounded by diamonds in a pleasingly old-fashioned setting.

"Something blue," he said.

"Oh, my lord," she said, in deep distress. It was such a beautiful, personal gift. "I could not."

"No," he said softly, "you could not refuse a wedding gift, could you? As a token of my—esteem, Samantha?"

"No." She still shook her head. "It is too—personal, my lord. I do thank you. Truly I do. But I could not accept it."

"Whatever would Hartley say if you refused it?" he asked.

"H–Hartley?" She looked at him, frowning.

He laughed suddenly. "My cousin," he said. "My cousin, Hartley. We practically grew up together. Has he not told you? And I have not, either, until now, have I? There are some things one assumes another must know; but there is no reason you should have. I am sorry. My mother and his father were sister and brother. I spent a large part of my youth in Yorkshire, at Highmoor."

She could remember that one year, when Jenny was to have made her come out and her engagement to Lionel was to become official, it had all been postponed because Lionel was in Yorkshire attending his uncle, who was gravely ill. And she remembered that it was some ghastly personal feud between Lionel and Gabriel that had thrown Jenny into the midst of such a dreadful scandal and had forced her to marry Gabriel. But she had never known or asked for all the details. Lionel was Hartley's *cousin*?

"The idea has taken you by surprise," he said. He was unpinning the brooch from its small velvet cushion inside the box. "But you see, you and I are cousins by marriage. And this is a *family* heirloom. You will not refuse it now, will you? And you really must have something blue."

"Yes," she said uncertainly. "Thank you, my lord."

She watched rather unhappily as he took the brooch from the box and reached across to pin it himself on her dress, just above her left breast. The pin was stiff. His fingers lingered for what seemed an eternity and burned her flesh through the thin muslin of her dress. One of his hands brushed downward over her breast, touching the sensitive nipple, when he was finished and was examining the effect of his handiwork.

"Yes," he said softly. "I knew this was where it belonged, Samantha. I could only wish that circumstances had been different, that you had been someone else's bride today. But I wish you every happiness, my dear." He made her an elegant bow, his eyes holding hers.

"Thank you, Lionel," she said, realizing only when it was too late that she had used his given name, something she had not done in six years. "I must go and find my husband."

"Your husband," he echoed. The sadness was back in his eyes. She turned and hurried in the direction of the house, though she was stopped and kissed by wedding guests no fewer than three times before she stepped indoors.

He had somehow got himself cornered by five elderly ladies, all of whom seemed pleased to reminisce about his father or his grandfather—"that handsome devil"—and all of whom agreed that it had been extremely naughty of him to hide himself away from the public gaze for most of his life.

"We will just have to hope that dear Lady Carew will effect a change in you," one lady said, startling him with the use of Samantha's new name.

"And really, you know," another said with unashamed lack of tact, "you need not hide away on account of a limp and a withered hand, Carew. Many of our war heroes have fared far worse. Young Waters, my sister's grandson, came home without one leg and with the other sawn off to the knee."

It was a great relief to see Samantha in the drawing room doorway, looking about her until she spotted him. Everyone she passed on the way wanted to talk to her and kiss her, but in five minutes' time she was at his side and smiling and talking easily with the dowagers, two of whom were not above giving her rather earthy advice about the coming

night and then cackling at their own wit and her blushes—
as well as his own.

Samantha had the social skills to extricate them easily
from the situation after a mere few minutes. He headed into
the hall with her, where some of their guests were finally
taking their leave. They had no time for private words for
some time to come.

He longed for privacy. He was the one who had wanted a
large wedding, and indeed he was not sorry. This would be
a day to remember for the rest of their lives. But he longed
to be alone with her. Even though there was a large part of
the day left and he would not be tasteless enough to try taking her to bed before it was time, nevertheless he longed for
just her company, just the two of them talking together or
perhaps even silently sitting together.

He felt a sudden nostalgia for those afternoons at Highmoor. Soon. Within a week they would be back there and
would proceed to live happily ever after.

He took her out to the garden eventually, past the thin-
ning crowds of their guests. He breathed in fresh air, tucked
her arm through his, and walked with her toward a small
rose arbor, which he hoped would give them a few moments of privacy. Fortunately there was no one there. He
seated her on a wrought-iron seat and sat at her left.

"Someone should have told me," he said, "that the person
one sees the very least on one's wedding day is one's bride."

"But this has all been so very pleasant, Hartley," she
said, turning to smile at him.

That was when he saw it for the first time. His eyes fixed
on it and he felt the blood drain from his head.

"Where did you get that?" he whispered.

"What?" She frowned. But her eyes followed the line of
his and she flushed and covered it with her hand. "Lionel—
L–Lord Rushford gave it to me as a wedding present," she
said. "He said it was a family heirloom. Of *your* family. He
said— I did not know he was your cousin, Hartley. I did
not know you were close. He implied that you would want

me to have it. He made a joke about it being something
blue. I had the other three things—my mother's pearls, my
new dress, Lord Francis Kneller's borrowed handkerchief.
I— Do you recognize it?"

It had been his mother's. One of her precious possessions, given her by his father on their wedding day—as
"something blue," she had always said. She had worn it almost constantly. She had told him when she was dying that
he was to have it and give it to his own bride one day. For
some reason that had stuck in his mind more than anything
after she died, and he had hunted for the brooch, asked his
father about it, asked his aunt, Lionel's mother, about it,
grieved over it almost as much, it had sometimes seemed,
as he had grieved over his mother.

He had never found it.

Lionel had had it. Perhaps he had taken it, or perhaps it
had been given him. But no one had ever told him, Hartley.
He had been left to search, far beyond the bounds of reason, for years.

And now the brooch had been given to his bride after
all—by Lionel.

"Yes, I recognize it," he said. "It was my mother's."

"Oh." She sounded enormously relieved. "Then it was a
very kind gesture, was it not, Hartley, for him to give it to
me? To give it back to you through me. It is a wedding gift
for both of us. It is yours as much as it is mine."

"It is yours, Samantha," he said, "just as it was my
mother's. It looks good on you."

She smiled at him and fingered the brooch again. But he
felt a deep and impotent fury—partly against himself.
Apart from her wedding ring, he had not yet bought her a
gift, he realized. His mother's lovely sapphire brooch, the
"something blue" for the wedding day, had been a gift from
Lionel.

What the devil had he meant by it?

Was it a peace offering?

The marquess did not for one moment believe it.

Chapter 13

She had often been a guest in other people's homes. She was accustomed to sleeping in strange bedchambers. Indeed, it could be said that she had had no real home of her own for a number of years. It was hard now to grasp the reality of the fact that this room was her own. She belonged here at Carew House as she belonged at Highmoor Abbey by virtue of the fact that she was married to the owner of both.

She wrapped her arms about herself, though she was not cold, as she gazed about the large square room with its high coved ceiling, painted with an idyllic pastoral scene, its warm carpet underfoot, its elegant furniture, its large, silk-canopied bed.

It seemed it was to be a normal marriage—there was no reason at all why it would not be, of course. He had said he would join her here shortly. Her mind touched on what Aunt Aggy had told her yesterday and on what Jenny had said in her letter. But she did not expect either extreme from her wedding night. She did not expect to find it fearsome and distasteful. Neither did she expect to find it beautiful and wonderful. She expected—she hoped—to find it pleasant.

She had been pacing, she realized when there was a tap on the door and she stopped. She did not call to him to come in. He opened the door and stepped inside and closed the door behind him. He was wearing a wine-colored brocaded dressing gown with a satin collar. He was smiling at her as he came across the room toward her, his hands reaching out for hers.

"I thought this moment would never come," he said. "I have been shamelessly looking forward to it all day. All month."

He was not wearing a glove. She found herself glancing down at his right hand as it clasped hers. It was paler than the left and thinner. His fingers were bent sharply at the joints. His wrist was bent.

"I wish I could be whole for you," he said.

"Whole?" She looked into his eyes. "You mean because of your accident? Do you think that makes a difference to me? Because you limp? And because you have lost some of the use of your hand? You are whole in every way that could possibly be of importance to me. I regret these things only in that they cause you distress."

She lifted his right hand to rub her cheek against his fingers. She turned her head to kiss them.

"Thank you," he said. "I was a little afraid."

She smiled at him—and blushed.

"You are nervous?" he asked.

"Not really," she said. "Just a little—embarrassed, perhaps." She laughed. "And I suppose nervous, too. But not afraid or reluctant."

He took a step closer so that he was almost touching her and set the backs of the fingers of his left hand against her cheek. "I have some experience," he said. "Which I say not as a boast but as some reassurance. I know how to relax you and how to give you pleasure. And I believe I will be able to minimize the pain of this first encounter for you."

He kissed her.

She was rather surprised, despite the fact that this was their wedding night and he had just come to her bedchamber, and despite the fact that he had kissed her at the Rochester ball—at her request. She had not expected him to kiss her tonight. Kissing was somehow suggestive of love and romance.

But she was glad. She set her arms about his neck and leaned into him. He was warm and comfortable and somehow familiar. He had said he knew how to relax her. He was doing it now. It would not have been relaxing to have been led immediately to the bed and to have been taken into the marriage act without further ado. She parted her lips as he had done and felt the increased warmth and intimacy of the meeting of inner flesh. She felt his tongue stroking the soft inside of her mouth.

She kept her eyes closed as he kissed them and her temples and her chin and her throat. His hair was soft and silky between her fingers. He intended for them to be lovers, she thought in some wonder, as well as friends and man and wife who had conjugal relations.

His mouth returned to hers. His hands were stroking up and down her back, relaxing her further. His left hand came forward to circle gently over the side of her breast. She turned slightly without conscious thought until her breast was cupped in his hand and his thumb was rubbing very lightly over the nipple.

Oh, he felt very good. She had known that he would feel good. How wrong Aunt Aggy had been——had her own marriage been so dreadful? This was lovely. Though this, of course, was not the marriage act.

"We will be more comfortable lying down," he said against her lips, as if he had read her thoughts.

She wondered if the time would come——she supposed it must——when all of this would be so routine that she would hardly think about it at all. But suddenly, as she lay down on the bed and watched him blow out the candles and waited for him to join her, she was glad this was the first time. Two of the most momentous experiences of her life—— her wedding and her first sexual encounter——were happening today, and she wanted to remember them for the rest of her life as also two of the most pleasant experiences of her life.

He slid his right arm beneath her head and drew her

against him before kissing her again. He was wearing only a nightshirt now, she could feel. He was very warm. She snuggled into his warmth. He felt solid and dependable. She was so glad it was he. She was so glad this was not an experience of wild passion and love. She would have been terrified. This she could enjoy. Thoroughly enjoy.

"Yes," she whispered when he touched her breast again. "That feels good, Hartley." His hand moved to the other breast.

She fell into a waking dream of contented pleasure. She was almost unaware that after a short while he undid the buttons at the front of her nightgown and slipped his hand inside so that he could stroke her naked breasts. Certainly there was no embarrassment.

"Beautiful," he murmured against her mouth. "Softer than silk."

She was a little more aware when he lifted her nightgown to her hips. But she was curiously unembarrassed. Had the time come, then? She was ready for it. But he did not do what she expected. His fingertips stroked lightly up the inner thigh of one of her legs and the backs of his fingers stroked down the other thigh. It was exquisitely pleasurable. She parted her legs slightly.

And then his hand moved higher and his fingers touched secret places, parting folds, stroking lightly through them. She tensed only slightly before relaxing again. He was her husband. He had the right. And really it felt very good. She would never have expected it. And then she tensed again as she both felt and heard wetness.

"No, no," he said against her ear. "You must not take fright. This is quite natural. This will help ease any discomfort. It is your body preparing itself for mine."

Aunt Aggy had not mentioned this. She relaxed. Though it was not quite relaxation, either. She felt—desire? No, not quite that, perhaps. She had no wish to feel desire or anything suggestive of passion. Her body had prepared itself for his and was waiting for his. Yes, he had described it well. Her body was ready.

And so, when he lifted himself over her and onto her, she welcomed his weight and his legs widening her own. Her breath quickened. She pressed her palms hard into the mattress on either side of her.

He was against her. And coming slowly and firmly into her.

It was—yes, it was by far the most wonderful experience of the day. Perhaps of her life. How foolish Aunt Aggy's warnings seemed now. There was no pain, except for one brief moment when she thought there would not be enough room and then felt him breaking through and realized that it had just been the loss of her virginity. There was no other pain, even though there was an unexpected tightness and stretching. He was far bigger than her imagination had anticipated. When he was finally fully embedded in her, she felt very—married, although she knew that this was not all.

"Have I hurt you?" His warm breath tickled her ear.

"No." She moved her arms to wrap them about his waist. "It feels good, Hartley."

"Slide your feet up the bed," he said. "You will be more comfortable. Wrap your legs about mine later if you wish."

Later. Just a few seconds there would be, Aunt Aggy had said, of movement that could be intensely unpleasant for the woman. It was best to hold one's breath and count slowly to ten—beyond, if necessary. Jenny had disagreed.

She bent her legs and braced her feet against the mattress on either side of his legs.

He began to move. Very slowly out and in again until a rhythm had been established. She could hear wetness but could understand now how it created ease of movement for him and pleasure instead of pain or discomfort for her.

It lasted a long time. When his pace increased slightly she remembered what he had suggested and twined her legs about his. His right thigh was as powerfully muscled as his left, she thought idly before her new position made her part of his rhythm and she gave herself up to pure enjoyment again.

She was sorry when she sensed that it was about to end. As far as she was concerned, it could have gone on all night. But he had slowed and his inward pushes had deepened. He strained against her while she tightened her legs about his, pulling him deeper, and even contracted inner muscles that she had been unaware of until now.

And then she felt a hot flow deep inside and knew that his seed had been released into her womb. He sighed against the side of her face and she sighed with contentment at the same moment. She was now in every way his wife. It was a lovely feeling, far lovelier than she had imagined. It was possible, she thought, to be lovers without feeling any powerful or destructive passion for each other.

Just this warm—uniting. She felt one with him at that moment and thought how accurate were the words of the wedding service. *One flesh.*

She was sorry it was over until tomorrow night. She did not want him to go away. She did not want to be alone again, even though she was tired. He was warm and relaxed and heavy on her. She wanted him to be asleep so that she could hold the comfort and the pleasure of her wedding day to her for a while longer.

But he was not sleeping deeply. After a mere couple of minutes he stirred.

"I am sorry," he said, lifting himself away from her. "I must be squashing you."

He did not immediately get out of bed. He lay on his side beside her. She turned to face him and smiled at him. She could see him quite clearly in the darkness. He slid his arm beneath her head again and smiled back.

"That was—"

"I did not know—"

They spoke together and stopped together. She waited for him to resume, snuggling close into his warmth again.

"I did not know it was possible to love so deeply," he said, "or to be loved so tenderly."

Love? Was he talking merely about the act they had just performed?

"I can still hardly believe it," he said. His voice was sleepy. "That you love me. I fell in love with you as soon a I set eyes on you, of course. You looked so lovely and so peaceful and so much as if you belonged, gazing down at the abbey from the hill. And then so startled and so guilty when I spoke. But then you are naturally beautiful and desirable—I have not failed to notice how many men here admire you. I will never cease to be amazed and grateful that you came to love me of all men. I am so very ordinary."

"You are not—"

But he laid a finger on her lips. "I am not fishing for compliments," he said. "I followed you to London because life at Highmoor without you was too empty and too painful. I thought that perhaps if I just saw you once more and perhaps spoke with you once more I would find ease for the pain in my heart. When I saw the gladness in your face and when you asked me to kiss you and told me you loved me . . . No, I cannot tell you how I felt, my love. There are not words to describe the joy."

Oh, dear Lord. Oh, dear Lord. No. Please, no. She would lose him. She was going to lose him. Feelings like that could not last. And feelings like that could not subside into affection or friendship. Only into hatred and pain. And despair.

He drew her closer until his lips almost touched hers.

"I love you," he whispered. "I am not sure I have ever said those words aloud to you, have I? They are strangely difficult to say. What a precious gift they were when you said them to me. I love you. I love you."

She gulped rather noisily and hid her face against his shoulder. "Hartley," she said. "Oh, Hartley." She was crying then, loudly and wetly, and could seem to do nothing about it. Everything was ruined. She had had no idea. If only she had. She could have prevented this from happening. But now it was too late. Why had she assumed that he felt as she did? He had never told her why he wanted to marry her. Only now did she realize that. And she had married him to escape from the terrors and insecurities of passion.

"Sweetheart." He was holding her very tightly, but his voice was gentle. "Darling, I know. Sometimes the heart is so full that it spills itself in surprising ways. It has been an emotion-filled day for you. Did I hurt you when I loved you?"

N—no," she said. "It was good, Hartley. I enjoyed it." They seemed inadequate words. But she did not want to use or feel anything more superlative. It *had* been good. She *had* enjoyed it.

She did not want him to love her. Not in the way he had just described. Romantic, delirious, passionate love. She remembered the feelings and the corresponding agony when they had let her down. If she had wanted passion again, she could have married Lionel and shared the feeling with him—for a while. Until it was over again.

"It will get even better," he said. "I wanted you to become comfortable with what happens this first time, my love. I wanted you to find it pleasant. But there is more. There is so much more for you to experience. So much more I want to teach you—and be taught by you. It will work both ways, you know, even if you do not realize it now. And we have the rest of our lives ahead of us."

Hartley, she thought, her eyes closed against his shoulder, *don't love me. I don't want you to love me.*

"Just a moment," he said as she sniffed rather wetly. "I have a handkerchief in the pocket of my dressing gown." He left the bed and felt around in the darkness. He sat on the edge of the bed as she wiped her eyes and blew her nose in his handkerchief.

"Don't leave me," she said, suddenly fearful. Though she did not quite know if she was talking about now, this mo-

ment, or about some vague future time in their lives. She
had felt so safe with him. Now she felt bewildered and
rather frightened.

"Leave you?" He bent toward her and tucked an errant
curl behind her ear. "I married you at least partly so that I
might sleep with you, my love. And I use the word not just
as a euphemism for making love, though that, too." He
smiled. "I want to sleep with you in my arms all night and
every night. I want to feel married to you. But we are both
very tired. I think we should sleep, don't you? Together?"

"Yes, please," she said. She lifted her head as he lay
down again so that his arm could come beneath her. She
curled in against him and breathed in the warm smell of
him. She felt almost safe again.

"Hartley." She could give him only one thing at the moment. "I did not cry because it was not good. I cried because it was very good. Because this whole day has been
very good."

"I know, love." He lifted her chin and kissed her softly.
"Do you think your body did not tell me your feelings? I
know it was good. Sleep now."

She was bone weary, she realized. She felt herself falling
immediately toward sleep. She was in this marriage now,
was one of her last thoughts. And she could not be as sorry
as she should be. Perhaps she could make him so firmly her
friend that he would never leave her or hurt her, even when
the love he now felt had died.

He had never believed in happily-ever-afters. They were
fine for stories intended for the delight of children. Children needed the security of a belief in lifelong happiness.
He knew that in reality life for most people was a series of
peaks and valleys, and that the best one could hope for was
that there would be more peaks than valleys and that they
would be higher than the valleys were deep.

Perhaps he still did not believe in happily-ever-afters. If
he had stopped, really, to consider the matter, basic good

sense would have forced him to admit that at some future time there would be troubles and problems and sadnesses in his life again. But he was so firmly on one of life's highest pinnacles that it seemed to him for two whole days after his wedding that he would never have to suffer again.

And he would never let his wife suffer. For the rest of his days, he would devote himself to her happiness.

It was an immature assessment of the future, he realized later. But it was understandable. He was in love with a woman who loved him and they were newly married. What more could life offer, except endless years together and children of their bodies?

He believed—though he had never discussed the matter openly with anyone—that it was considered decorous to love one's wife once a night and perhaps not even that often. What was a pleasure for men was said to be an unpleasant duty for women. If one needed a woman more often than decorum allowed, then there were women enough who were only too glad to provide a service for a suitable fee.

He cared nothing for decorum. Allowing him his marital rights was no unpleasant duty to Samantha—he had known that from the very first time. And he had no wish for any other woman but his wife for the rest of their lives. It was not so much that he needed a woman more often than strict decorum allowed. It was that he wanted his wife constantly.

On their wedding night, tired as they both had been when they fell asleep, they woke together just before dawn, smiled sleepily at each other, and sank toward sleep again. But desire had kept him awake, and he had made love to her once more after she had assured him that she was not sore. He had made it long and almost languorous, all interior play with no foreplay. He had held back his release until he felt her relaxed pleasure.

They went walking in the park during the morning, when it was almost deserted, keeping to the quieter paths that gave the illusion of being in the country rather than in the middle of a city. There were even deer grazing among the trees, as there were at Highmoor. They held hands when it seemed they would be unobserved, and talked about their surroundings and about Highmoor. It was always so easy to talk with Samantha. He was fortunate, he thought, to have a friend as well as a lover in his wife. She glowed when she talked to him and smiled a great deal. She *liked* him as well as she loved him, he thought, and derived amusement from the rather peculiar thought.

They drove out into the country in an open carriage during the afternoon, taking a direction that would be unlikely to bring them into company with others. They sat with clasped hands and talked very little as they gazed about at the wonders of nature. And that was another thing about Samantha, he thought. They could sit silently together for hours and still be comfortable. It seemed almost as if their minds worked along the same lines, though they rarely compared notes to be sure.

The *ton* would have been shocked at what he did when they arrived home at teatime. They did have tea, but then he took her to bed and loved her again. Of course it was not in bad taste, she assured him with a smile that was almost impish when he suggested it. She was his wife. She was his for the asking. And he certainly would not have to beg.

He loved her twice during that night. The next day followed much the pattern of the day before, except that it rained soon after luncheon and they spent the whole afternoon in bed, first loving, then sleeping, then talking about Highmoor and what they would do there during the summer. The day after tomorrow they would start their journey, he told her. He had intended starting back earlier, but he did not want to end this idyll with her too soon. Travel was tedious and inn beds not nearly as comfortable for love as this bed was.

He loved her three times during the night. He really must allow her some rest in the coming day and the following night, he decided with a smile as he held her and watched dawn lighten the room while she slept. Not that making love was a great deal of exertion for her. She enjoyed physical love with him. He did not doubt that. But so far hers had been a largely passive role. She had lain quiet and receptive as he worked in her.

He could bring her to climax. He could arouse passion in her and build it to a crescendo and then coax her over the edge. He could teach her to be as active in their lovemaking as he was. He could teach her to make love to him and in the process intensify her own pleasure. And he would do it. He longed for it.

But not yet. She was not ready yet for passion. He would not have been able to put into words how he knew. It was something he sensed. Because he loved her. Because he knew her well despite the fact that they had been acquainted for a relatively short time. Because—Dorothea had once told him this—he had the rare skill of being able to read the messages of a woman's body.

He knew that his wife was not yet ready for passion.

And so he waited patiently for her. It was no hardship. They loved dearly. And they both drew deep enjoyment from their sexual encounters.

For the three days and nights that started with his wedding day, the Marquess of Carew would have said that he was living happily ever after, even if a part of him would have known that there is no such thing in this life.

All of him knew it the next day.

Chapter 14

They were to leave for Highmoor the next day. Samantha could hardly wait. To go back there and know it was to be her home—the thought was still unreal. She would not believe it until she was there. And all of the summer would remain to wander about the park, to see perhaps the construction of the bridge over the lake—Hartley had said he would start with that. And there would be Jenny and Gabriel and the children to see again. She was to be their close neighbor. And Hartley had said they were his friends.

She longed to be on the way. The sooner they left, the sooner they would arrive. But there was one bad part about leaving so soon. The honeymoon was at an end. She had several people to call on in order to take her leave of them. Hartley had similar errands and some business to do. And so they went their separate ways that day after a late and lingering breakfast together.

Some of her fears had been allayed. He had talked of love that first night and had frequently told her since that he loved her. He almost always called her by some endearment rather than by her name. But he was invariably kind to her and gentle, and they were still friends. They could still talk and laugh together endlessly, or be silent together without any awkwardness or boredom.

Perhaps, after all, she had nothing to fear. Perhaps she was safe. After all, Jenny and Gabriel loved, and they still seemed perfectly happy—and each other's friend—even after six years of marriage.

Perhaps she need no longer punish herself for the sin of kissing and of falling in love with Jenny's betrothed all those years ago. And for wishing that the betrothal could somehow be ended. And for being secretly glad when it was, despite the terrible suffering and humiliation Jenny had had to face.

Perhaps, after all, she could allow herself to be loved.

She had been happy for three days—and three nights. Wonderfully, unexpectedly happy. He was the friend and companion she had hoped for when she had agreed to marry him. And as a lover he was—oh, how could she use any superlative? She had no one with whom to compare him. He was gentle and considerate and patient and thorough. He was good—he was very good. She had come to adore his body and the skilled way he used it to give her pleasure. She never minded being wakened during the night, tired as she might be—and sometimes she was the one to do the waking, though she did not believe he realized it yet. And she never minded being taken to bed during the day, even though it was very obvious to her that the servants *knew*. Let them know. Let them be envious.

She had looked forward to the physical side of marriage and had hoped that it would at least be pleasant. It was far more than pleasant. It bound them together in a tie deeper than mere friendship. She could not put a word to the bond. But after three days she felt very much his wife. And she hugged the feeling to herself as perhaps her most precious possession, even if it was intangible.

She called on Lady Brill first and the two of them made a round of calls. Her uncle told her that he had been pleased to discover that, after all, she had a wise and sensible head on her shoulders in choosing a husband with a superior title and seventy thousand a year. Her lady friends hugged her and lamented the fact that she would be gone for the rest of the Season and wished her well. Some of them looked faintly envious. One of them—though she had never been a close friend—remarked apropos of nothing, or so it seemed, that it was a pity the richest men never seemed to be also the handsomest men.

"Not that I was insinuating—" she said, looking at Samantha in dismay, one hand flying to her mouth.

Samantha merely smiled.

Lady Sophia, her newly mended leg elevated on a satin pouf, looked Samantha over from head to foot and nodded in satisfaction.

"She is looking like the cat that got locked in with the cream pot, Aggy," she said. "Carew must have done his job on her and done it well." She cackled at her own joke and Samantha's hot blush.

"You are in need of exercise and fresh air, Sophie," Lady Brill said briskly.

And so they drove in the park, the three of them. The weather was warm and sunny again after yesterday's rain. The *ton* was out in force. The barouche in which they rode moved at snail's pace, when it was moving at all. People came to inquire after Lady Sophia's health. Friends came to greet and chat with Lady Brill. And Samantha drew quite as much attention as she had ever done. Perhaps more today. She fancied that everyone was looking at her with curiosity and interest. It was doubtless her imagination, she told herself, but the knowledge of how she had been spending her nights—and her afternoons—since the *ton* saw her last set her to blushing a great deal of the time.

Lord Francis, dashing in puce riding coat and skintight black leather pantaloons and Hessians, rode up to her side of the carriage, distracting her attention from the conversation the other two ladies were holding with a couple at the other side. He leaned one arm on the door of the carriage and looked at her closely and appreciatively.

"Well, Samantha," he said quietly, "never let it be said that marriage disagrees with you."

"*I* certainly would begin no such rumor, Francis," she said. But she could not prevent the telltale blush.

"Lucky dog," he said, more to himself than to her. "You love him, then, Sam?"

It was the first time he had used Jenny's name for her. But his question jolted her. There must be something in her face. But what could show in her face apart from her blush?

"Why else would I have married him, Francis?" she asked. She had meant the question to be lightly, teasingly phrased. She heard too late the earnestness in her voice. She wanted him to believe that she had married for love, she realized. Hartley deserved that. "Of course I love him."

"Yes, Sam," he said, his smile slow in coming. "It is there in your eyes for all to see, my dear. And so I must begin the search for another incomparable to inspire my devotion. You will be hard to replace."

"Oh, nonsense, Francis," she said, but fortunately Lord Hawthorne rode up at that moment and the couple who had been talking with her aunt and Lady Sophia drove away. The privateness of the moment was gone.

Was there really something about her eyes? Samantha wondered in some alarm as they drove from the park a short while later. She could not think what it could be, except perhaps a certain vacantness occasioned by the fact that her mind kept wandering to Hartley, wondering how he was spending his day, wondering if he would be home when she returned, hoping that he would be, longing to see him again, dreaming about the past three days—and nights.

She must not start daydreaming. It had never been one of her shortcomings. And it was very ungenteel to daydream in the presence of others about her husband.

Finally her own carriage set her down outside Carew House and she hurried inside with eager steps. It was after six already. The day was gone. She hoped he would be home. She hoped some of his friends had not persuaded him to dine at one of the clubs on his last evening in town. How dreary it would be to have to dine alone and wait until perhaps late into the night for his return. And then perhaps he would be foxed, though she had never known him to drink to excess. Or else he would sleep in his own bed because of the lateness of the hour and his reluctance to wake her.

Her foolish fears fled faster than they had crowded in upon her as soon as she stepped into the hall. He was standing at the far side of it, his left arm behind his back, his feet braced slightly apart. He looked—handsome, she thought, smiling. The library door was open behind him. He must have heard the carriage and come out to greet her. But he had not hurried toward her. And so, just in time, she checked her impulse to rush toward him and offer her mouth to be kissed. There were two footmen in the hall, and despite what they must know, all open signs of affection must be reserved until he and she were behind closed doors.

"Hartley," she said, untying the strings of her bonnet, pulling it off, and shaking out her flattened curls, "did you have a good day?"

Tell me you missed me. No, wait until we are alone.

"Thank you, yes," he said. "Will you join me in the library?"

So that we can close the door and put our arms about each other and bemoan the waste of a day apart?

She pulled off her gloves. "Give me time to wash my hands and comb my hair?" she asked, still smiling. *So that I can be beautiful for you.*

He inclined his head to her.

"Will you order tea?" she asked, hurrying toward the staircase. "I am parched."

She turned her head to look down at him as she climbed the stairs. And stopped for a moment. What was it? He looked his usual self, neat and tidy, but not in the first stare of fashion. He was watching her with no particular expression on his face.

What is wrong? she was about to ask. But there were the servants. She would wait until she came back down and they were in the library.

Her steps quickened. She would be as fast as she could. She did not even bother to ring for her maid. She washed her hands and face in cold water and brushed quickly at her curls to bring the spring back into them. The need to hurry, to waste not one more moment than was necessary, was strong on her.

But the brush paused as she caught herself feeling the urgency. The need to be with him. In his arms.

What was happening?

She peered suspiciously at her eyes in the looking glass. *Were* they different from usual? They looked like the same old eyes to her. She grinned at herself.

And went hurrying from the room and running lightly down the stairs. A footman crossed to the library door and held it open for her. She smiled at him in passing.

He went to White's with Bridgwater for luncheon, and they were joined by Gerson and a few other acquaintances. It was a very pleasant way to spend his last day in town, even though he had missed Samantha from the moment of handing her into his carriage and waving her on the way to Lady Brill's.

He endured a great deal of teasing, much of it decidedly ribald. It was all good-natured, he knew, and perhaps fueled by a degree of envy. Besides, he admitted to himself that he really was feeling rather smug. No one else, after all, had just married the loveliest lady in London. No one else was loved by her. And, truth to tell, he had been every bit as randy during the past three days as his friends accused him of being, though he had been more respectful of his wife's body than a few of them dared to suggest.

They were enjoying a few drinks after luncheon, and he was trying to calculate in his mind the earliest hour he could expect to find Samantha at home, when Lionel appeared in the doorway of the dining room, paused there, and came inside.

"Hart," he said, walking toward him, right hand extended, his smile warm. "How is the new bridegroom? Retreated to your club to recuperate from certain, ah, exertions, have you?"

He squeezed the marquess's right hand rather painfully while the others chuckled and offered their own answers to the question. Friends, it seemed, never tired of reminding a newly married man of how his nights had suddenly changed for the better, even if they had become more sleepless.

The marquess got to his feet and drew his cousin a little apart from the crowd. The noise there was getting louder in direct proportion to the amount of alcohol that was being consumed. He swallowed his dislike of Lionel and smiled back at him. Perhaps it was time. They were grown men. The stupidities of boyhood and the excesses of young manhood were behind them. At least he must believe so. He was rather ashamed of his reaction to Samantha's wedding gift.

"I have to thank you, Lionel," he said. "It was a kind and generous gesture."

Lionel's handsome brows rose. There was some amusement in his eyes, the marquess thought.

"The brooch," the marquess said. "You must know that it is more precious to me than just its market value. Mother always wore it and it is somehow associated with my fondest memories of her. I suppose Father gave it to you as a memento after her death, not realizing that she had intended . . . But it does not matter. It was a precious wedding gift you gave us. I thank you."

"Perhaps you misunderstood, Hart." There was definite amusement in Lionel's eyes now. "It was a gift for your bride alone. A gift from me to her. In appreciative memory of times past. Did you not know about us?"

The very thought of Lionel and Samantha's being referred to as "us" was somehow nauseating.

"We were an item six years ago," Lionel said. "Indeed we were indiscreet enough to be a partial cause of the breakup of my betrothal to her cousin—Lady Thornhill, you know, your neighbor. We were what you might call in love, Hart. Deeply, head over ears in love. I had to abandon her because Papa had the notion that my absence was more desirable than my presence, and I would not embroil her in my disgrace. She was still an innocent, you see. I am sure you found her satisfyingly virgin on your wedding night?"

He raised his eyebrows but did not wait long for an answer.

"I do believe I broke her heart," he said. "I rather fancy that she blamed me. And perhaps she was right. It is a shameful thing for a man to be responsible for breaking his own engagement, is it not? She would have nothing to do with me when I returned this spring. And yet she was frightened by the power of the feelings she still had for me. Strange, is it not, Hart, that a woman of such exquisite beauty was still unmarried at her age? You came along at the right moment, old chap. She ran to your arms, where I daresay she feels safe. Rightfully so, I would imagine. You are looking after her well, I presume? But of course you would."

Regrettably it was not a story he could brush off as a product of a malicious imagination. Though the intent in telling it was utterly malicious, of course.

"Yes, I am looking after her well, Lionel," he said quietly. "You will, of course, leave what is past in the past from this moment on."

"Why, Hart," Lionel said, chuckling, "if I did not know you better, I could almost imagine that that was a threat."

"You were doubtless on your way somewhere when you spotted me through the doorway," the marquess said. "I will not delay you any longer, Lionel. Thank you for your good wishes."

"Ah, yes," Lionel said. "You remind me of my manners, Hart. My good wishes for your continued happiness."

He smiled warmly at his cousin and at the noisy group of men still gathered about the table, then left the room.

"It is time for me to leave, too," the marquess said to his friends, dredging up a smile from somewhere inside.

"The bride must not be left to pine alone for one moment longer than necessary," a tipsy voice said from the midst of the throng. "A toast to you, Carew. A toast to your continued stamina. Still able to get to your feet after three days. Jolly good show, my good fellow."

"But flat on his stomach again as soon as he has raced home," someone else said, raising his glass in acknowledgment of the toast.

"I'll come with you, Hart," the Duke of Bridgwater said, getting to his feet.

"There is no need," the marquess said. "I am going directly home."

But his friend clapped a hand on his shoulder and accompanied him downstairs, where they retrieved their hats and canes, and out onto the pavement.

"I overheard," he said. "I did not mean to eavesdrop, Hart. At first I did not realize it was a private conversation."

"Hardly a conversation," the marquess said.

"He was always a scoundrel," the duke said, falling into step beside him and adjusting his stride to the more halting one of his friend. "And for what he did to Lady Thornhill—and to Thornhill, too—he deserved to be shot. Thornhill showed great but lamentable restraint in not calling him out. The lady had been put through enough distress already, of course. I have been glad to see since then, whenever they have been in town, that the two of them seem contented enough with each other."

"More than that," the marquess said. "I never did know quite what happened, Bridge. And I do not want to know now. It was a long time in the past."

"Except that the scoundrel has managed to bring it into the present," the duke said. "There was never a breath of scandal surrounding Lady Carew's name, Hart. I would advise you not to give any credence to anything he said. He obviously fancied her himself this year and was annoyed when she chose you—London is full of men who are annoyed about exactly the same thing. Fortunately all the others are honorable men. Kneller, for example. He has been wearing his heart on his sleeve for more than one Season. She chose you, Hart. She might have chosen any of a dozen others, all almost as well set up as you."

The marquess smiled. "You do not have to plead my wife's case, Bridge," he said. "I am married to the lady. I know why she married me. I respect her and trust her. And I do not choose to discuss the matter further with you. Marriage is a private business between two people."

"And I would not intrude," his friend said unhappily. "But if you could see your face, Hart."

"I am going home," the marquess said. "I would take you out of your way if you came any farther, Bridge."

His grace stopped walking. "And I would not be invited inside if I did come farther," he said ruefully. "Well, Hart." He extended his left hand. "Have a safe journey and a good summer. Give Lady Carew my regards."

They shook hands before the marquess turned and limped away.

He tried not to think. He had known from the age of six on that Lionel was not worth one moment of suffering. For some reason—he supposed the reasons were pretty obvious—Lionel had marked him as a victim ever since they were young children together. Nothing had changed. Lionel would do anything and everything in his power to hurt him or belittle him. But Lionel could have that power only if it was given him. The Marquess of Carew had done no giving since the vicious "accident" that had left him partly crippled.

He was not going to reverse the lesson of a lifetime now. It was as Bridge had said. Lionel had returned to London, set his sights on Samantha—whether for marriage or mere dalliance only he knew—and had been severely humiliated when she would have none of him. Humiliation had turned to spite and the vicious need for revenge when she had married his far less personable cousin, the apparent weakling who had always been his victim.

But thought could not be kept at bay. He retired to his library as soon as he reached home, with the instruction to the footmen on duty that Lady Carew was to be asked to join him there on her return. He paced as he waited for her. But it was a wait of three hours.

She had been hurt in the past. He had known that. He had even spoken of it to her. Six years ago she would have been eighteen. Probably in her first Season. A ripe age for a romance with a man of Lionel's looks and practiced charms. And of course she would have met him on a number of occasions. He had been betrothed to her cousin at the time. And she had been living with her uncle, Lady Thornhill's father.

She had been hurt so deeply that in six years she had not married, though he knew that she had spent each Season in London, and since his arrival this year he had seen that she had a following unrivaled by any other young lady of *ton*. He had seen, too, that a number of those followers—yes, Lord Francis Kneller was among them—had a serious attachment to her. But she had not married.

It must have been a far worse than ordinary heartbreak. If she had been partly responsible for the breakup of her cousin's engagement . . . She loved her cousin. And it seemed from the little he knew that the incident had brought terrible and painful scandal to Lady Thornhill. And if then, after it all, the object of her love had left the country, abandoned her . . . Yes, for someone as sweet and sensitive as his wife, such events might keep her from love and marriage for six years.

And inexplicably this year she had fallen headlong in love with him. With a man who was apparently no more than a traveling landscape gardener. With a man about whose looks the kindest thing that could be said was that he was not quite ugly. With a man who limped so badly that sometimes people turned their heads away in embarrassment. With a man with a claw for a right hand.

What a gullible wretch, he would have said of himself if the story had been told to him of someone else. What a romantic fool!

Lionel had returned to England this year. Perhaps—no, *probably*—that had been their first meeting, at the Rochester ball. They had been waltzing together, looking incredibly beautiful together. He would have used his charm on her again—Lionel would have been unable to resist the temptation to exert power over a beautiful woman who had once loved him when he was forbidden territory. And she would have felt a resurgence of her long-suppressed feelings for him. She would have tried to resist them. She would have been very upset.

If she had rushed from the ballroom after the set was over, rushed onto the landing outside the ballroom and run into someone she had never expected to see again, someone with whom she had struck up a friendship a month or two earlier, she would have greeted him with delight and relief. She would have seen him almost as a savior. She would have begged him to take her outside where there was air. She would have tried to forget with him. She would have asked him to kiss her. She would have told him she loved him. . . .

And if she was still upset the following day, and if the friend called upon her to make her an offer, having mistaken the cause of her ardor the night before, she might have impulsively accepted him. She might have tried to escape from herself and to have avoided having her fragile heart rebroken by accepting the offer of someone safe.

She had never once since their marriage, he thought, told him that she loved him. He had said the words to her numerous times. She had never shown any sign that she wanted passion with him.

He was her friend. No less and no more than that.

He wondered how far off the mark all his guesses were.

Not far, he believed. As far as the sun is from the earth, he hoped.

He could not bring himself to hope.

She came, finally. He heard the carriage and stepped into the hall. She was like a little piece of the summer sky in her pale blue muslin dress and straw bonnet trimmed with yellow flowers. She was flushed and smiling.

Something blue, he thought.

And even then he had to wait. She wanted to go upstairs and wash her hands and comb her hair, though it looked lovely enough to him. She paused on the stairs and looked down at him. But she continued on her way.

She could have been no longer than ten minutes. It seemed like ten hours. But he heard the door of the library open behind him eventually and turned as she came in. Fresh and lovely and still smiling.

His wife. His love.

The door closed behind her and she stopped suddenly. He had thought she was going to walk right across the room into his arms.

"What is it?" she asked him, her head tipping to one side and her smile dying. "What is the matter, Hartley?"

"Why did you marry me?" he asked her.

He watched her eyes widen with surprise and—with something else.

Chapter 15

The light went out of the day. She did not understand the question—and yet she understood one thing very well. She understood that the dream was fading, that she was waking up. That she was being forced to wake up.

"What?" she asked. She was not sure that any sound got past her lips.

"Why did you marry me?" he asked again. "Because you love me, Samantha?"

The ready lie sprang to her lips but did not make it past them this time. She stared at him, the man above all others whom she would protect from hurt if she could. "What has happened?" she asked him.

"You counter one question with another," he said. "Was mine so difficult to answer, Samantha? A simple yes or no would have sufficed."

The light that had been in his eyes since the night of the Rochester ball had died. Oh, fool not to have realized before it was too late that it was the light of love. It was gone.

"Tell me something," he said. "And let there be honesty between us. Do you still love him?"

Something died inside her. Something that had been blooming unnamed and almost unnoticed since her wedding day.

"What has he been telling you?" she asked.

His eyes grew bleaker, if that was possible. "I notice," he said, "that you do not ask to whom I refer."

"What has he been telling you?" Her hands sought and

found the handle of the door behind her back. She clung to it and moved back against it as if it could protect her from pain.

"About six years ago," he said. "And about this year."

"And you believe him?" she asked.

"I will believe *you*," he said. "Tell me what happened six years ago."

She closed her eyes for a few moments and drew deep breaths. What did six years ago have to do with this moment? But of course it had everything to do with it.

"I was very young," she said, "and fresh from the schoolroom. And he was handsome, charming, experienced. I did not like him. I thought him cold. I even told Jenny so. But that was before he kissed me one evening and declared his passion for me. There was nothing else except melting looks from him and fiercely unhappy glances and the suggestion that if we were ever to know happiness together, I should speak with Jenny and have her end the betrothal. He could not do so as an honorable gentleman."

"Did you think him honorable, Samantha?" he asked quietly.

"No!" she said sharply. "But I thought him unhappy and in love and desperate."

"As you were?" he asked.

"I would not do as he asked," she said. "I fought my feelings for him. And I felt sick for Jenny, about to marry a man who did not love her. I prayed for an ending of the betrothal so that she could be saved and he and I could be together, but when it happened it was horrible. Oh, dear God, it was horrible. The terribly public disgrace for Jenny. Uncle Gerald caning her and preparing to send her away. And worst of all—or so it seemed at the time—Gabriel forcing her into marriage. And it was all my fault."

"But it was not," he said.

"No." She had her hands over her face. She drew a deep breath again. "But I have never been able to stop feeling guilty. If I had not presented Lionel with the idea of a way out . . . He did not love me. He had tried to use me. He laughed at me when I approached him after Jenny's hasty marriage. He made me feel like a silly child, which is just what I was, of course. I have hated him ever since."

"Hated," he said. "Hatred is a powerful emotion, Samantha. Akin to love, it is said."

"Yes." Her voice was dull. "So it is said. I still hate him. Today more than ever. Why would he want to hurt his own cousin?"

"It amuses Lionel to hurt people," he said. "Tell me about this spring."

"There is nothing to tell," she said. "I saw him in the park the day before the Rochester ball. I had not known he was back in England. I was terrified. And then he appeared at the ball and asked me to waltz with him. I did. That was all. Oh, and he called on my aunt and me the next afternoon."

"Before I called?" he asked.

"Yes."

"You were terrified," he said. "Of what? That he would harm you?"

"No." She felt suddenly weary. She would have liked nothing better than to sink to the floor and fall asleep. But there was the necessity to talk. He was not going to let it go. And now she must reap one of the rewards of the friendship she had wanted with him. Friends were open and honest with each other. "No, not that he would harm me. That he— That I would find that my hatred—"

"—was merely a mask for love?"

"Yes." Her hands had found the handle of the door again.

"And was it?" he asked.

"No," she said more firmly. "For a while I thought it just possible that he was sincere. He tried to persuade me that he had loved me all the time, that he had hurt me in order to protect me from his own disgrace, that he had come back with the intention of wooing me again and making me his countess. I was confused. And afraid. But I did not want to believe him or love him. I did not trust him and would never have been able to. I know now that my instinct was right, that he is still as contemptible as he ever was. Why did he want to hurt you?"

"When you asked me to walk in the garden with you," he said, "and when you asked me to kiss you and told me that you loved me, you were reacting to the turmoil of emotions he had aroused in you, Samantha? And the next afternoon when I came to offer you marriage, the same thing?"

"Oh." She gazed at him unhappily. "I was so very happy to see you. Those afternoons at Highmoor with you had been among the happiest times in my life."

"With plain, ordinary Mr. Wade," he said. "Who had defects to add to his ordinariness. Who was the very antithesis of a Don Juan. Who would never confuse you or hurt or abandon you. Who would be your little puppy dog. You would be very safe with him. And so you married him."

The horrifying thing was that there was truth in his words. But only some of the truth. Not all of it.

"Hartley." Her grip on the doorknob became painful. "Don't belittle yourself. Oh, please don't do this."

"Then suppose you tell me," he said, "why you married me. Tell me, Samantha."

"Because I wanted to," she said. "Because you were sweet and kind and, and—"

"—and very rich?" His voice was hardly recognizable. She had never heard sarcasm in it before.

His face swam before her eyes, and her jaw felt suddenly cold as a hot tear dripped off it onto her dress. "Oh, don't, Hartley," she begged him. "Please don't. You *know* that I was unaware of that fact. I married you because I wanted to, because I liked you more than any other man I have ever known, because I felt s—"

"—safe with me." There was harshness in his voice. "I would be so ecstatic to win such beauty for myself that I would be unlikely ever to stray from you. Well, you were right there, Samantha. I have what is perhaps an unfortunate belief in fidelity in marriage—on both sides. No mistresses for me, no lovers for you."

"Hartley—"

"Listen to me, Samantha," he said. There was a harsh command in his voice that frightened and distressed her. "You lied to me. You let me marry you believing that lie. And it was a momentous lie. I have never wanted a loveless marriage, and yet now it seems I am irrevocably in one. But it *is* a marriage. Never forget that. You are *my wife*. You had better sort out your feelings for *my cousin* once and for all. If it is love, put it from your heart. If it is hatred, let it go. I will not have you always afraid to see him lest you find yourself in love with him. And I will not have you beneath me on our bed, dreaming that I am he."

"Hartley!" Her mouth fell open and she gasped for air.

"There may never be love between us," he said. "It is strange how my own has shriveled to nothing in the course of a few hours. But there will never be shadows. Or secrets. Is that understood?"

"You are being unfair," she said. "You are being cruel. I have never—"

"I *asked* if you understood." His face was stony, his eyes opaque. He was unrecognizable. She did not know this man.

"Yes," she said.

"If your maid has started packing your things," he said, "you may tell her to unpack again. We will be staying here."

"No." She was shaking her head against the door. "I want to go home, Hartley. Please let us go home. Oh, please."

"We will be staying here," he said. "You can enjoy the rest of the Season, as you usually do. I can occupy myself in any number of useful and useless ways. We need not be in each other's company any more than either of us would wish."

"I want to go home," she whispered. But she knew it was

useless. He was implacable, this stranger who still stood across the room from her, his back to the empty fireplace.

"If you have taken leave of all your friends," he said, "you may now boast, Samantha, that you begged to stay and that your besotted bridegroom bowed to your wishes. I will not contradict you. It is late. You will wish to change for dinner. If you will excuse me, my lady, I will be taking dinner at my club."

She turned without another word and fumbled at the handle of the door before getting it open. She hurried, head down so that the footmen would not see her face, up the stairs to her room.

It was all ruined, she thought. Her marriage. Her life. Everything.

It seemed she had been wrong to forgive herself at last.

There was to be no happiness for her.

Only three days and three nights. Pure joy, now worth less than nothing. Yes, less. It would have been far better if she had never known it.

She did not know how she was going to live through the pain. It was worse than the last time. Oh, far worse. Because this time she—

Well, this time she was the one who had done most of the hurting. And therefore her own pain was inconsolable.

He lifted his left arm to the mantel and rested his forehead on it. He did not know himself or this strange, unexpected anger that had had him lashing out to hurt as badly as he was hurt. He had intended only to talk with her, to have the truth in the open so that somehow they could patch something together out of their marriage and move on.

He had not intended to become angry—he *never* lost his temper. Never until today. And with the person he loved most dearly. And he had never felt the desire to hurt. Until today. He wanted to put a bullet between Lionel's eyes— No, that was too quick and probably painless. He wanted to pound him to a bloody pulp. And he had wanted just now to reduce Samantha to tears, to have her begging for what he would not grant.

He had succeeded admirably.

He drew a deep and ragged breath through his nose. But it was no use. He wept with painful, chest-wrenching sobs.

He froze when the door opened behind him again. He kept his head where it was. She came close to him before speaking.

"Hartley." Her voice was very quiet, very calm. If she had touched him at that moment, he would have gathered her to him with such force that he would have crushed every bone in her body. "I want you to return it to Lord Rushford, if you please. Or if you wish to keep it because it was your mother's and is precious to you, then please do so. But I do not want it and I don't want ever to see it again. This 'something blue' has ruined my marriage."

He lifted his head and looked at his mother's sapphire brooch in her palm. He took it without a word.

He felt her looking into his half-lowered face for several silent moments before she turned and left the room again.

He closed his fingers over the brooch and tightened them until the diamonds cut into his hand rather painfully.

He was late coming home. She lay on her back, staring up into the darkness beneath the canopy of her bed as she had done for several hours, listening to the sound of the door to his room opening and closing more than once, to the distant hum of his voice and his valet's. To silence.

She gazed upward and imagined him leaning against the tree on the hill at Highmoor, watching her look downward toward the abbey, catching her trespassing. If only she had turned and hurried away at that moment. Back to Chalcote and safety.

But she had not.

Her dressing room door opened softly and a faint beam of candlelight shone across the room, across the lower half of her bed. She did not move her head or close her eyes. He came and stood beside the bed.

"You are awake, then," he said after a few moments. His eyes must not be as accustomed to the darkness as hers were.

"Yes."

Please talk to me. Please tell me you did not mean those cruel things. Tell me I did not really lie to you. Take me home tomorrow.

She did not move. She continued to stare upward.

He was removing his dressing gown and climbing into bed beside her. And turning to her and starting to make love to her.

Say something. Not in silence like this.

He was slow and gentle and patient. His hands—not his mouth—worked their skilled magic on her body, until they both knew she was ready for him. And then he came inside her and slowly, skillfully worked the same magic there, until she was wonderfully relaxed and strangely aching all at the same time. He released his seed, hot and deep inside her.

It was all right, she told herself. Everything was going to be all right. But she knew that nothing at all was right. He had loved her as he usually did, though there was never a sameness about his loving. But there was something missing. Something undefinable. Something essential.

She could smell liquor on his breath, though she did not believe he was foxed.

She held him against her, her legs still twined about his, willing him to sleep. But he never slept on her for more than a minute or two at the longest. He was too considerate of her comfort to squash her beneath his full weight for too long. He lifted himself away.

And up to sit on the side of the bed. He got to his feet after a few moments and put his dressing gown back on. He looked down at her in the darkness.

"Thank you," he said. "Good night, Samantha."

She was too miserable to reply. She gazed upward again. Moments later the beam of light from the doorway narrowed and disappeared. She was in darkness once more.

Ah, dear God, she was in eternal darkness.

Lady Carew, the *ton* were soon agreed, had got just exactly what she wanted. She had made a brilliant match to a wealthy and indulgent husband who was willing to cater to her every whim. He had been about to drag the poor lady back to his own dull life at remote Highmoor in the middle of the Season. But she had easily talked him out of that foolishness. And so they had remained, she to dazzle society with more charm and wit than ever, he to follow in her wake or to pursue his own quieter pleasures until summer came.

It appeared to be a thoroughly successful marriage. They were both happy—no one had ever seen Lady Carew more vivacious than she was in the weeks following her marriage, and no one had ever seen as much of her husband. He was almost always smiling.

Lucky dog, the gentlemen of the *ton* thought, looking with some envy and some surreptitious lust at his wife. There was more than one thing to be said for being worth upward of fifty thousand a year.

Fortunate woman, the ladies of the *ton* thought. Her husband was not much of a man, perhaps, but he was wealthy and besotted and kept her on a very loose leash—if there was a leash at all. Give her a year to produce his heir and next spring they would watch with interest to see whom she would take as her first lover. She could hardly have done better for herself.

Samantha was pregnant already. She knew it, even though she was only one week late and her newness to sexual activity might be the reason for the irregularity. But she knew she was pregnant. There was something relaxed—she could not quite put a word to the feeling—deep inside her, rather like the feeling she always had at the end of the marriage act. She knew it was their child starting life in her womb.

She did not know how she would tell him when the time came. She did not know how he would feel about it. He would be glad, she supposed, as she was. She would be able to stay at Highmoor. He would not be able to force her to come back next year for the torture of another Season. Perhaps, if he continued relations with her after the birth of the child, she would conceive again. And again. Perhaps she would be able to stay at Highmoor for the rest of her life.

It seemed to her, perhaps irrationally, that Highmoor was her only hope for any measure of happiness. No, never that. Of peace. She could live out her life if only she could find some peace.

They spent a fair amount of time together, almost all of it in company with other people. Almost the only time they spent alone together was the half hour or so he took to make love to her each night. A silent half hour except for the courteous thanks at the end of it. Thanks for services rendered.

He accompanied her to most evening entertainments. Even balls. He would see her into the ballroom, stand with her until the first set began and she had taken the floor with her first partner, and then disappear into the card room or somewhere else until it was time to escort her home.

He always smiled in public. She always sparkled.

The perfect couple, perfectly in love but perfectly well-bred—they did not live in each other's pockets.

They saw Lionel almost wherever they went. They avoided him and he seemed content to look alternatively amused and lovelorn—the latter if he caught her eye across a room when Hartley was not with her. She perfected the art of moving out of a room or attaching herself to another gentleman—usually poor Francis—if she suspected he was moving her way.

She hated him. And despised him. And she was no

longer afraid of the hatred. She knew that it was just that and that it was poles away from love.

She hated him, not so much for what he had done to her—innocent as she had been, she had partly asked for it—but for what he had done to Hartley. His own cousin.

For what he had done to Hartley she could cheerfully kill him. With slow torture.

She did not know how to put right what was wrong with her marriage. If only they could go home to Highmoor, she thought. Somehow it seemed as if everything would be fine if only they could go there. And there would be a baby early in the new year. A new start for them, perhaps. But he had not said anything more about going home.

And she was afraid to ask again. Or perhaps too proud to ask.

They were to have attended Lady Gregory's ball. The invitation had been accepted. But he did not feel like going. He was weary of the constant going, the constant pretense. He told Samantha that he would stay at home, that she should pen a note to Lady Brill to accompany her and he would have it sent over.

He went into the library after dinner—she had gone to dine with Lady Brill. He sat in his favorite chair beside the fire, a book in his hands though he did not open it. He set his head back against the chair and closed his eyes.

He was so weary. He wanted to go home. He did not know what to do about his marriage. It had all been his fault, this estrangement. Perhaps she had not married him for love, but the lie had been inadvertent. And he had not told her of his own feelings until their wedding night. Many people married for reasons other than love and had perfectly successful marriages. And theirs had started well. She had enjoyed his company and his lovemaking—he had ignored those facts in the first hours of blinding hurt. She was not the sort of woman who would give less than her whole devotion to a marriage. She would have been a good wife to him for the rest of their lives if he had not ruined things.

He did not know how to put things right. He did not know if things *could* be put right. Perhaps all was ruined forever.

He wanted to go home. Perhaps things would be better there. He would tell her tomorrow to pack again. No, he would *ask* her. Perhaps she no longer wanted to go there herself. She always seemed happiest when they were in company.

He turned his head when the door opened without there having been a knock. It was Samantha, dressed neatly in an evening dress but not in a ball gown. She was carrying her embroidery bag.

"I did not want to go to the ball," she said, not quite looking at him. "Do you mind if I sit in here with you, Hartley?"

"Please do," he said. He felt almost like crying when she sat quietly across from him and drew her work from her bag and began to sew. He had dreamed of evenings like this. Evenings of quiet domestic contentment with his wife. He wanted to say something to her, but he could not think of anything meaningful to say. He pretended to read.

It was only when she got up from her place some time later and left the room without a word that he realized he had been staring into the fire, rubbing his right palm with the thumb of his left hand, straightening the fingers one by one. His hand was stiff and aching.

He should have talked to her. Perhaps she would have stayed. What was the matter with him? Was he determined to drive her away even when she had been perhaps offering an olive branch? But she had left her embroidery and her workbag behind.

And then she returned, something in her hand. She did not say anything to him or even look at him. But she drew a footstool up beside him on his right side, undid the top of the little bottle of oil he could see now in her hand, poured some of it into her palm, and rubbed her hands together. She reached out and took his right hand in her own and began gently massaging the oil into his palm and out along his fingers. Her touch was firm and sure despite the gentleness. He put his head back and closed his eyes.

He thought she was finished, but she was just applying more oil to her hands. The massage was incredibly soothing. No one had ever done that for him before. Not even his mother. His mother had not been able to bear to touch his wounded parts. Or even to look at them. She was the one who had first made him gloves.

Incredibly, he was almost half-asleep when he felt his hand being lifted and felt the softness of her cheek against the back of it. She must have thought him fully asleep. She turned her head and kissed his knuckles. And kept his hand where it was.

She did not move when he rested his left hand very lightly on her curls. He gently smoothed his fingers over her head beneath her hair.

"Samantha," he said. "Forgive me."

"You have done nothing," she said. "It was me."

"No," he said. "You were good to me during those three days, and have been patient and gentle since. And you were right—I *was* cruel. Forgive me."

"I married you," she said, "because I wanted to. I really wanted to, Hartley."

"Sh," he said. "You never gave me reason to believe otherwise. Shall we go home?"

"To Highmoor?" She looked up at him then, her eyes shining with tears.

He nodded. "Home. Shall we go?"

"Yes." She smiled at him. "Yes, let's go home, Hartley."

"As soon as possible. Three days," he said. "There are a few things we are really obligated to attend. Three days and then home." He closed the gap between their mouths and kissed her softly—for the first time in several weeks.

"Thank you, Hartley," she said, and laid her cheek against the back of his hand again. It no longer ached or felt stiff, he noticed.

Chapter 16

Lady Stebbins was the Duke of Bridgwater's aunt. Her ball, always one of the great squeezes of the Season, was one they felt obligated to attend, though neither wished to go. They did not say so to each other—he knew that she enjoyed dancing, and she knew that the duke was a particular friend of his. His grace had been best man at their wedding. They both knew, though, that their longing to be home was mutual. They talked about Highmoor frequently again—it had scarcely been mentioned in the weeks that had succeeded their all-too-short honeymoon.

One more ball could be endured, they both thought, quite separately.

Word had spread once more that they were leaving London early in order to return to Yorkshire. Word always spread among the *ton*, even if one confided the news to almost no one.

A few people commiserated with Samantha.

"Alas," Mr. Wishart said. "Have you lost your influence with your husband already, Lady Carew? Is he forcing you to miss what is left of the Season? It is a downright shameful thing."

"I have not lost my influence at all," she said, laughing lightly—it was easy to laugh these days. "Why do you think we are going to Highmoor, sir?"

"*You* want to go?" he asked in some astonishment.

"*I* want to go," she said. "Hartley has bowed to my wishes."

He was no longer in the ballroom. He had gone to observe the proceedings in the card room, as he usually did.
But he had not left before signing his name in her card next
to the supper dance. She had raised her eyebrows and
smiled at him.

"No, I am not going to make a spectacle of myself," he
said, returning her smile. "But I want to be the man to lead
you in to supper, Samantha. Will you mind sitting out a
set? Or *walking* it out? Shall we stroll in the garden? The
evening is warm."

"I will look forward to it," she had said. It would remind
her of their first meting in London—how long ago that
seemed now. Perhaps they could relive it with better re-
sults. Perhaps she would find a quiet spot to lead him to
and would ask him to kiss her again. And perhaps she
would—oh, perhaps she would repeat the words she had
spoken to him then.

She would mean them. Not quite in the way that she
thought of as love, perhaps. But there were many kinds of
love. And one of those kinds described her feelings for
Hartley. Perhaps she would tell him.

He had kissed her hand in a courtly gesture that she
knew was being observed by many people around them.
She was glad. She wanted everyone to know that they had a
close relationship. She had told herself that she did not
mind that people believed she had married for position and
wealth, and in many ways she did not mind. But for Hartley's sake, she would like it to be known that she cared for
him. Not for any of his possessions, but only for him.

Sometimes she wished she had told the story of the
rather shabby landscape gardener who had come calling
and proposed marriage to her. It would have amused the
ton. Especially the part about her accepting before she discovered her mistake.

"I will meet you outside?" he had said.

She had nodded and he had taken his leave.

Lionel arrived late. She was dancing a country dance

with Jeremy Nicholson at the time and inadvertently met Lionel's eyes across the room. He gave her a burning glance. She looked hastily away. The next set was a waltz, she knew. A dangerous dance. As soon as Jeremy had escorted her back to the group, she linked her arm through Francis's and smiled brightly at him.

"Our waltz next?" she said, though in fact no one had yet solicited her hand.

He looked casually about the ballroom. "Ah, yes," he said lazily. "I would have been out of sorts for the rest of the year if you had forgotten, Samantha."

"Thank you," she said later when they were safely dancing.

"If you were my wife," he said, "I would have challenged the bastard to pistols at dawn long before this, Samantha. Pardon the language."

"But why?" she asked. "He has done nothing but hover ever since my marriage, Francis. You do look splendid, though a little shocking, in that particular shade of pink, by the way."

"I wanted to powder my hair the same color," he said, "but my valet threatened to leave without notice. He is too good a man to squander. I can see my face in my boots when he polishes them."

"How pleasant for you," she said, grinning at him.

"Saucy wench," he said. "And clever wench. You can always divert my thoughts by appealing to my vanity. I do not like the looks he gives you, Samantha. Is Carew willing to tolerate them?"

"We are going home the day after tomorrow," she said.

"Running away?" he asked.

"How dare you, Francis!" she said indignantly.

"Sorry," he said. "I am sorry, Sam. Truly. It is none of my business."

"No," she said, "it is not. How could you make your hair pink when it is so dark a brown?"

He chuckled. "With a couple of tons of powder," he said.

"I think it rather a shame that we have outlived those days. Men of a few decades ago used to know how to dress, by Jove. I abhor the trend toward black. Ugh!" He shuddered theatrically and almost lost his step.

Samantha laughed. "You almost have me believing you," she said. "For shame!"

He looked at her with pursed lips, then threw back his head and laughed. "Pink hair," he said. "And you almost believed me. Sam, Sam."

The evening seemed interminable. Perhaps if Hartley's name had not been scrawled—his left-handed writing was anything but elegant—in her card for her to see every time she glanced at it, she could have lived through the evening with greater patience. As things were, she looked forward to their stroll and to having supper with him just as if she were a girl planning her first rendezvous with her first beau. He was her husband of more than a month. She was increasing with his child—surely she could not be wrong about that. There was still no sign of bleeding.

She did not wait for the supper dance to begin. As soon as Mr. Carruthers had led her off the floor following a quadrille, she made an excuse to her group and dashed from the ballroom out onto the balcony and down the steps into the garden. There was no one down there, even though it was quite well lit. Everyone would want to dance the supper dance, she supposed, and stroll outside afterward before the dancing resumed.

Hartley had not come out yet. She found herself smiling in some glee. She would find her secluded spot now and lure him to it as soon as he came down the steps. She would greet him with open arms and ask for his kiss. Would he realize what she was doing? Would he know that she was obliterating old memories and replacing them with new? Would he know that she meant it this time, that she would not be in any way motivated by an upheaval of emotions?

There was a small stone fountain, the water shooting out of the mouth of a fat cherub, in the middle of the garden. A willow tree overhung it on one side. It was the perfect spot. She moved into the shade of the drooping branches and turned to watch the steps from the balcony, just visible from where she stood.

But she had already missed him. He must have come down the steps when she was still moving into her hiding place. He came up almost behind her. She whirled around to face him, a smile on her lips, mischief in her eyes. She half lifted her arms.

"An invitation I have long dreamed of," he said, his voice husky with mingled amusement and desire. "And one I have had the patience to wait for."

Her smile froze. She took one step back, but that one step brought the backs of her legs up against the stone wall of the fountain.

"Go away," she said. "Go away."

"I believe it is time you stopped fighting it, Samantha," Lionel said. "It has been me from the start, has it not? You married Hartley because you were afraid of your feelings for me. But you must have grown mortally tired of him after more than a month of marriage. He is not much of a man, is he? I cannot imagine he has what it takes to satisfy someone of your passions. You need someone like me for that."

She could not lean back far enough to avoid his long finger stroking along her jaw.

"Go away," she said.

"After you led me out here?" He laughed softly. "It was in a garden such as this that we shared our first kiss, Samantha. It is time we repeated it."

"I will vomit," she said, "if you come any closer."

For once he looked nonplussed. "You and Hartley," he said. "I do believe you deserve each other, Samantha. I seem to remember that six years ago, too, you lacked the courage to reach out for what you wanted. I must taste, though, what you have been giving my cousin for the past month."

He had her backed up against the fountain. She could go no farther. But she was boiling with rage. It had been a foolish threat. Though she might *feel* like vomiting, and it would serve him right if she did it all over him, it was not something she could do at will. But she was not going to let such a snake steal any kisses without putting up a decent fight.

She brought her knee up sharply before he got quite close enough to make it impossible. He grunted with pain and surprise and folded over, presenting his face as a tempting target before he dipped too low.

"That was for Hartley," she said, feeling a wonderful sense of exhilaration. "And this is for Jenny." She stung her hand so sharply across his face that she almost cried out in pain herself. But she was not quite done. "And this one is for me." She snapped his head the other way with a slap to the other cheek. "Now, what was that you had to say about tasting?"

"I think," a quiet voice said from the shadows, "my wife has made herself perfectly clear, Lionel."

Lionel was a little too preoccupied with his pain to respond.

Samantha turned her head, the exhilaration dying as quickly as it had come. "I did not arrange a meeting with him," she said. "I came out here to meet *you*, Hartley."

"I know," he said.

"Do you need any help here, Carew?" another voice asked from a short distance away.

They both turned to see Lord Francis Kneller.

"I saw him follow Samantha—Lady Carew—outside," he said. "I thought she might need my protection."

"You may escort her inside, if you will, Kneller," the marquess said.

"No, Hartley," she said quickly. "Take me home. I want to go home now."

"My lady?" Francis was offering her his arm, just as if she had not spoken.

"Go with him, Samantha," her husband said.

What was he planning to do? Lionel was already straightening up. Obviously she had not done a great deal of damage. Lionel would pluck Hartley limb from limb. She opened her mouth to argue. And snapped her teeth together again. She had recognized the tone. She guessed she would hear it from time to time down the years, and her children, too. It was the tone that said he was to be obeyed without question. And she could not argue with that tone before witnesses. She could not humiliate him like that.

She took Francis's arm and he led her with firm steps toward the ballroom. Music was playing, she realized. The supper waltz was in progress. Everything at the ball was normal. No one else appeared to be down in the garden.

"Francis." She pulled on his arm. "What is happening? He is not being foolish, is he?"

"Good Lord, Samantha," he said, "I hope not."

Which was about as ambiguous an answer as anyone had given to any of the questions she had ever asked.

"Smile," he said, smiling down at her. "We are about to be on view, Samantha."

Her teeth were beginning to chatter. Her hands were stinging. Hartley was out there being murdered, at the very least.

She smiled.

"Well, Hart." Lionel leaned a hand on the wall of the fountain and clenched the other hand in an obvious attempt to control his pain. "You have taken an admirably heroic stand. I am sure Samantha and Kneller were marvelously impressed. Are you about to slap a glove in my face? Or would you prefer to keep it on, to hide your deformity?"

"I'll meet you at Jackson's tomorrow morning at eleven," the marquess said quietly. "Be there, Lionel. And come prepared to fight. Until one of us is insensible."

Lionel looked at him incredulously for a few moments and then threw back his head and burst into laughter.

"By God, Hart," he said when he finally had his amusement under control, "I hope you invite a large audience. It is going to be more amusing than a public hanging. Someone will be lugging raw meat back to Samantha's arms."

"Perhaps," the marquess said curtly. "And then again, perhaps not. Choose your second and bring him with you. Though I daresay Jackson himself will set down the rules and see to it that we abide by them. It will be just as well. I might kill you, else."

His words occasioned another roar of laughter.

"You had better reconsider before morning, Hart," Lionel said, still chuckling. "Before this reaches a point from which you cannot back down. I will think no worse of you. I will hold you in the same esteem I have always held you in. You had better go inside now and tell Samantha and Kneller that you wagged your finger at me and scolded me roundly for trying to steal a kiss from your wife, and that you left me drowning in tears of remorse. Tomorrow you can crawl home to the safety of Highmoor and live there happily ever after. I'll not come after you—or Samantha. I thought it would be amusing to revive old emotions, and I was right. It was. But she bores me now. She is all yours, Hart, my boy. Run away now like a good little boy."

The marquess inclined his head. "Good night to you, Lionel," he said with quiet courtesy. "I shall see you tomorrow morning. At eleven sharp." He turned and made his way back to the ballroom.

Lionel's laughter followed him.

He made his way as quickly and unobtrusively as he could around the edge of the floor—amazingly, the supper dance was still in progress—and out through the nearest door. He found the Duke of Bridgwater in the card room, watching a game in progress. He sent up a silent prayer of thanks that his friend was not dancing, as he had been most of the evening.

"Bridge." He touched the duke on the sleeve and drew him to one side. "I need your services."

His friend grinned. "I thought you were slinking off into the garden for a secret tryst with Lady Carew," he said.

"I need a second tomorrow at Jackson's saloon," the marquess said. "I have challenged Rushford to a bout—until one of us is unconscious, if Jackson will allow it. Will you stand by me?"

His friend merely stared at him.

"He was molesting Samantha in the garden," the marquess said. "She gave a good account of herself, but it was not enough."

"No," his friend said quietly. "No, it would not be. Yes, you can count on me, Hart."

"And on me." The marquess had been half-aware of Lord Francis Kneller entering the room and coming to stand a short distance away. "I'll second you, too, Carew, if I may."

"Thank you." His lordship nodded curtly. "Where is Samantha?"

"Dancing with Stebbins," Francis said. "He led her out despite the fact that the set had already begun and he was wheezing and as red as a lobster from the evening's exertions."

"My uncle could never resist treading a measure," his grace said, "especially with a pretty partner."

"She is smiling and sparkling and holding up like a trouper," Francis said. "What time tomorrow, Carew?"

"Eleven," he said. "If you will excuse me, I'll catch the end of the waltz and then take Samantha home. It has been a trying evening for her."

His friend and Samantha's stood where they were as he limped away. Then their eyes met.

"It is going to be a massacre," Francis said. "But he had no choice."

"I am not so sure," the duke said, frowning. "About the massacre, I mean. He will be beaten, of course, but maybe not quite as badly as one might think. For the last few years he has been having private sessions with Jackson. Jackson would not waste his time on nothing, would he? I have no idea what has been going on between the two of them, but it appears that tomorrow morning we will find out."

"I'll respect him in future," Francis said, "however humiliating the outcome is for him tomorrow. I must confess I have thought him a weakling. That bastard has been stalking Lady Carew since he came back to England."

"No, not a weakling, Kneller," his grace said. "Hartley has a quiet dignity that does not need to assert itself in swashbuckling. But he has a wife now whom he loves. He is not the type to stand by and see her insulted."

"Good," Francis said. "If he had not challenged Rushford, you know, then I would have. And that would not have been quite the thing, would it?"

"Most unwise, my dear chap," his grace said. He raised one eyebrow. "Though I am sure that if you look hard enough you will find some other lady with quite equal charms who would welcome your gallantry and your devotion and your willingness to rush to her defense."

"By Jove," Francis said, "I do believe you are warning me, Bridgwater."

"My dear fellow," the duke said, rearranging the lace folds of his cuffs over the backs of his hands, "I would not dream of it. I am merely suggesting that you avoid, ah, making an ass of yourself, shall we say? She is very lovely, but then so are many of the ladies who grace our ballrooms and drawing rooms if we but take the trouble to look. I am famished. Shall we make an early sortie into the supper room?"

"Lead the way," Francis said, brushing an invisible speck from his pink arm.

"Hartley?" She leaned across her empty breakfast plate and set her hand flat on the table, close to his.

He had been glancing through the morning paper. He looked up, set it aside, and smiled at her.

"Hartley," she said, her best wheedling look on her face

and a matching tone in her voice, "I have been thinking. My trunks are almost packed and I daresay yours are, too. The weather is good. Do we need to waste another day? Could we not start on our way home this morning?"

She wanted to be out of London. She did not believe she would ever want to come back, though she supposed that feeling might pass in time. She wanted to be home, back in that wonderful place where it had all started—her love affair with friendship. And with Hartley. She could not bear the thought of waiting even another day.

He covered her hand with his own—his right one, thin and crooked and ungloved. She had asked him not to wear his glove at home. There was no need, she had assured him, taking his hand in her own and raising it to her cheek and kissing it—it was the morning after she had massaged it for the first time. She had done so each day since.

"It will have to wait one more day," he said. "I have a couple of pieces of business to attend to first. Tomorrow will come eventually, my love. And then we will have Highmoor and the summer to look forward to."

She sighed. "And no one else can attend to this business for you?" she asked.

"I am afraid not." He patted her hand. "And you will wish to say good-bye to Lady Brill."

"I seem to have done nothing but say good-bye to her in the past month or so," she said.

"Poor Samantha." He smiled at her. "Take her shopping with you. Buy her something pretty, and yourself, too, and have the bills sent to me. Lady Thornhill has been known to complain, you know, even in my hearing, that there is nothing fashionable to be bought in Yorkshire."

"You will be sorry," she said. "I will spend your whole fortune."

He chuckled and got to his feet before offering her his hand. "I will have to be going," he said. "I have an appointment for which I cannot possibly be late."

She pulled a face. "And so a mere wife has been put

firmly in her place," she said. "All she is good for is tripping out to shop for baubles."

He chuckled again. "Scold me all day tomorrow," he
said. "You will have a captive audience in the carriage.
Now I really must be going."

Men and their mysterious "appointments," she thought a
few minutes later, alone with her maid in her room, preparing to call on her aunt. He had probably promised to meet
the Duke of Bridgwater and Lord Gerson at White's for
luncheon, and that was more important than making an
early start for home. Or than giving in to a wife's best
wheedling.

She did not really want to go out today. She dreaded that
she would perhaps run into Lionel. Not that she would stay
indoors merely to hide away from him. She had been rather
proud of the way she had handled him the evening before—
and enormously relieved to see later that Hartley was un-
harmed. She had rather expected a shattered nose and two
black eyes, at the very least.

He had been very reticent about what had happened out
in the garden after he and Francis between them had removed her from the scene of her triumph. He had merely
assured her that she need not worry about Lionel's harass-
ing her ever again.

He had not—as she had half expected—asked her if she
had finally got her feelings for Lionel sorted out. Perhaps
her actions in the garden had spoken louder than any
words.

And he had not—it had been a terrible disappointment—
come to her bed last night. It had been the first time since
their wedding. She had shed a few tears of self-pity and
anger—he *did* believe she had gone out there to meet Lionel, despite what he had said at the time. Why had he not
said so, then? She had done the unthinkable eventually. She
had gone through to his room—she had never even set foot
in it before—and stood by the side of his bed, shuffling and
clearing her throat until he woke up. He had been *sleeping*.

"What is it?" he had asked, sitting up.

"I went out there to meet *you*," she had said, her voice more abject than she had intended. "I was finding a secluded spot so that you could *kiss* me there."

"Ah. I know, love," he had said. And he had reached out and lifted her bodily over him and onto the bed beside him. There had appeared to be no lack of strength in his right arm. He had covered her with the blankets. His bed was soft and warm. "I did not doubt you for even a moment."

"Then why—?" she had asked.

"I thought you would be as tired as I was," he had said. "I did not realize my not coming would upset you."

"It did not—" she had begun, but he had shushed her and then kissed her.

He had not made love to her.

It had not mattered. She had been asleep within minutes.

Well, she would go out, she thought now. The day would crawl by if she stayed at home. She would do as he had suggested and take Aunt Aggy shopping. She smiled and met her maid's eyes in the looking glass. The girl smiled back. And she would spend a fortune, too. She was *never* a spendthrift. But today she would be. She would punish him horribly.

"No, my straw bonnet," she said when her maid handed her a more subdued and more elegant one.

This was going to be a day of gaiety. She was going to enjoy her last day in London. Her last day for maybe a long, long time. This time next year she was going to be nursing a baby—no wet nurses for her, even if Hartley tried using his I-must-be-obeyed-without-question voice. And the year after next—well, she was sure the nursery at Highmoor must be far too large for one child. Probably even for two.

Chapter 17

He was gazing downward, trying to block out both sight and sound, trying to concentrate. It was not easy. This particular sparring room in Jackson's boxing saloon was crowded with eager spectators. He had told no one and Bridge and Kneller had just assured him that they had not. But Lionel, of course, would have no reason for keeping quiet about the fight and every reason to publicize it.

Barefoot and stripped to the waist, he felt woefully inadequate. He knew that in appearance, even apart from his twisted foot and hand, he was laughably inferior to Lionel, tall and splendidly built and beautiful in his corner with Viscount Birchley, his second. He was flashing his grin on all comers and loudly greeting every new arrival.

"It is a good thing you are punctual," he called gaily to someone who had just arrived. "It will not be a lengthy entertainment. But then neither is a hanging."

He had obviously liked that analogy the evening before and had thought it worthy of repetition.

Jackson had agreed—reluctantly—to a fight that would end only with the unconsciousness of one or other of the combatants. Normally very strict and very gentlemanly rules applied to the sparring bouts at his establishment. He had just finished explaining to both of them and their seconds and anyone else who cared to listen—there had been a dead hush in the room—that there would be a limitless number of rounds, each to last three minutes. There were to be no hits after he had called the end of a round or before he had called for the beginning of the next. All hits were to be cleanly above the waist.

"Pipe down, Jackson," someone had called from the back of the room. "Your instructions are taking longer than the fight will last."

Gentleman Jackson had fixed the offender with an iron stare and invited him to take his leave. It was a measure of the power he wielded within the doors of his saloon that Mr. Smithers rather sheepishly slipped away through the door and did not come back.

And now the fight was about to begin. The Marquess of Carew tried to concentrate, to remember everything he had learned over the past three years—though he had never expected to be using his skills in actual combat.

"Defend with your right and attack with your left," Lord Francis Kneller advised him rather urgently. "Protect your head."

"You will need to get in close, Hart," the Duke of Bridgwater said. "He has a longer reach than yours and powerful fists. But protect your head. Keep your chin tucked in."

"Go get him," Lord Francis said. "Think of your wife."

Poor advice. Very poor. He tried to concentrate on the fight itself. A fight he could not win, perhaps. But one in which he must give a good account of himself.

"Round one," Jackson said. "Begin, gentlemen."

The marquess looked up and stepped forward to a swell of sound from the onlookers.

"Daniel and one of the lions," some wit said.

"David and Goliath, more like," someone else shouted from the other side of the room.

Lionel was grinning and dancing and waving his fists in a most unsportsmanlike way. He was making very little pretense of defending himself.

"Time to draw your slingshot from your belt, Hart," he said. "See if you can get me right between the eyes."

The next moment he was flat on his back on the floor while a roar of mingled astonishment and amusement went up from the crowd. And then murmurings of outrage and calls of "Foul!" and "Shame!"

Lionel roared with wrath as he scrambled to his knees. "What the bloody hell!" he shouted.

"Disqualification, Jackson," Viscount Birchley cried. "The verdict goes to Rushford."

"By God, Hart, splendid hit, old chap," the duke said.

The bout appeared to have stopped.

"You were not listening, gentlemen," Jackson said crisply. "The rule was that no hit was to be below the belt. That hit was full on the chin. The rule did not state that hits can be made only with the fists. The foot is a permitted weapon within the rules of today's bout. Proceed, gentlemen."

"I am not fighting a bloody contortionist," Lionel said scornfully.

Since he was still on his knees, it took the marquess little effort at all to twist his right leg high enough to poke Lionel on the chin again hard enough to send him sprawling.

"Then yield," he said coldly, "while you are still conscious. Before all these witnesses of yours, Rushford. And be stripped of what little honor you have remaining."

Lionel scrambled to his feet and put himself in a far more respectful attitude of defense than before.

"Come on, Carew," he said. "If one of us can kick, the other can, too. If you choose to fight dirty, then dirty it will be. But do not expect mercy of me. I might have spared—"

His speech was cut short when the sole of the marquess's foot caught him on the shoulder and sent him reeling, though he managed to keep his feet this time.

Before the end of round one it became obvious that the Earl of Rushford was not going to be able to use his feet in the fight. The only time he tried it he kicked his cousin almost in the groin and received a severe warning from Jackson. He swore again about contortionists, but he had not had the hours of exercise and practice that the marquess had had in turning his body and throwing out his leg to the height of his own head. Nor had he had the training and experience of using that leg and foot as a weapon quite as powerful as a fist.

There had been little if any betting before the start of the bout. What was the point of betting when the outcome was a foregone conclusion? The only betting there had been was on how many seconds the fight would last. At the end of the first round the real betting began. At the end of round two it was as fast and furious as the round itself had been.

After four rounds the marquess was feeling sore on every square inch of his body and weary in every muscle, even muscles he had not known he possessed. He had been down twice, Lionel three times, not counting those first two falls in the first round. Lionel had succeeded a few times in grabbing his leg and twisting it, throwing him off balance and causing excruciating pain. But Jackson had warned him about holding and it had not happened in the last round.

Lord Francis was squeezing a sponge of cold water over his head and down his back. It felt delicious. Bridge was waving a towel energetically before his face.

"Keep it up, Hart," he said. "Show him a thing or two, old chap."

"Think of your wife, Carew," Lord Francis said quietly.

He had begun to think of her. Of the innocent, eager eighteen-year-old who had fallen prey to Lionel's cynical scheming. Of the heartbreak his cruel rejection had caused her and—worse—the guilt that had been left behind to blight her life for six years. Of the woman of four-and-twenty who had feared that he would still have a power over her she would be unable to resist and who had turned to him—to Hartley Wade—to protect her and keep her safe from ugly passions for the rest of her life. He thought of her last night, lashing out with her knee and her hands and even then lingering to throw defiance in Lionel's teeth. He thought of her beside his bed last night, miserable because she thought *he* had rejected her, too. He had been refraining from sexual relations in order to conserve his energy for this morning.

He had promised her last night that she would never have to fear Lionel again. And there was only one way to ensure that. He knew that he had won the respect of his peers this morning, even if he was rendered unconscious in the very next round. And perhaps he had won his own respect, too, finally doing more than just enduring Lionel's taunts, finally challenging him and facing him man to man.

But it was not enough. It was no longer enough merely to give a good account of himself in this fight. He had to win it.

He *had* to win it. And it no longer seemed an impossibility. Lionel was sitting across from him, in the opposite corner, gazing at him from one open eye and one swollen and half-closed one. His breathing was labored. And for once—and at last—he was looking with quite open and naked hatred.

"Time, gentlemen. Round five," Gentleman Jackson said. "Begin."

It was easier, of course, to tell oneself that one had to win than to do it. In round nine the marquess finally knew that he not only could do it, but would. Lionel was swaying on his feet. His guard was low, so it was possible to punish his face with both left fist and right foot. One of his eyes was a mere slit in swollen flesh. The other was half-closed. His nose looked as if it were broken.

His own strength had all but been used up. He was proceeding on sheer willpower and determination. And on the image of Samantha's face that constantly swam before his tired vision.

There was very little noise now in the room, though it appeared that no one had left except the unfortunate Smithers.

"Think of her, Carew. Think of her," Lord Francis said to him insistently at the end of the round, as he had said at the end of the round before, and the round before that. He was squeezing a sponge down over his chest. "Think of her, dammit, and don't you dare let up."

Kneller was in love with Samantha, he thought sluggishly. He had known that all along. But Kneller was an honorable man. Well, he would avenge her for both of them.

"It has to be this round, old chap," the duke said, still vigorously fanning as he had between all rounds. "You are close to exhaustion. You will collapse in round eleven. This is round ten. This is the one, Hart. Go to it. There is not a man here, with the possible exception of those two opposite, who is not pulling for you. *This* round, Hart."

It took him two and a half minutes to do it. But finally Lionel was swaying on boneless legs, his hands in very loose fists at his sides, looking at him—though perhaps not really seeing him—with implacable hatred. He would have fallen unaided and been unconscious by the time he hit the floor. And it was tempting even then to have a modicum of mercy on him.

But the marquess saw an image of himself at the age of six, his child's body shattered and in indescribable pain. And an image of his mother, who could not endure the sight of pain, especially when it was being suffered by her beloved only son. And of Samantha begging him to kiss her, telling him she loved him—and *meaning* it at the moment she spoke—because she had been frightened by Lionel's reappearance in a life he had made unhappy for six years.

He gathered together his last remaining shreds of strength and jabbed out with his right leg. His last blow, like the first, landed squarely on Lionel's chin, snapping back his head and sending him crashing backward.

He groaned once and then lay still.

There was noise then. Deafening noise. Men talking to him, laughing, thumping him on the back before Bridge roared at them all to keep their distance and Kneller swore at them to stand back and give Carew air or he would start laying about him with his own fists.

"Well, lad," Jackson was saying from somewhere above him—someone had pulled him down onto the stool in his corner, "I feel compelled to say that you are perhaps my best ever pupil. But if you had just remembered to keep up that right hand—how many *times* have I told you?—your face would not be looking quite as raw as it does. Some people are a glutton for punishment."

Viscount Birchley was fanning Lionel, who was prone on the floor, and yelling for someone to fetch some water. No one was taking a great deal of notice.

"Go and give him a hand, Bridge," the marquess said, not even daring yet to flex sore muscles or to try to get to his feet. His legs had turned to rubber.

The duke gave him a speaking glance, which he did not even see, and went.

Lionel was still on the floor, groaning with returning consciousness as Birchley sponged his face carefully and the Duke of Bridgwater waved the inevitable towel before his face, when the marquess finally got to his feet with Lord Francis Kneller's help and limped stiffly from the room to retrieve his clothes and make his way back home.

There was going to be no keeping the morning's events from Samantha as he had hoped to do, he thought ruefully. He did not think any story of walking into a door was going to convince her. Well, perhaps she would be happy to know that he had avenged her.

Perhaps she would even be proud of him.

She had spent a veritable fortune—far more, at least, than she had ever spent in a single day before. And she did not feel even a moment's guilt. If he had taken her home today as she had asked, she would not have spent a single penny. He would not have had anything to grumble about. Not that Hartley would grumble anyway. She could not quite imagine him grumbling about anything.

Besides, he had told her to go out and buy Aunt Aggy and herself something pretty. Like a good little wife she had obeyed.

She bought her aunt a delicate ivory fan, laughing at Aunt Aggy's protests that she was too old for such a pretty little trinket. And she bought her a pair of kid gloves, too, since her aunt had been saying all spring that she simply must buy herself new ones. She bought Hartley a snuffbox, though he never took snuff, because it was pretty and irresistible and because the silver lid was inlaid with sapphires and she had the sudden idea of giving it to him as a belated wedding present—though he was going to pay for it. It would be their "something blue" to replace the other horrid thing. She had not asked if he had kept it or given it back. She did not want to know.

She almost forgot to buy herself something, but remembered just in time and bought some silk stockings and a new bonnet so bedecked with ribbons and flowers that she half expected that her neck would disappear into her chest when she tried it on. But it was as light as a feather and looked so dashing and so very—extravagant that she had to buy it, though she was not sure if it was the type of bonnet she would wear in Yorkshire. She also visualized herself wearing it when she was huge with child and had to swallow her laughter lest she have to explain to Aunt Aggy and the milliner.

Despite herself, she was enjoying her last day in London.

And then, after they had stopped for luncheon—although Aunt Aggy had protested that it was extravagant to eat out and not quite proper without a gentleman to escort them— Samantha spotted Francis farther down Oxford Street and lifted her hand gaily and waved to him and smiled.

He came hurrying toward them.

"Samantha," he said. "Lady Brill." But he turned back to the former. "Were you not at home when Carew arrived?"

"Now?" she said. "Recently? Is he at home already? I thought his business was to keep him out all day."

He took her arm and lowered his voice. "I believe he may need you," he said.

The tone of his voice and the look on his face alerted her. "Why?" she asked fearfully. "What has happened? Lionel? Did—?"

"Yes," he said.

Her eyes widened in terror. "Hartley *challenged* him last night? Is he *dead*?" But even as she clutched at his sleeve she remembered his just saying that Hartley might need her. Would a dead man have need of her?

"No," he said. "Deuce take it, but I have bungled this. It was fisticuffs, Samantha. At Jackson's. And your husband *won*."

"Your timing and your sensibilities leave something to be desired, my lord," Lady Brill said as Samantha clung to his sleeve with both hands. "She is all but fainting. Come. Help her to the carriage. I will convey her to Stanhope Gate without any further delay. Carew won, did you say? But against whom, pray? And in what cause? It will be a story worth listening to, at any rate. And I do not doubt it will be the *on dit* by this evening. There, dear, in you go. Lord Francis will help you."

Samantha smiled rather wanly down at him after she was seated. "No, do not apologize, Francis," she said. "Thank you. I might not have heard, otherwise. I might have been gone all day. Oh, Hartley." She fumbled in her reticule for a handkerchief.

"He may be battered and bruised, Samantha," he said, "but you may tell him from me that he is the most fortunate man in England. And more worthy of you than any other man I know. Good-bye."

He closed the door before she could make any response more than a rather watery smile.

He had bathed and changed, and his valet—looking quite smug and satisfied—had rubbed ointment into the rawer of his wounds. And he had limped his way downstairs to the library to sit by the fire he had had lit despite the warmness of the day outside. There was probably not a joint or a muscle in his body that was not screaming at him. Miraculously, both eyes had escaped, but they were about the only part of him that had.

He wished Samantha would come home and massage his hand.

He wished he did not have to face her for a week.

He had won. He set his head back and closed his eyes, but the euphoria built in him like an expanding balloon of excitement. He had *won*. He had set the score right. He had avenged her—and himself, too. He allowed himself a smile of pride. He had never realized that a smile could physically hurt.

And then the door crashed inward. He turned in time to see a little whirlwind rush inside, the yellow flowers on its straw bonnet nodding violently. But she snatched the bonnet from her head even as he watched and hurled it to one side without even checking to see that there was somewhere other than the floor for it to land. Someone closed the door quietly from the outside.

"I could *kill* you," she said. "With my bare hands. Hartley! You did not even *tell* me. Business indeed. Business to attend to. He might have *killed* you. I could kill you."

"Perhaps it is as well," he said, "that a man can die only once."

"Hartley." She came to stand in front of him and then went down on her knees and rested her hands on his knees. "Oh, Hartley, your poor face. Why did you do it? Oh, I know why. You did it for me. You should never have done anything so foolhardy. But thank you. Oh, thank you. I do love you so."

"For those words alone it was all worth it," he said, smiling carefully. "It was partly for me, too, Samantha."

"Because in insulting me he insulted you?" she asked, gazing up at his shiny, reddened face.

He was never a handsome man, he thought, but now he

must look grotesque. And yet she was gazing with something that looked almost like adoration in her face.

"Yes," he said. "And because of this, Samantha." He held up his right hand. "And my foot. He was the cause of both. It was no accident. He pushed me—a child of six."

Her eyes brightened with tears. "Oh, Hartley," she whispered. "Oh, my poor love. Francis said that you won. Does Lionel look worse than you?"

"Considerably," he said. "He will spend the rest of his life with a crooked nose, and I would wager his eyes will be invisible and blind for at least the next week."

"How delicious," she said, grinning unexpectedly. "I am so glad. Well done, sir."

"Bloodthirsty woman," he said.

"Hartley." She rested her chin on his knees and continued to gaze up at him. "I have been terribly foolish. I have realized it only during the past few days, and only last night and today has it become fully apparent to me. I have been mistaking the meaning of a word."

He chuckled. "Foolish indeed," he said. "What word?"

"I think you are in terrible pain," she said. "Would it be quite impossible to sit on your lap?"

He was in pain. Even the pressure on his knees hurt. He reached his arms down to her. She curled up against him, her head on his shoulder.

"It is the word 'like,'" she said. "I did not know that what I had always thought was liking was really love. I have been very foolish."

He felt rather as if someone had just punched him in the stomach again. He felt robbed of breath.

"Give me an example," he said, risking further pain by lowering his cheek to the top of her head.

"When I met you at Highmoor," she said, "I liked you so terribly much, Hartley. After each meeting I lived for the next time, and when I had to leave early with Aunt Aggy, there was a dreadful emptiness in my life where you had been. I thought you my best friend in the world, and I thought I would never know such friendship again. Town and the Season were flat because I did not have my friend to share them with. And then when I saw you again, I was so *happy* that I thought I would burst. I wanted you to kiss me and I wanted to say what I said to you afterward and I wanted to marry you—because I liked you so much. After we were married, for those three days, I—I have never been so happy in my life. I was delirious with happiness. Because I liked you so much. And afterward I wanted to die, I wanted the world to end because I thought you did not like me any longer."

"Ah, love," he said.

"Have I given you enough examples?" she asked. "Do you see what I mean?"

He swallowed and rubbed his cheek against her hair.

"You see," she said, "when I went through that horrid experience during my first Season, I called it love. I thought that was what it was, that horrible obsession, the dreadful guilt, the—oh, everything. And all I have clung to since is the conviction that I wanted nothing more to do with love. I saw Jenny and Gabriel together and other people, too, but I did not believe in it for myself. So when I met you, I think I was afraid to call my feelings what they were. I thought everything would turn ugly. I wanted to like you and you to like me so that we could be happy together."

"I like you, sweetheart," he said.

"And I *love* you," she said. "You see? I have said it and no thunderbolt has fallen on our heads. Hartley, you are everything in the world to me. Everything and more. You always have been, from the moment I first saw you. You put sunshine back into my life."

He swallowed again, and then, without thinking of the pain he was going to cause himself, he moved his head, found her mouth with his own, and kissed her.

"It is not too late?" she whispered.

"It is never too late," he said. "I love you."

She sighed and reached for another kiss. But she broke off after a few moments and smiled at him. "I have a gift for you," she said. "I bought it and have had the bill sent to you." She laughed gaily. "And it is not even something you use, Hartley. But it was so pretty that I could not resist it. And it is blue. Something blue. A belated wedding gift." She leaned down from his lap and retrieved the reticule she had dropped to the floor.

"I have a gift for you, too," he said. "It was the first matter of business I spoke of at breakfast this morning." He chuckled. "It is something blue. To help you forget the other." He had slipped it into a pocket before coming downstairs. He reached for it now.

"Oh," she said, looking at her sapphire ring a few moments later. "Oh, Hartley, it is beautiful. Oh, my love, thank you." She held out her hand to him and he slipped the ring on next to her wedding band. She held the hand farther away, fingers spread, to admire the effect.

He smiled down at his snuffbox. "Shall I take up the habit," he asked, "and learn to sneeze all over you?"

"You do not like it?" she asked doubtfully. "It was a foolish idea, was it not?"

"I shall wear it next to my heart for the rest of my life," he said. "I shall treasure it as much as a certain green feather I once won. Thank you, Samantha."

"Do you want another gift?" she asked. "It is not blue or a green feather and cannot be put in your hands—yet. But I think you will like it." She was looking at him with luminous eyes.

"What?" He smiled and set his head back against the chair.

"I think . . . ," she said. "Actually, I am almost sure. I think we are going to have a baby, Hartley."

He was glad his head was back. He closed his eyes briefly. "Oh, my love," he said.

"I think it must be so," she said. "In fact, I feel that it must be so. I want to go home to Highmoor, Hartley. The baby will be born in the new year and I will nurse him or her next spring and summer, and then before you can have ideas to bring me back here to enjoy another silly Season, we will have another and squash the possibility again. That is my plan, anyway." She was smiling warmly, a little impishly at him. "Do you not think it a wonderful plan?"

He smiled at her and cupped her cheek with his right hand. "I think *you* are wonderful," he said. "I cannot grasp this reality yet. I am to be a father? Am I really that clever?"

"Yes, you are," she said. "Hartley? Do you remember telling me there was more to learn? That you would teach me and that I would teach you?"

"Yes," he said.

"I do not know what I could possibly teach you," she said, "but will you help me to learn?" Her eyes were warm, wistful, full of love. "And to teach? I want everything there can be with you. And I want to give you every happiness there is."

He drew her head down to his shoulder again and nestled his cheek against her head. "Starting tonight, love," he said. "And continuing through the rest of our lives."

There was a contented silence for no longer than a few moments.

"What is wrong with this afternoon?" she asked him.

Nothing except a whole bodyful of aching joints and sore muscles and raw flesh. Absolutely nothing whatsoever.

"Nothing that I can think of," he said. "Your room or mine, my love?"

"Yours," she said, springing to her feet and reaching down a hand for his. "For a change. Your bed felt deliciously soft last night, Hartley, even though all we did was *sleep* in it."

"Well," he said, hauling himself somehow to his feet and offering her his left arm, "we will certainly have to rectify that little omission before another hour has passed. Never

let it be said that all I ever did in my own bed with my wife
was sleep with her."

She chuckled merrily and laid her arm along the top of
his, just as if he were about to lead her into a dance.

"This is certainly going to be more enjoyable than shopping," she said. "Thank heaven I ran into Francis. Oh, by
the way, I am to tell you from him that you are the most
fortunate man in the world."

"Amen to that," he said, opening the door and leading
her through to the hall and up the stairs.

"I, of course," she said, "am the luckiest woman in the
whole *universe*. I am in love with and married to my dearest friend. My *special companion*."

 SIGNET REGENCY ROMANCE

HEARTWARMING ROMANCES BY MARY BALOGH

☐ **CHRISTMAS BELLE** When a beautiful London actress and a notorious rake meet after several years have elapsed, they discover that there are painful wounds that never heal—and burning passions that refuse to die.
(179544—$3.99)

☐ **TEMPTING HARRIET** She had resisted scandalous seduction once before, six years ago. But now she was no longer that young and innocent girl. She was Lady Harriet Wingham, beautiful wealthy widow. The libertine who had almost taken her virtue then was the Duke of Tenby. He still wanted Harriet—not as a wife but as his mistress. (179528—$3.99)

☐ **DANCING WITH CLARA** Clara Danford had illusions about Frederick Sullivan, a rake whose women were legion and whose gambling debts were staggering. She knew why he wished to wed her. It was not for the beauty and grace she did not have, but for her fortune. Clara might have no illusions to lose—but she would have to be careful not to lose her heart.
(178734—$3.99)

☐ **A PRECIOUS JEWEL** Sir Gerald Stapleton wants Miss Priscilla Wentworth to be his most favored favorite—his mistress. Although they both believe that they know the ways of the world and that their fling could never turn into love, they know all too little about the ways of the heart. (176197—$3.99)

*Prices slightly higher in Canada

Buy them at your local bookstore or use this convenient coupon for ordering.

PENGUIN USA
P.O. Box 999 — Dept. #17109
Bergenfield, New Jersey 07621

Please send me the books I have checked above.
I am enclosing $_____ (please add $2.00 to cover postage and handling). Send check or money order (no cash or C.O.D.'s) or charge by Mastercard or VISA (with a $15.00 minimum). Prices and numbers are subject to change without notice.

Card #_____ Exp. Date _____

Signature_____

Name_____

Address_____

City _____ State _____ Zip Code _____

For faster service when ordering by credit card call **1-800-253-6476**

Allow a minimum of 4-6 weeks for delivery. This offer is subject to change without notice.

 **SIGNET REGENCY ROMANCE**

DAZZLING ROMANCES BY MARY BALOGH

☐ **SECRETS OF THE HEART** When Sarah is reunited with her former husband, she counts on passion to melt the barriers between then. "A winner!"—*Romantic Times*   (152891—$4.50)

☐ **COURTING JULIA** Can Miss Julia Maynard ever become the bride of the arrogant, cavalier Earl of Beaconswood no matter how irresistible he might be ... no matter how foolish her heart behaves when he takes her in his arms to teach her the dangerous delights of desire?
(177398—$3.99)

☐ **THE NOTORIOUS RAKE** Lady Mary Gregg was surprised to find herself the object of Lord Waite's desires. But even more surprising was her reaction to his shocking advances. How could she remain a lady with this man who knew so well how to make her feel like a woman ...?
(174194—$3.99)

*Prices slightly higher in Canada

Buy them at your local bookstore or use this convenient coupon for ordering.

PENGUIN USA
P.O. Box 999 — Dept. #17109
Bergenfield, New Jersey 07621

Please send me the books I have checked above.
I am enclosing $_____ (please add $2.00 to cover postage and handling). Send check or money order (no cash or C.O.D.'s) or charge by Mastercard or VISA (with a $15.00 minimum). Prices and numbers are subject to change without notice.

Card #_____ Exp. Date _____
Signature_____
Name_____
Address_____
City _____ State _____ Zip Code _____

For faster service when ordering by credit card call **1-800-253-6476**

Allow a minimum of 4-6 weeks for delivery. This offer is subject to change without notice.